God is an Astronaut

God is an Astronaut

a novel

Alyson Foster

BLOOMSBURY

NEW YORK · LONDON · NEW DELHI · SYDNEY

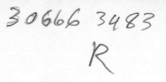

Published by Bloomsbury USA, New York

Bloomsbury is a trademark of Bloomsbury Publishing Plc

All papers used by Bloomsbury USA are natural, recyclable products made
from wood grown in well-managed forests. The manufacturing processes
conform to the environmental regulations of the country of origin.

LIBRARY OF CONGRESS CATALOGING-IN-
PUBLICATION DATA HAS BEEN APPLIED FOR.

ISBN: 978-1-62040-356-3

First U.S. Edition 2014

1 3 5 7 9 10 8 6 4 2

Typeset by Hewer Text UK Ltd, Edinburgh
Printed and bound in the U.S.A. by Thomson-Shore Inc., Dexter, Michigan

Bloomsbury books may be purchased for business or promotional use.
For information on bulk purchases please contact Macmillan Corporate
and Premium Sales Department at specialmarkets@macmillan.com.

For Michael

From: Jessica Frobisher <jfrobisher@umich.edu>
Sent: Thursday, March 13, 2014 8:57 pm
To: Arthur Danielson <danielsav@umich.edu>
Cc:
Bcc:
Subject: Not sure there is one

Arthur,

Discovered your card in my mailbox early this morning. I'm
guessing it arrived sometime last week, but as you know, I make a
habit of checking my box as infrequently as I can get away with it.
Earlier this semester the department hired a new admin
coordinator. She looks practically pubescent, certainly not old
enough to be administrating or coordinating anything. Her name
is Mackenzie. She calls my office approximately once a month to
leave a snippy message on my voice mail informing me that my
box is full and *any additional mail received will be disposed of.* I
couldn't care less if they throw my mail away, but I listen with
great admiration to her use of italics. I'd like her to teach me to
inflect like that—it would probably be quite effective in getting
Jack and Corinne to chop-chop—but I'm on her shit list. It will
never happen.

My first thought was that you had heard what happened. I don't
know how quickly news reaches you up in the wilds north of

Winnipeg. Depends on how often you decide to emerge from the conifers and go hunt down a signal, I guess. (Here I imagine you licking your finger and putting it up to the wind, listening for an elusive high-decibel hum, a telltale resonance in the pinecones overhead that would tell you where to set up camp with your laptop.) Then I opened up the card, saw the question about the greenhouse, and realized that you couldn't have. You probably still haven't heard unless you've somehow seen the *Times* or the *Post,* both of which have been running articles about the accident nonstop since it happened four days ago.

We got the call from Arizona on Sunday night. It was Liam's friend, his best Spaceco buddy, Tristan. I was down with a case of bronchitis; my voice was an octave low. When I picked up the cell from the nightstand and said "Hello" into it, I heard Tristan say, "Liam, we're fucked. We're fucked, Liam," back to back, just like that. I didn't even respond. I just rolled over and handed the phone to Liam. Then I got up, went down the hall to check on Corinne and Jack, and made my way downstairs to put on some tea. I'd never felt anything quite like it, that thrumming nerved-up calm. Like having bees in your ears. Do you know the kind I mean? I watched my hands as they wiped down the counters and shook out the tea bags with a brisk efficiency I'd never realized they possessed. When that was done, I started on the refrigerator. I opened all the drawers and began, very methodically, purging their contents. All the vegetable artifacts—the frizzled-out leeks, the calcifying carrots, the strawberries encrusted in what looks like barnacles. All the questionable relics tarnishing in glass jars. Action, drastic action, seemed required; nothing was spared. Not until the next morning did I realize that I'd thrown away Jack's science fair project. (A potato/Play-Doh hybrid? Should I be concerned that my son seems to lack a basic understanding of the scientific method? Aren't his ten-year-old Chinese counterparts already practicing the genetic modification experiments that will help them take over the world and bring us to our knees? When

Jack discovered my blunder at breakfast, a scene ensued. Corinne joined in with her own wailing dirge, and nothing, nothing, not my futile trash-picking, not all my ardent repenting, could salvage that catastrophic morning.)

At last I heard Liam's footsteps on the stairs, I stepped back and put both hands on the counter behind me. I was literally braced—a little cold—besides that, nothing but expectant. I held stiffly onto the granite slab and watched Liam run his hands down his face, one then the other, while he delivered the news.

It was this: that just a half an hour earlier, Spaceco's 6:30 p.m. shuttle launch had exploded twelve seconds after liftoff. The two crew members and four passengers inside the *Titan* had been killed instantly. A piece of debris from the blast, carried unexpectedly far by the high winds that evening, landed within fifty yards of eastbound I-8, and traffic in both directions was shut down for more than four hours.

That. That is what happened.

What happens next is what we're still trying to figure out.

More later? I haven't decided yet.

Jess

From: Jessica Frobisher <jfrobisher@umich.edu>
Sent: Saturday, March 15, 2014 10:42 pm
To: Arthur Danielson <danielsav@umich.edu>
Cc:
Bcc:
Subject: The long answer

Arthur,

How's the greenhouse coming, you asked. After I e-mailed you
yesterday, I folded up your card and stuck it in the pocket of my
blue jeans, where I carried it around all day. More than once I
found myself pulling it out and rereading the single line of your
question like a riddle, studying your familiar script, the listing
masts on your h's and t's—the tell of a left-hander. Liam is
left-handed too. Not by genetic predisposition—it's an
adaptation. The end of his right thumb was blown off in an
accident with a bottle rocket when he was eight. I don't know if
you noticed when you shook his hand. Most people don't. He is
Liam, after all.

How's the greenhouse coming? After sifting through all the
possible implications of this benign (?) query, I settled, true to
form, on the most insulting one. Meaning: Have I finally, for once,
undertaken what I said I would?

Well, fuck you, I have. I think I've mentioned the door in the back
corner of our house—the one off the dining room where the
ground slants down so that it opens out into empty space. All
right, not *empty space*, not the desolate, star-spangled void that
entrances Liam—it's a plot of incorrigible wild grass, our own
little brambly wilderness. Though at night, if you steel yourself
and push open the door, *space* is exactly what you think of—the
distant windows of the neighbors trembling through the trees like

4

satellites, the jungle beneath your feet suddenly vanished into the dark. It has an unsettling effect, like if you stepped out, you would simply drift away into the darkness. In the five years we've been living here I've never seen Liam so much as glance at that door, but I've caught both Jack and Corinne lurking around it, and after I came downstairs one night and found the two of them perched in the open doorway, their toes lined up along the edge of that six-foot drop-off (I never was able to determine who was daring whom), I drilled two deadbolts into the frame at shoulder height. The previous owners had intended to build an addition, but they were waylaid by financial difficulties, and then some other mysterious tragedy that our realtor staunchly refused to reveal. "I don't have the details," she said in a meaningful tone that made us understand that (A) she was lying, and (B) if we knew what was good for us, we wouldn't ask. So we didn't.

And so it's here I decided to get to work, Arthur, to put something in the place of nothing. It was beautiful here on Sunday morning—the day of the accident—one of those balmy, deceptive days that seem to be, but are not, a prelude to spring; there's still a long ways to go. I spent nearly all of it outside, carving away the winter-thinned thicket around the back of our foundation with a chain saw I rented from Home Depot to make a twenty-by-thirty-foot footprint for my greenhouse. The ironic nature of my undertaking was obvious to me long before I went inside for lunch and listened to Liam's cracks about the marauding botanist laying waste to the local flora. The truth is, I could hardly hear them—the cracks, I mean. After the first hour or so spent in the din of that raging saw, I felt as though my own head had turned into a silo—my thoughts boomeranging around inside its walls, everything on the outside diminished to faint and muffled reverberations. And here I will confess to exactly what I once angrily denied: that I thought of you, and not just in passing, but over and over again. I thought of you until I couldn't think of anything else, and eventually, I stopped thinking at all.

Nothing I've ever done in my life has been as hard as slinging that chain saw around. The sap was surging up in all the branches and shoots, and every one of them fought back. As the afternoon passed, I felt the sky slipping down notch by notch, settling like a gray slab onto my shoulders, but even with that reminder I still forgot. I forgot to look up. In our kitchen, there's a bulletin board with a calendar hanging on it. All the Spaceco launch dates are emblazoned with Technicolor rocket stickers—Jack and Liam's handiwork. Counting off the days between the launches and sticking them up there started out as an exercise to help Jack keep better track of time. (He still seems, without fail, to end up shortchanged by week's end.) Jack has an unnerving, almost autistic devotion to this ritual. Those stickers *have* to go up on the first day of the month when we change the calendar page; otherwise he gets spectacularly anxious. Why this is, he can't, or won't, tell us. We forgot one time, a couple of months ago in February, *I* forgot. I flipped the page without thinking. The next night I came downstairs and found him sleepwalking through the kitchen in his softball T-shirt and his underwear. Every single drawer and cupboard had been opened, and his hands were full of rubber bands and thumbtacks. Corinne is the only one who seems to understand this superstition. Corinne, of all people—who would win World's Most Pragmatic Five-Year-Old if such an award existed. She promised to explain it to me once, in strictest confidence, and then, when I squatted down next to her, she cupped both hands around my ear, deliberated for a moment, and then leaned forward and whispered: "It's very complicated. I don't think I can tell you."

But I'm guilty too. Somewhere in there, I fell into my own superstitious ritual. On launch mornings, while Jack and Corinne are squabbling over the selection of cereal (all of it nutritious, all of it ho-hum), I linger in the kitchen, staring out the window up into Michigan's infernal never-ending cloud cover. I press my thumb against one of those stickers, like a talisman, the symbol of the day's coming gamble. It is as close as I will come to acknowledging that our state of grace might not last. Maybe you won't admit it, but I think you'll understand. I certainly know better. It's like knocking on wood, like throwing salt over your shoulder, like holding your breath as you jam down the accelerator and sail through an intersection while the light turns red. As though a gesture could save anyone—in this universe where even the smallest pieces are hurtling away from one another at the speed of light.

That's all, then. Or all I can say right now.

What say you?

Rhetorically,
Jess

From: Jessica Frobisher <jfrobisher@umich.edu>
Sent: Monday, March 17, 2014 11:57 pm
To: Arthur Danielson <danielsav@umich.edu>
Cc:
Bcc:
Subject: One more thing

Hey,

I just thought you might want to know that there's something wrong with your out-of-office message. The auto-reply is bouncing back a stream of gobbledygook—lines of numbers and &s and antiparentheses))((. It looks like the code Liam used to write for rockets on his old hulky mad-scientist computer, back when it was a labor of love for him, when we were living on beautiful hypotheticals. The language of spaceships, Li used to tell me, has a God-like logic, a rigorous, elegant syntax. It contains subsets inside subsets inside subsets that loop on into infinity. Every query is paired with an answer, every *if* with a *then*.

But not anymore. Arthur, yesterday morning, while I was brushing my teeth, I looked out the window and discovered three TV vans parked at the end of our driveway. Right at the bottom of the hill—they were clearly visible through that tree cluster there, which is still bare and leaves us exposed. One of the vans was from FOX News. Talk about adding insult to injury. I couldn't stop staring at them. I stared at them while I tapped my toothbrush against the sink for five minutes, and then I went downstairs to stare at them from the sidelight next to the front door. You know how mirages disappear when you get closer to them? These didn't. The CNN crew had some sort of miniature grill out, and they were barbecuing what appeared to be breakfast sausages.

Out of everything in that surreal moment, it was the sausages, for some reason, that assured me I wasn't dreaming. It was still five-something out in Arizona where Liam is now doing triage, so after I texted him, I went around the house lowering all the blinds, starting at the front of the house and working my way around. Then, when the Fair and Balanced cameraman had gone out for a Dunkin' Donuts run, I squirreled Jack and Corinne into the back of the Acura and went to Home Depot to return the chain saw. I had kept it five days longer than I was supposed to, and there was a zillion-dollar replacement charge on Liam's AmEx.

By the time we came back, the vans were gone, but there's no telling for how long.

Look, I'm going to come out and just say it now: Arthur, will you please, please write me back?

Over and out,
~J

From: Jessica Frobisher <jfrobisher@umich.edu>
Sent: Wednesday, March 19, 2014 2:09 am
To: Arthur Danielson <danielsav@umich.edu>
Cc:
Bcc:
Subject: Corrections

Dear Arthur,

So two auto-replies got bounced back from my last e-mail, a day's space between them—the garbled original version followed by a corrected version with every comma perfectly in place. I take this to mean that you are checking in, that you are alive and reading this, even if you won't write me back. Fair enough. I haven't forgotten that silence was our agreement, or our disagreeable understanding. Just remember that you broke it first.

Of course, maybe it means no such thing. Maybe all it means is that some technocrat puttering around behind the scenes found and deleted an error in a line of code, or that someone, somewhere rebooted a server. These kinds of processes are, and remain, stubbornly mysterious to me. It's my own fault. All those times I tuned out Liam's explanations. All those wasted meetings with holier-than-thou IT Bob—remember those? Back in the planning stages of the BioSys database when he wanted to elaborate on his theories about the "architecture" of the information? I would try to care for about five minutes, and then I would just give up. Now it's too late, and I just have to fake it.

But then I wonder about a lot of things these days, now of all times—"when thinking is pretty much useless." That last line is a direct quote from Paula. A woman who makes her living from scanning people's brains, who shuts them up in a tube and then commands them to add 1,552 and 397 and list synonyms for the word *sad*. When she saw me setting down my coffee mug and opening up my mouth to respond, she hurriedly added: "I mean *your* kind of thinking, Jess. Sometimes people just need to concentrate on putting one foot in front of the other and forget everything else." Ever the dutiful sister, Paula has taken a few weeks off from work, abandoned her beloved MRI machine, and driven up from South Carolina to minister to us in our hour of need. This ministering takes the form of cleaning our out-of-control closets and tending to our incessant phone, a full-time job in and of itself these days. Reporters and anonymous busybodies don't scare Paula a whit. She taught Corinne and Jack the phrase "No comment," and they love it. It's bulletproof, new in the repertoire, better than the threadbare "I'm rubber, you're glue," the tired "I know you are but what am I," and the reliable old standby, "I forgot."

But "pretty much useless" or no, that doesn't stop me. I don't believe I've been to Zingerman's since last year, when you and I used to get coffee there, but last Friday, between classes, I walked over to Kerrytown. By the time I climbed the stairs and stepped into the deli's half gloom, I'd completely forgotten what it was I'd come there for. I fingered the golden bottles of imported olive oil, the dusty bread rounds. I dallied in front of the dessert case, eyeing all those jeweled fruit tarts while people streamed in and out of the door behind me, my arms tucked behind my back, shuffling my feet in a silly, adolescent, pining sort of way. A man behind the counter was flaying a salmon in knife flashes so deft, so graceful, that the gestures looked a work of art—the slithering red flesh between his fingers, the silvery scales raining down around his ankles and collecting in the cuffs of his blue jeans. I am not pining away for anything. I would like to make that clear. But I never did remember what I wanted. Finally I gave up and bought a $10 rosemary baguette and a weedy gladiolus from the display by the door. Plants are like puppies to me—as you know. It's impossible for me to pass them by, especially the scruffy, rough-around-the-edges ones.

I was walking back to campus, baguette under one arm, gladiolus under the other, when a woman wearing a blue velvet jacket accosted me on the sidewalk. "Jess?" she said. "Jess, is that you?" I had never laid eyes on this woman before, I swear to God, but there she was, holding onto my sleeve and pinning me down as if she had some sort of claim on me. Paula was right. If I hadn't been distracted by all those useless thoughts, I might have been quick enough to sidestep her, but it was too late, I was trapped. I know I'm paranoid about people thinking I'm standoffish, but it's not intentional. Remember that time we went out to lunch a few years ago? That time you snuck a tortilla chip onto the shoulder of my sweater while we were walking back to campus, and I traipsed along like an idiot for I don't know how many blocks before I looked down and noticed it there? Well, laugh if you will, but it's only gotten worse, and in the past couple of weeks I stopped even caring—when I see people coming for me all I want is to get away, before someone tells me something else I don't want to hear.

So I didn't even bother to feign recognition, to try to feel my way into the conversation, groping discreetly for clues, the way you're supposed to. I just stared blankly at her. Blue Velvet Lady was positively shimmering in that jacket, but it was waaaay too cold for something that thin. My baguette knuckles were turning bright red.

"Jess, Jess," she said, shaking my elbow as though she were trying to resuscitate me. "I heard what happened. I read that article in the *Post*, and when I saw how they quoted Liam, I told Mike—"

"I'm sorry," I cut her off. "I think you've mistaken me for someone else. My name is Priscilla." Priscilla is the name of Corinne's latest imaginary friend, the newest member of her coterie—an exceptional collection of individuals, so my daughter tells me. I have no idea what possessed me to say it. But I didn't wait for a response. I just put my head down and kept walking into the wind. By the time I got back to my office, the baguette was nearly broken in half—I'd been throttling it that hard. So I threw it into the trash, that stupid ten-dollar loaf of bread.

"Well, who was she?" Liam said later that night. We were on our way to Detroit—running late for Liam's nine p.m. flight to Tucson. I was the one behind the wheel. Everyone on 94 drives like they want desperately to die; they can't even be bothered to hide it, and I prefer my own scuttling, tail-between-my-legs defensiveness to Liam's go-for-broke maneuvers, thank you very much.

"I just told you I don't know," I said. "If I knew who she was, why would I have told her my name was Priscilla?"

"Well, she's sure as hell going to wonder about that the next time we run into her," Liam said. "Jesus Christ, Jess."

Which is true, but this is the least of our worries. It was only the beginning of a disastrous conversation, which became more disastrous with each passing mile. We were discussing what we should tell our children—whether to lie to them, whether to come clean, and if so, how much. Corinne is still safe, I think, but someone will say something to Jack—a teacher, some little know-it-all runt on the bus. It's only a matter of time.

There's something about trying to sum up your own take on a terrible truth, when you have to pare it down to something a five-year-old and a ten-year-old can—I was going to say "understand," but that isn't the right word, it isn't even close. It reminds you that you don't know shit. I was in favor of "Certain things are nobody's fault." Liam was more in line with "Human error inevitably makes its way into all our best efforts." Barreling along at seventy miles an hour on the freeway, we were going round and round about semantics and I don't even want to think about what else until Liam finally slammed his hand on the dashboard and said, "Tell them whatever you want, Jess, tell them whatever you want."

Pretty much useless, all this, I guess. I wonder how you are, you and your elegant pines. That adjective is yours, and I think of it from time to time. Pines *are* elegant—none of that deciduous fuss and muss. The days up there are probably still—what?—seven hours long, but the sap has probably already started rising. You might tell me, you know, if you felt so inclined, but maybe you don't.

Anyway.
Jess

From: Jessica Frobisher <jfrobisher@umich.edu>
Sent: Saturday, March 22, 2014 5:46 am
To: Arthur Danielson <danielsav@umich.edu>
Cc:
Bcc:
Subject: Re: synonyms for sad

There are forty-four, according to Merriam-Webster. You fell way short of that, and I beat you by two—only after *dolorous* came to me in a flash of inspiration during my drive home. It's probably best if we don't compare lists and don't go back to see exactly which ones we missed, no? There was no insinuation in that deciduous remark of mine, none whatsoever. Ha! Seriously though, Arthur, watching the trees, I am struck by what a messy and arduous business it is. That's all I meant. Forcing those buds out every spring, thousands of them, only to lose them all when the fall rolls around again. Not for the faint of heart.

I did put your question to Paula. There was a man once who came up with fifty-one synonyms, she said. That's the record. He was forty-three years old, she said, and in the throes of such despair that he was no longer even able to tie his own shoes. When they stuck him in the MRI machine they saw that the topography of his brain was riddled with dark pockets, like shantytowns—whole neighborhoods that had just gone off the grid. My sister delivers anecdotes like these with an admirable matter-of-factness.

Glad to hear the work is going well, O man of few words.

From the woman of many.

~j

From: Jessica Frobisher <jfrobisher@umich.edu>
Sent: Monday, March 24, 2014 11:02 pm
To: Arthur Danielson <danielsav@umich.edu>
Cc:
Bcc:
Subject: Re: marauding and other activities

Believe it or not, yes. If Liam had time these days to be anything other than frantic, he would probably be mildly annoyed to discover that the greenhouse is the one thing I've actually made progress on during the past week. I wrote myself a greenhouse to-do list and taped it up on the calendar, smack dab on top of all of Jack's rocket stickers. (I can't look at those gaudy little spaceships without feeling queasy.) Every day I force myself to accomplish one thing on that list, even if it's nothing more than running outside after dusk and scooping up a few armfuls of that brush I chain-saw-massacred back on the day of the accident, stuffing it into a Hefty, and lugging it down to the bottom of the hill so the trash guys can come haul it away.

For a while there, Arthur, I didn't even need a flashlight. The news vans out on the street had set up these floodlamps at night, and they would emanate this unearthly light through the trees, like a space station straight out of one of Jack's sci-fi books. Thank God that's over. (They did have this certain eerie allure, but the ambient lighting was starting to wreak circadian havoc. I was forced to buy blackout curtains for Jack, whose room faces the street, the heavy-duty kind they market to truckers and ER doctors.) What with that and all the traffic, we're probably on some sort of neighborhood hit list.

I guess the point of this is to say, I'm working hard to get back in the habit of keeping promises to myself. I just had no idea it was going to be this difficult to get back on the wagon.

Quitting now,
Jess

From: Jessica Frobisher <jfrobisher@umich.edu>
Sent: Tuesday, March 25, 2014 2:49 pm
To: Arthur Danielson <danielsav@umich.edu>
Cc:
Bcc:
Subject: Speaking of Sasquatch

Liam's not a fan of the greenhouse. I was pretty sure you knew that already. The plans I drew up were, yes, a little extravagant, and my husband isn't crazy about extravagant ideas unless they're his, in which case he's all for them. Back when I pitched the greenhouse to him, when I cornered him in the bathroom while he brushed his teeth and told him that I wanted to pull a few grand from our IRA to build it, he listened patiently to all my selling points and their exclamation points (fresh lettuce in December! heirloom tomatoes all year round! a space to breed my own orchids!) and then let out a long sigh. "I don't know, Jess," he said. "It's not such a great time to take on that kind of big project, is it? Don't we have a lot of things going on right now?"

"If by 'a lot of things' you're referring to my second job as a minivan chauffeur," I said, "the answer is yes."

"I'm talking about your work. Your *science*." Liam leaned over and spat matter-of-factly into the sink. "It's just not the most practical thing. That's all I'm saying. Not to mention that the seals around all those glass panes are going to hemorrhage heat in the winter. Even with the best insulating you can find, I can't imagine what it

16

will do to our energy bills. We'll have a Sasquatch-size carbon footprint. I thought you loved the environment."

"Never mind," I said, turning around to leave.

"Jess," he said. "*Jess.*" He was saying my name in that way I hate, that tone of voice that makes it sound like a call to reason, so I just waved my hand and kept walking.

"I'm not saying no," he called after me. "For the record."

For the record, I have to go. Go forth and give those trees some tough love.

Jess

From: Jessica Frobisher <jfrobisher@umich.edu>
Sent: Thursday, March 27, 2014 11:01 pm
To: Arthur Danielson <danielsav@umich.edu>
Cc:
Bcc:
Subject: Bad fences

But you have to admit that he has a point about the carbon footprint. I haven't figured out a way around that problem. I don't think there is one. This issue takes us back to our good old discussion about selfish gratification versus hypothetical greater good—that one where we were pretending to have a debate about the climate change problem while we were actually talking about something else. I'm tired of that conversation. We're not going to agree. We're not even going to be able to agree to disagree. Can we please talk about something else?

For example: I think our paparazzi friends are gone for good. The last of them pulled up stakes yesterday, leaving our street with an eerily abandoned feeling.

I finished clearing out the thicket behind our dining room door, and yesterday I began stripping off the sod. Winter hasn't decamped entirely. You could see these silver glints of deep freeze in the grass's roots, like little shards of granite. But I managed OK. I sectioned it off in pieces, handed over the smallest strips to Corinne and Jack, and they ran back and forth between the wheelbarrows, their arms full of rumpled squares of terra firma, like green and brown quilts, while Paula watched us skeptically from the dining room window. I've told Jack and Corinne that we're going to have our own jungle garden. Orchids and orange trees and gardenias and roses hanging from the ceiling. It gets more lavish with each iteration. Butterflies will be considered; parrots have received the parental veto. The realization of such a thing cannot possibly be as beautiful as its imagining, of course. I'm perfectly well aware of this fact, and I do not need Paula to point it out to me. I just think we should enjoy whatever diversions we can find these days, wherever we find them. If this is an indication of some deeper lurking pathology, so be it. I picked Jack up after school this afternoon. When I pulled up into the parking lot, I saw him between the school buses before he saw me. He was standing with one hand on the playground hurricane fence, face turned toward the sky. He was tracking the path of a distant jet overhead with a troubled expression. He'd forgotten to zip up his backpack; everything was avalanching out of the sides of it, and the kids were running past, flick, flick, flick, like he wasn't even there.

We had almost finished, and I was bent over the wheelbarrow, loading up the last of the dirt, when I heard Corinne say, "Hi, Mrs. Hollins." I looked up, and sure enough there was our neighbor, coming out of the trees at the edge of our yard. At the sound of

Corinne's voice she sucked in her breath, straightened up, and stepped backward, as though she were going to try to pull a Glinda the Good Witch disappearing trick and shimmer away into the camouflage of the maple trees. (This is, I think, Corinne's most longed-for superpower.)

Our neighbor kept shifting around like she was under some sort of duress. You could tell that there was nothing more than sheer bred-in-the-bone midwestern politeness holding her there, like a knife at her back. Saint Beth, I used to call her, at least until Liam started making catty meowing sounds when I said it. I think it's the combination of her painterly red-gold ringlets—her highlights really do look gilded—and her overwhelming (perhaps creepy?) sincerity. Beth has a trampoline and five or six nieces and nephews that look as though they've been mail-ordered from a J.Crew catalog. She and her husband Jim are sans children, and Arthur, you don't have to know the two of them for longer than five minutes to understand that this state of affairs is one of life's Disappointments with a capital D, the kind of thing you don't get over.

Beth barely looked at Corinne. This from a woman who *couldn't get enough* of my daughter last Halloween. (Have I told you this story already? Corinne was Sleeping Beauty and Beth was Cinderella, and I thought I was going to be stuck there on the stoop listening to the princess powwow all night. Finally I had to orchestrate our getaway by looking at my watch and reminding Corinne that midnight was only four hours away and we had to let Beth get to the ball before her Toyota Corolla turned back into a pumpkin. *Meow, hiss*, said Liam when I told him.)

It was clear that Beth didn't want to make eye contact with me either, although you had to hand it to her, she was making a valiant effort. She said brightly, "Oh, hi, Jess. I didn't see you guys."

"Everything OK?" I said, because I could tell by her wavering gaze that it wasn't. I was wondering if I should offer an apology for the TV van jamboree that had been going on for the past couple of weeks, the spectacle that's been clogging up our neighborhood thoroughfare and impeding the eight-to-five commute of our respectable fellow citizens. (We seem to be surrounded by attorneys.) I was under orders from Liam not to—apologize, that is. "Those neighbors are surrounded by TV cameramen," he said. "For God's sake, don't say anything that could be misconstrued."

Only here I was, Arthur, looking at Beth, and thinking we'd played our hand wrong.

"It's nothing," she said. "Ollie got out again. He must have pulled the stake on his chain out. I'll find him."

"Ollie ran away?" Jack said. His voice gave a mournful little quaver at the end of the question. He's been moody—by Jack standards, which is to say *extremely*—since the accident, and I couldn't tell whether he was getting warmed up for the next calamity or just picking up on our sweet neighbor's sudden coldness.

"I'm sure he's around here somewhere," I said. Ollie, Arthur, is an English bulldog with a decidedly American obesity problem. I was thinking that it would have been impossible for him to *run* anywhere. He couldn't have pulled off anything faster than a double-time waddle, tops. I started peeling off my gardening gloves in an effort to appear helpful and neighborly. "You want us to help look for him? Jack could run down to the end of the street and see—"

"Please don't bother," she interrupted me. "I'm sure you're busy. Jessica—" She dropped her voice. "I hope you realize that we're all praying for you. With all our hearts." And with that, she turned around and disappeared back into the trees.

"What's *her* problem?" said Corinne, but I couldn't answer. My face was frozen in a tight smile, and I had to put down the wheelbarrow with exaggerated care in order not to dump it.

Look, I'm going to stop here and try calling Liam again.

More later, perhaps?

jf

From: Jessica Frobisher <jfrobisher@umich.edu>
Sent: Saturday, March 29, 2014 6:59 am
To: Arthur Danielson <danielsav@umich.edu>
Cc:
Bcc:
Subject: Re: report from the front lines

I know! I had no idea my neighbors were up to such a thing. Here I was thinking that Liam and I were living in an enclave of staunch secular humanists and rabid Dawkins-style atheists.

I'm joking, of course, but all of this is about as funny as a punch in the face. What do people think? They think we've blown a bunch of innocent people to smithereens—that's what they think. And they're right, aren't they? The hows and the whys don't matter. Like any good liberal, I'm a firm believer in mitigating circumstances, but more and more, Arthur, I think it's possible that we're beyond those now.

Not that I know squat about those hows or whys. I'm not sure how much Liam does either—he's probably still knee-deep in spaceship rubble. So to answer your (carefully neutral) question: no news. Calls from Li these days are like catching a train. If you miss one, there's nothing you can do but wait for the next one. Remember that year when Liam was practically living in Tucson—how I used to kid about performing my own modern-day rain dance? Only instead of rain, I'd dance for phone calls? It was barely a joke. There were evenings when I'd be downstairs in the kitchen, practically doing a little shuck and jive with the phone in one hand, beseeching the satellite dish gods up there in the heavens to shower me with phone calls from Liam.

Now it's even worse. I'm so completely at the mercy of that stupid phone. I have it with me and on at all times. I put it on the toilet tank while I'm showering, and on the dashboard while I'm driving, and on the podium during class while I'm doing what you used to call (fondly, I think?) my hector and lecture. I put it on Liam's pillow while I'm sleeping, and as soon as I lurch awake, I grab it and stare at its evil little eye, waiting for it to blink with a message that's almost never there. I feel like Janus—like I've grown another set of eyes and ears, a face always trained somewhere else, somewhere I am not.

Now that I've written this, I realize that, of course, this comparison is apt in more ways than one.

But I have to go.

Jess

From: Jessica Frobisher <jfrobisher@umich.edu>
Sent: Monday, March 31, 2014 10:14 am
To: Arthur Danielson <danielsav@umich.edu>
Cc:
Bcc:
Subject: Turning of the screws

Goodbye, gymnosperms. In Botany 102, it's now all angiosperms,
all the time, for the next four weeks. I have a captive
audience—157 warm undergraduate bodies this semester—and I
am free to impose my tastes mercilessly upon them. Back in my
own undergraduate days, I took this dreadful intro lit class. The
professor was about a hundred years old and he made us read
nothing but Henry James for, well, it *felt* like months on end.
When the semester was finally over, I ripped out the pages of
Portrait of a Lady one at a time and used them to mulch a tray of
begonias. That was before I discovered orchids. Those begonias
were extraordinary—a purple so intense that looking at them
could make you ache. I still remember the painful feeling things
like that used to give me—like there was this certain
overwhelming profuseness to the world, a certain too-muchness.
I was twenty years old and torn between the desire to devour it all
and the need to avert my eyes, to look away.

And now look at how things have changed. Last year, someone
complained on one of my 230 evaluations that I have a tendency
to belabor some of my points—"beating a dead horse" was how it
was put, I believe. Yes, well, OK. I'm still using Mauseth's ancient
third edition; yesterday in class I made everyone open up to page
427, and I read the passage about endogenous rhythms out loud to
them, the entire page: "If the plants are placed in continuous dark,
the leaflet position continues to change, returning to the up
position about every 24 hours. In many flowers, the production of
nectar and fragrance is also controlled by an endogenous rhythm

and occurs periodically even in uniform, extended dark conditions." Do you know what this tells us? I said to them. It tells us that there's this mechanism, that plants have an innate sense of time. That they track its passing even in the dark, even out in space, I said, *and we don't know how they do it*. Think about that, I said.

I doubt any of them did, beyond taking snarky mental notes about my blunders—my repetitions, my breathless, unprofessional enthusiasm. Here's something I don't think I've ever told you: one morning last spring, maybe a week before I went out to Arizona to watch Liam get shot up into space, I snuck into the back of one of your Plant Bio lectures. I only meant to hunker down in one of those clanky, threadbare seats for five minutes or so and then be stealthily on my way. I ended up staying the entire hour. I watched you stroll unselfconsciously from one end of the stage to the other, rubbing your nose thoughtfully from time to time as you spoke. You were talking about evolution. "A dialectic process" is what you called it. *Lecture* isn't really the right word for what you were doing. It was more like watching someone thinking out loud, or like walking through the park early in the morning when the sun's coming up. You know how you see those people running lay-ups? That singular rhythm they fall into with the ball, skimming back and forth across the lines when the courts are empty and they think no one else is there? That's what I remember—how generous you seemed, how candid, nothing overdone, nothing withheld. *Organisms find a way to the light, or they learn to produce their own light, or they teach themselves to survive without it.* You were wearing a pale blue dress shirt with a grass stain on the tail. A completely extraneous detail, but I kept recalling it later that night when I couldn't sleep. Pangs of self-doubt kept me propped up on my elbows, checking the clock on the nightstand. And Arthur, I know you won't believe me—as glaringly obvious as it was, I still failed to grasp the exact nature of the problem.

There's something else I wanted to ask you, but I don't have time now, so

mORE LATER,
jESS

From: Jessica Frobisher <jfrobisher@umich.edu>
Sent: Tuesday, April 1, 2014 12:46 am
To: Arthur Danielson <danielsav@umich.edu>
Cc:
Bcc:
Subject: Re:

_____

That wasn't what I was going to ask you, but it's funny you guessed that. I'm sitting in it right now, writing you this, diligently ignoring the forty-seven lab notebooks I have left to grade. Your office was supposed to be on loan to a visiting scholar from Taiwan . . . I'm drawing a blank on his name. The one who published that amazing paper about luminosity in mushrooms in _Nature_ and then he bailed and two GSIs were trying to get dibs on it, but that fell through too, so right now it's _inocupado_. Which is hard to believe given that it's prime Angell Hall real estate with all that professorial early morning light. I still have that key you illegally copied for me, after my office flooded, and so I've been sneaking in here, looking surreptitiously over my shoulder while I unlock the door and let myself in. It's like time has stood still in here—there are the boxes of pinecones you've left behind, and the single Guinness bottle hidden at the bottom of the recycling bin, under a bunch of last year's syllabuses. There's my fisherman's sweater, which I'd hung on the back of your door, and completely forgotten. There's your half-scribbled Post-it notes, one of which just has the word _fuck_ written on it and underlined twice, and I go

25

back and forth between thinking I know exactly what you were thinking when you wrote it, and then thinking no, I don't. I'll admit that I do touch your things, Arthur, but I'm always careful to put them back.

I had been priding myself on my stealth, thinking I'd gone a semester and a half without anyone once seeing me go in or out, but yesterday morning I was sitting in here, leafing distractedly through one of your books, when suddenly someone knocked on the door. The sound of it startled me completely out of proportion to what it should have. I froze in your desk chair, with my feet on your desk. Then I told myself not to be ridiculous and I marched over to the door and flung it open.

There stood Moira. I can't quite describe the look she had on her face. I'm well versed in your complaints about Moira—the way she holds us hostage at those interminable staff meetings, that she forces us all to wear "Hello My Name Is _____" nametags at the welcome week barbeques. I actually don't give a shit about those nametags. No, what gets me about Moira is that unnerving way she has of noticing things that have nothing to do with her. I don't know if you remember that holiday party a few years ago, the one I brought Corinne to. She must have just turned two. I had passed her around to about a dozen people, and she had taken it like a champ—completely unfazed by all the manhandling, the scratchy velvet dress, the strangers snagging her tights with the clasps of their wristwatches. And then you came up to me—you reached out with your most irresistible smile to take a turn—and my angelic toddler let out an enraged scream and grabbed my neck in such a punishing chokehold that for a second I really thought she was going to strangle me. Remember? Moira was standing right behind you, glittery-eyed with merlot, and she started laughing. "Look at him blushing," she said. "You'd better watch out, Arthur, she's onto you." I was struck by a sudden paranoia; I couldn't bring myself to look up

26

and see if you were blushing or not. I didn't know if you'd even heard her. You never mentioned it.

"Hi Jess," Moira said. "I thought I might find you here. There was a student hanging around your office, hoping to catch you. You want me to send him over here, or tell him to come back later?"

"I'll be there in a sec," I said. My office hours had been over for forty-five minutes, and unlike you, Mr. Two Time Golden Apple Award Winner, I make it a point not to be at my students' beck and call. But I was discomfited into being obliging. It wasn't just that I had been caught squatting in your office either. The day before yesterday, I was bcc'd on an e-mail thread—accidentally, I think. I'm getting paranoid again. Since Liam and I don't have the same last name, not everyone is aware of my connection to the accident. Most of the talk right now is focused on three crème de la crème computer science kids who were supposed to graduate from U of M's engineering school a year ago but signed with Spaceco instead. I couldn't tell who else exactly had gotten the e-mail, and I was wondering if you had seen it. I'm afraid to ask anyone else.

Did I mention that I'm paranoid?

Moira had already started off down the hall ahead of me, but then she turned around again. She tucked her hair behind her ear. All her nails were perfectly done, and that, for me, is always a strike against a woman. Go ahead and tell me that's petty. "Oh," she said. "I've been meaning to ask you, and I keep forgetting. How's Arthur doing?"

"I hear he's great," I said. I looked down and realized I was still holding the book of yours I'd been flipping through. Of all things: Mary Oliver's *New and Selected Poems*. "Global warming's been hell on the pines."

27

Well, Arthur—how are you? Inquiring minds want to know. I have forty-seven ungraded lab notebooks and miles to go before I sleep, so that's all for now.

Over and out,
~j

From: Jessica Frobisher <jfrobisher@umich.edu>
Sent: Wednesday, April 2, 2014 3:17 am
To: Arthur Danielson <danielsav@umich.edu>
Cc:
Bcc:
Subject: Fw: Fw: Have you seen this?!

Well, in that case, here it is. Scroll all the way down. The link's at the very bottom.

The truth is, I haven't either. Read much about it, I mean. I keep starting to and then I have to stop. My home page was set to Google's news site, but I changed it a day or two after the accident when *Spaceco* started showing up as one of the most-searched terms—every time I saw it I would break out in a cold sweat. I guess that's why it took me so long to see this.

Spaceco records all its launches. There are thirty-four video cameras mounted around the site at different locations. Most of them are surveillance-type jobbies with no audio. They render the Arizona desert in austere gradations of moony silver, like one of those old nitrate photographs, and everything in them has a surreal, poetic clarity to it. The spire of the shuttle looms in the distance, like a tower in a fairy tale. Every now and then, an anomalous rodent or a lizard creeps along the bottom of the

28

screen. I remember how you once dismissively spoke of space—*nothing grows out there*—but if you'd seen what I'd seen, Arthur, you would understand, you would have to acknowledge the force of this awe, like it or not, and the brilliant human will behind it.

Those cameras captured the disaster from thirty-four different angles but it all occurs in absolute silence, in pristine flashes of light, like a star rupturing in a distant galaxy or a flower unfolding in one of those time-elapse sequences. It's strangely undramatic. I suppose that's why CNN bought this footage from one of the space groupies who was there at the time. There's a club that comes to the launches—thirteen or fourteen men, all retired engineers and pilots. I saw them when I was out there last spring with Liam. They park their vans along the Spaceco property line, pull out lawn chairs, eat sandwiches, count down, and chat with one another in their bewildering lingua franca of Mach numbers and thrust. Someone posted it on YouTube and there it is, you can't get away, you can't escape: the jarring blue sky swings back and forth, the dust actually shakes loose, rushes up from the earth. "Oh shit," says the cameraman, "oh shit," and someone else runs through the shot with his arms over his head like the world is ending. It *is* ending. You can hear the sky fucking falling around them in these weird, unearthly pitches, like mortar shelling—but never mind, you don't need me to tell you. Watch it for yourself.

I don't even know who Terrence Katz is. I had to look him up in the directory. He's an adjunct in the Physics Department. I don't know what he's doing, mass-forwarding his colleagues this kind of unsolicited carnage. Aren't we all already up to our ears in calamities? The e-mail showed up in my in-box ten minutes before my 126 lecture.

Instead of heading out to class, I settled down into my chair and began drafting a scathing reply about the appropriate use of university e-mail. I spent half an hour, honing all the sentences in my diatribe, like a set of knives. I copied Bill Delaney and one of the policy people over in IT, and Dori Jackson over in Legal. But then I didn't send it. I got afraid. I think that's the right word. I have this feeling, Arthur, that I no longer have a leg to stand on.

I'm going to try sleeping again. You know what they say. If at first you don't succeed, try a Nyquil-and-single-malt-scotch cocktail.

Just kidding.

Jess

----- Original Message -----
From: Terrence Katz <terrlkatz @umich.edu>
Sent: Tuesday, March 23, 2014 10:02 am
To: Patricia Freer <frepatric@umich.edu>
Cc: Stan McKeldin <stanlmckel@umich.edu>, Virginia Nguyen <nguyenvir@umich.edu>, Elinor Dupree <duprelin@umich.edu>
Bcc: Jessica Frobisher <jfrobisher@umich.edu>
Subject: Fw: Fw: Re: Fw: Have you seen this?!

>Just curious—was I the last person in the world to see this?
> Words fail . . .

>> ----- Original Message -----
>>From: Mark Veizaga <mark.l.veizaga@gmail.com>
>>Sent: Tuesday, March 25, 2014 8:02 am
>>To: Rachel Willis <willisra@umich.edu>
>>Cc:
>>Bcc:
>>Subject: Fw: Re: Fw: Have you seen this?!

>> My darling metaphysician,
>>
>>I know you've been up to your ravishing neck in elegies, so I
>>thought I would send
 >>you this, just in case you somehow missed it. Remember
>>Trevor's kid? He was one of the wunderboys who signed w/
>>Spaceco last Apr. The last time I saw him, he was a gangly kid
>>doing backflips off the trampoline. None of us could have
>>predicted that he would go on to a brief & brilliant career of
>>blowing up spaceships.
>>
>>Can't wait to see you. Don't forget to tell the Reverend Donne
>>that you've got other plans this weekend. I don't care if it
>>makes him jealous. I hope it does.
>>
>>xoxoxo (and then some),
>>Mark

>>> ----- Original Message ------
>>>From: Mark Veizaga <mark.l.veizaga@gmail.com>
>>>Sent: Monday, March 24, 2014 11:47 pm
>>>To: Daniel Smallwood <Daniel.Smallwood@stanford.edu>
>>>Cc: Meenakshi Argawal <argawal47@nyu.edu>, Christine
>>>Liddel <littlechristie@comcast.net>, Russ Krauss <russell.
>>>krauss@mit.edu>, Ramona Gomez <rgomez@ngs.org>,
>>>Adam Foulds <afoulds@spaceadventures.com>
>>>Bcc:
>>>Subject: Re: Fw: Have you seen this?!

>>>Dan,
>>>
>>>Yup. Supposed to be class of '09, but Spaceco lured them away
>>>early with a signing bonus. An *undisclosed* amount. I don't
>>>know any more than that.

>>>
>>>The wheels of the gossip mill out there must be pretty
>>>gummed up if you're slumming around on Wikipedia. Next
>>>thing I know you'll be asking me for dirt on the SA deal. I
>>>don't know anything about that either, so better luck next
>>>time, pal.
>>>
>>>Tell Carol I say hey.
>>>
>>>mv

>>>>> ----- Original Mess
>>>>>From: Daniel Smallwood <Daniel.Smallwood@stanford.
>>>>>edu>
>>>>>Sent: Monday, March 24, 2014 11:31 pm
>>>>>To: Jennifer Scriber <scribegirl@yahoo.com>, Mark
>>>>>Veizaga <mark.l.veizaga@gmail.com>, Meenakshi
>>>>>Argawal <argawal47@nyu.edu>, Christine Liddel
>>>>><littlechristie@comcast.net>, Russ Krauss <russell.
>>>>>krauss@mit.edu>, Harry Ingram <ingramharold@gmail.
>>>>>com>, Ramona Gomez <rgomez@ngs.org>, Adam
>>>>>Foulds <afoulds@spaceadventures.com>
>>>>>Cc:
>>>>>Bcc:
>>>>>Subject: Fw: Have you seen this?!

>>>>>Think some of these spaceco guys are/were affiliated with
>>>>>U of M, but haven't been able to
>>>>>confirm yet. The Wikipedia spaceco page keeps >crashing.
>>>>>Mark—have you heard >>>yay or nay?

>>>>>What a f@*#ing horror show. If I were in Ann Arbor, I'd be
>>>>>buying a new suit and prepping for my Senate hearing,
>>>>>because that's where this is headed if the FAA is getting

>>>>>involved. Maybe they'll >>>televise it. Good tv—a refreshing
>>>>>change of pace!
>>>>>
>>>>>www.youtube.com/watch?v=sF42MelkZyKw

From: Jessica Frobisher <jfrobisher@umich.edu>
Sent: Thursday, April 3, 2014 9:16 pm
To: Arthur Danielson <danielsav@umich.edu>
Cc:
Bcc:
Subject: Re: some things, say the wise ones

Sure. If you give me the address, I'll send it. Hell, I'll even splurge
and send it first class. Media mail will take weeks. And I think it's
safe to say that by that time, anything could have happened.
Anything at all.

Jess

From: Jessica Frobisher <jfrobisher@umich.edu>
Sent: Saturday, April 5, 2014 1:32 am
To: Arthur Danielson <danielsav@umich.edu>
Cc:
Bcc:
Subject: Re: unnamed threats

Sorry. I didn't mean to sound so melodramatic. After Jack and
Corinne went to bed last night, I couldn't sleep, so I went

downstairs, steeled myself, and turned on the TV. I've been avoiding it for the last three weeks—not even the mindless enticement of *Dancing with the Stars* could tempt me to turn it on—and since I've been playing the role of *Mommy tyrannis*, no one else has been allowed to turn it on either. I know Paula's been sneaking it on when I'm not here, probably trying to assess the exact extent of the damage, maybe getting an idea of how well the TV cameras can see us from their vantage point down on the street. I know because I was standing next to the TV after I came home last Thursday, taking off my coat, and it shocked me on the elbow. Hard. When I put my hand on the screen, I could feel hot and prickly emanations.

"Who had the TV on?" I demanded. Corinne and Jack exchanged one eloquent, sidelong glance. Their telepathic exchange only took about a second, and then Corinne said, "No comment." I'd been totally outmaneuvered.

A correction here: I *thought* I had steeled myself. The shock hasn't even begun to wear off yet. When I was flipping past MSNBC and heard Lawrence O'Donnell saying the name of my husband's company, I felt a sickening thrill that made me jam my thumb down on the remote and go back. By that time one of the guests had interjected, a middle-aged guy sporting blue-rimmed glasses who looked frighteningly apoplectic, even by pundit standards, which should tell you something. He was practically yelling at O'Donnell and a silvery-haired woman with a severe expression who might have been Elizabeth Warren, but probably wasn't, and he was saying something along the lines of this:

"There are a million examples, but this whole Spaceco debacle is a perfect one. I'm not saying that people don't have the right to spend their money as they please. But doesn't part of you just want to say, 'Come on'? Do you really not have enough things here on Planet Earth to keep you entertained? Are you really that hard up for things to spend your money on? And it's not enough that they're doing this for kicks, they're putting innocent people at risk while they're doing it. That piece of wreckage fell within—what—fifty yards of I-8? Can you imagine if the wind had been blowing five to ten miles an hour harder? Maybe these people were fine with gambling their lives away, but that poor woman who was driving her kids home from day care after her shift at the Walmart, maybe she'd rather not be blown to smithereens by falling spaceship shrapnel—"

"Look," said the Elizabeth Warren doppelganger. "I get it. We are all seriously concerned about this. I have personally been in touch with the FAA, and an investigation is under way—"

There was more, but I was too nauseous to hear it. Instead I lay down on the floor and stared up at the ceiling. There were cracks up there I had never noticed before. They had an interesting pattern. They looked like rhizomes, Arthur, one shooting off into another.

"Hey," said Paula from the doorway, startling me. "Don't you have pay-per-view or something?" I'm not the only one who has problems sleeping. Insomnia runs in the family, or *insomno-mania*, as Liam likes to call it. When I can't fall asleep, I repot plants. When Paula can't fall asleep, she cooks. She'd been in the kitchen blasting the tops of half a dozen perfect miniature crèmes brûlée with a tiny torch of Liam's that she'd found in the garage.

"We need to paint in here desperately. How come you didn't say anything to me?" I said. "I know you noticed it. Blue or yellow? You tell me. You're the one with the good taste." I had to take a deep breath in order to cut off my own rambling and get to the point. Paula has zero tolerance when it comes to aimless yakking, a quality that's a little surprising in someone who spent five years working as a shrink. "Oh, and by the way. They're talking about a federal investigation."

"She's a politician, Jess." Paula flopped down on the couch and flung out her legs. She had pilfered a pair of my blue jeans to wear while she and Corinne were papier-mâché-ing, and they were rolled up and spattered in a way that looked charming instead of like a disaster. My sister has lovely ankles, and whatever the elusive gene for that is, I did not inherit it. "Demanding investigations is part of the job description. Haven't you noticed that? It keeps them busy, so they don't have to actually *do* anything. If there's nothing to find, then they're not going to find it. " Her feet turned around and started heading back through the doorway. "Burgundy."

"What?" I said.

"I said, paint it burgundy. Now get off the floor and get it together."

Sound advice, Arthur, and I'm doing my best to take it.

Your
insomniac Jess

From: Jessica Frobisher <jfrobisher@umich.edu>
Sent: Monday, April 7, 2014 6:12 am
To: Arthur Danielson <danielsav@umich.edu>
Cc:
Bcc:
Subject: Re: cold turkey

So no more news just like that, huh? I find it hard to believe—you were such a junkie. Aren't your hands shaking? Don't you wake up in a cold sweat in your DNR cabin in the middle of the night, jonesing for a hit of Politico or the Huffington Post? I guess you weren't kidding. You really have turned over a new leaf. Congratulations. I think.

I suppose going cold turkey is easier when you're on the fringes of civilization. Despite my efforts at TV abstinence, we're still somehow absorbing the story, walking through an invisible cloud of it every day, like pollen, taking microscopic particles of anecdotes in through our pores.

Even Jack isn't immune. Earlier tonight while we were eating dinner, he looked up abruptly from his plateful of peas and said, "Did Dad know Oliver and Sam?"

Since you're going cold turkey, you probably won't know, but Oliver Keller and Samuel Allen were the two crew members aboard the *Titan* shuttle when it exploded. What took me aback wasn't that Jack had nailed down the names. It was the way he said them, "Oliver and Sam," like he knew them.

"I'm pretty sure he didn't, sweetie," I said. Which wasn't exactly true. Oliver was one of the guys who took Liam up into space last year. They were acquainted enough that Liam knew that Oliver had a golden retriever named Arnold. That, Arthur, was the only thing he said to me the night of the accident. We had both crawled back into bed, sometime around two a.m., and we were lying there staring at the ceiling. And out of nowhere, Liam said, "You know Oliver had a golden retriever named Arnold?" And neither of us said anything else. We just went back to staring at the clock.

Spaceco tried to hold on to the names of the victims as long as possible. They claimed it was because they wanted to make next-of-kin notifications. But it took about two hours before the press got hold of the names. Kelly Kahn, media mogul. Joseph Connelly, trust fund playboy. Daniel Goldstein, retired investment banker. And Uri Katamatov. Out of all of them Katamatov has been getting the most press. He was a twenty-eight-year-old tech genius who had been developing <u>these Internet glasses</u>—basically some sort of smartphone you wear that allows you to beam Yelp reviews and Wikipedia entries straight into the air in front of you. Omniscience at the touch of a button, like something out of one of Jack's beloved sci-fi books.

Goldstein's posthumous attention has been less glowing, thanks to an unfortunately-timed article that came out in the *Atlantic* the day after the accident, detailing his work in credit default swaps and their connection to the 2008 financial crisis.

So now you're up on all the details. More or less.

Until later,
Jess

From: Jessica Frobisher <jfrobisher@umich.edu>
Sent: Thursday, April 10, 2014 5:45 am
To: Arthur Danielson <danielsav@umich.edu>
Cc:
Bcc:
Subject: rude awakenings

Mary Oliver's winging her way to you as we speak, along with a (very small) bottle of Jack. When the lady at the post office asked me about liquid and perishable substances, I looked her straight in the eye and lied, thereby committing a federal offense. She said the package should be in Manitoba w/in a week. Look for it in your box.

Liam was supposed to fly back from Arizona on Monday night, but he was held up by some more unforeseen developments in the investigation ("Too complicated to get into," he said in a tight voice that translated into "Don't ask"). Then an ice storm hit early Tuesday morning, coming out of nowhere. Things were a little chaotic. I had made the mistake of predicting that school would be closed, but it wasn't. The Ann Arbor school system was opening right on time, never mind the solid half inch of ice on the roads. The bus was coming in twenty minutes, and Arthur, all of us looked like complete wrecks. I only had one sock on. Corinne's half-braided hair was unraveling. Jack smelled like little-boy funk. Getting him to take a shower is an ordeal to end all ordeals these days. I practically have to pick him up by the scruff of the neck, throw him into the bathroom, and slam the door shut behind me before he can claw his way back out.

Anyway, it was right then—with full-blown panic mode set in—that Corinne said something that made us forget all about the bus. She was standing at the upstairs window, twirling a Barbie around by its ratty hair, like a nunchaku. She said, "What's that?"

"Honey, we really don't have time—," I started to say, but Paula went to look too, and then Jack. Gritting my teeth, I brought up the rear. Sure enough, just where the driveway broke through the trees at the bottom of the hill, there was the front of a huge . . . something. A van maybe. A cloud of exhaust rising, silently, troublingly ghostlike, above the tree line told us someone was inside, and had been for quite sometime.

"It's just *sitting there*," Jack said.

Corinne had stopped twirling the pantsless Barbie. "Maybe it's a spy," she said.

"If he is, he's a pretty bad one." With her elbow, Paula wiped the window clear. All our speculations were fogging things up. "Do you think he knows we can see him?"

Jack was worming his way under my elbow by then, trying to get a better look, but I grabbed his arm and steered him away. He was still in his Transformers T-shirt, sporting holes in both armpits. All his hair was standing up in tufts. He looked like an urchin, a little boy straight out of *Oliver Twist*. "Go get dressed, Jack," I said.

"Why can't I see?"

"Go get dressed." I was squeezing him harder than I meant to, and I had to force myself to let go. I turned to Paula. "I'm going to see what it is."

"Hmm," was all she said, but even Paula's single syllables are expressive. "Should I arm you with a steak knife? Maybe we should just sit tight, Jess."

"Like prisoners? In our own house? For no good reason?" I was already thundering down the stairs. Liam has a monolithic pair of boots. They must have been manufactured in about 1965; the insides are slippery, polished by decades of man-sweat and wool socks. Wearing them is like walking around with bricks strapped to your feet—you feel an instant, crushing power with every step. I had already stepped into them and was yanking the salt-stiffened laces as tight as I could make them go. "I'll be back in two minutes." I made a V with my fingers and brandished them at Jack, who was glowering at me from the doorway. "Two minutes, Jack."

The driveway was a death trap, too treacherous to even attempt, so I clumped my way straight down the hill, through the lawn, shattering the grass under my feet. My hands were balled up in fists inside my pockets. Maybe it was the boots—it was like I was channeling Liam, the way he has of walking, the shortest distance between two points, shoulders thrown back. When I got to the trees at the bottom of the hill—a stand of unwanted birches that thrives unapologetically in our drainage ditch—I just plunged straight through them. All the branches were glittering like diamond chandeliers around my head, swinging perilously right at their breaking points. I was trying to push my way through them when I lost my footing, and away I went—slithering ungracefully out the other side onto the street. I barely managed to get my hands out in front of me to catch myself as I slammed against the side of the Hummer parked there. It was like body-slamming a tank.

There was a long, loud horror-movie scream with an absolutely exquisite trill at the end, and for a second I thought it had come from me, that both my wrists had shattered on impact—I keep accidentally reading articles about early-onset osteoporosis—but no, it wasn't. It was a woman inside the car, who I had scared the bejeezus out of. She threw open the passenger-side door and leaped out feetfirst. When she hit the pavement, she nearly lost her footing on the ice and went down before she caught herself, just in time. For a second neither of us could do anything. We just stood there, clutching our chests, gasping melodramatically, and staring at one another. She was taller than I am, a waifish woman in blue jeans, with a pixie cut and tiny silver studs, like braille, adorning the curves of her ears. She looked like a Sarah Lawrence graduate student. Not a trench coat in sight. All in all, a pretty disappointing spy.

She was the first to regain the power of speech. "I'm sorry," she said. "Oh my God. That was so unnecessary. Screaming like that. What a junior high school stunt. Are you OK?" She slapped the Hummer's monstrous hood a couple of times and whistled out between her teeth.

I said the first thing I could think of. "Nice Hummer."

"Thanks." She was either oblivious to my sarcasm or pretending to be. "Believe it or not, there was a screwup at the rental-car place. I thought I would go with it. Because hell, who *doesn't* want asphalt-crushing power?" She shrugged her shoulders. "You know what they say. Desperate times, desperate measures."

"So I'm told." I pointed to the black-and-orange No Trespassing sign hanging on the birch next to the mailbox. Paula bought it a couple of weeks ago at Walmart. It really adds something to the place—a certain *Deliverance* feel that I hadn't realized was lacking. "This is private property. You can't park here."

"Exactly," she said. "It's clearly marked, which is very helpful. That's why I made sure to keep all four tires on the street. I didn't go over, not by an inch. It was no easy feat. I had to get out and check several times. You know those ads where the Hummers are careening around out on some godforsaken dried-up lake bed? You know how you watch them and think, Why, why the hell are they doing that? After you drive one of these bad boys, you understand. The drivers didn't end up out there on purpose. They don't actually *want* to be there. They just accidentally drove off the shoulder of the road, and they didn't notice until it was too late. It looks like a joyride, but really they're just frantically trying to find their way back to civilization. . . . Jessica Frobisher, right? It's Dr. Frobisher?"

I had been starting back up the driveway, but I stopped at the sound of my name. I turned around and looked at her again. She was older than I had first pegged her to be, and she was smiling a little at me. Not unkindly, but a little alarm started pinging right then, very quietly in my ear.

"My name is Melissa Kramer," she said. "I'm with the *New York Times.* I've been working on the Spaceco story. I was wondering if I might be able to ask you a couple of questions."

Too late, I remembered where I was supposed to be, Arthur. Which was back in the house and not talking to strangers. I attempted to take a couple of steps back, but the pavement was tilted in a way that caused me to slide forward instead of back. It was like the ice and I were working at cross-purposes.

"No," I said. "Absolutely not." It must have looked odd, me shaking my head emphatically while I steadily glided toward her. I had to brace one hand on the Hummer to stop myself. "Loose lips sink ships"—that was the little slogan Liam liked to say back during Spaceco start-up days, when they were signing everyone to confidentiality agreements, and now it's practically become our official family mantra. "There's a number they set up for media inquiries. You're a journalist, right? So I'm sure you know the drill. If you have a pen, I'll give it to you: 888-727—"

"I got it, thanks." Even cutting me off mid-sentence, the woman managed somehow to sound perfectly agreeable. She had her head tilted, sizing me up. Something about her look at that moment made me think of you, of your face when it's wearing my least favorite expression. You know which one I'm talking about, so don't pretend you don't. It's the expression that says any number of things is being read between any number of lines, but you are not, you are never, going to tell me what they are. "I've called it. Several times, actually. The people I've talked to have been very pleasant and . . . How should I say it? Less than forthcoming." She shoved her hands in her jacket pockets and flung them out, a gesture that looked like an apology, but wasn't. "That's why I'm here. And in answer to your question, yes, I do know the drill. The drill is, when the door doesn't open, you find a window and start knocking obnoxiously on that instead."

"Well, you guys keep picking the wrong window." I had been backing up, moving toward the grass, heel, toe, heel, toe, but I stopped then and turned to meet her head-on. All the blood was surging to my head. It felt good to let someone have it, like something I'd been waiting for for a long time. "You're not even in the right state. Maybe flyover country all looks the same to you, but I've got some news for you, Melissa. You're about two thousand miles off. If you want to talk to my husband, you're going to have to get back in that Hummer and drive until you see cactuses. No one here knows a thruster from a hole in the ground, and last time I checked nobody had added me to the Spaceco payroll as a company spokesperson. Now, if you'll excuse me."

I started to turn around, but there she was, right next to me, as though neither one of us had moved at all.

"That's too bad," she said. "If you asked me, I'd say they need all the spokespeople they can get, Dr. Frobisher." Another step, and still she was right at my elbow. "Dr. Frobisher. Do you know anything about Norell Ops?"

"No." We took another three strides perfectly in tandem. Someone watching us from across the street could have mistaken us for dance partners, and damn good ones at that.

"You should. You should ask your husband about it. If you don't hear about it from him, someone else will tell you."

That faint pinging alarm, which had fallen quiet, began to ping again, a little louder this time. I stopped, but something kept me from turning around. "Like you?" I said. Up in the frozen trees somewhere, one lonely, mysterious bird was singing—an all-clear, maybe, or a warning. Someone savvier than me would have been able to name it, but oh, Arthur, there are so many things I don't know. I closed my eyes and tried to concentrate.

"I have a contact at NASA," Melissa said. "We lived in the same dorm freshman year at Princeton, believe it or not." She was standing just behind me, talking quietly into my ear. She knew I was listening. "I'm sure you already know, there's a lot of back-and-forthing between NASA and the commercial space people. Everyone in that field is specialized to the nth degree. Anyway, Cam was the one who first told me about Norell Ops. They're a contractor based in Dayton. Computer equipment. They manufacture switches in a lot of aircraft control panels. NASA looked into using them a while back, but they ended up passing because of what he called, in quotes, 'concerns' some of the engineers had. There were some anomalies on the readouts, a couple of glitches they couldn't seem to kill. A year or so later, he heard a rumor that Spaceco had signed a deal with Norell, but he couldn't say for sure. Do you see where I'm going with this?"

"I think I get the gist, yes," I said. I opened my eyes. I looked up the hill toward the house. It's hard to explain, Arthur—it was like I was staring at it from a long ways off, just like a stranger watching it flash onto one of those TV screens on which it had no doubt appeared. I was free to my rightful judgment of what I saw there. The listing blue shutters. The slovenly piles of sod, stripped away from the foundation of my fabulist greenhouse. The rosebushes I had brutally shorn down last fall, when I was at my most bitter, and then trussed up in intricate twine nets, telling myself I could impose a new and more sensible arrangement upon them, that all my scratches and scars would be my proof and my painful consolation. There was the stained-glass window above the front porch, glimmering its baroque purples and reds. I call it the zinnia window, because that's what it looks like. The person who made it went a little overboard with all the petals and tracery. It was the handiwork of some kind of savant, or else someone saddled with profound compulsions. It all seemed to me then, standing there, unable to look away, like the most damning of evidence.

45

"Dr. Frobisher," Melissa said. Her voice was weirdly gentle, almost kind in its cajoling. "You have to trust me. I've been in this business long enough to know. Insinuations, questions that go begging for answers, they're worse. They inflict far more damage than the truth, no matter how bad it is. You have to put me in touch with your husband. I have to talk to him."

But by then I had snapped out of it. "Thanks," I said. Or at least I think I did. *Loose lips sink ships.* Thank you, Liam. "I'll give him the message." I shook her off my shoulder and began making my treacherous way back up the hill. Behind me, I could hear the school bus hurtle past.

I met Paula at the front door, putting on her jacket. "I was just coming to get you," she said. "Who *was* it? We've been up here imagining the worst."

"That's what you think." I pushed past her into the foyer. "Are Jack and Corinne ready? We're late. We have to go. We have to *go now.*" My italics would have given admin assistant Mackenzie a run for her money, and I wasn't even trying. I wasn't aware of raising my voice, of my inflection having changed at all, but suddenly everyone was following my orders, jumping into their coats, racing for their backpacks, even Corinne. Liam once said Corinne was physically incapable of the verb *hustle,* that she would be unable to hurry even if the world were ending in fire or ice. He was wrong about that one too, and I thought maybe now would be a good time for me to start a list. She was making a strange little hiccupping noise, like she'd been crying, but I couldn't ask her what was wrong. We were out of time. Also: I was afraid. I thought if I stopped, I might not be able to start moving again.

The drive through town was harrowing. I braked, and the car kept going. I turned the wheel to the left, and the car slid right. I kept starting to curse and then catching myself just in time on the letter *f*. In front of the houses, crocuses were frozen inside their ice carapaces, tiny, painful anachronisms, and my eyes kept stinging. The roads were eerily empty. "Where is everyone?" Jack asked.

Meanwhile, Corinne was worrying out loud about being late. That day was her day to feed the kindergarten hamster, whose name is, of all things, Mr. Munchy. She was missing the Pledge of Allegiance. Neglecting this small, gravely important ritual was the final straw, and she was on the verge of breaking down for real. I told her I would say it with her. I thought maybe it would steady me while we made our way down Saline Road, cheating death at every stop sign. *I pledge allegiance to the flag. Of the United States of America.* It didn't. Have you ever heard a five-year-old recite the Pledge of Allegiance, Arthur? It's creepy as hell. Their enunciation is perfect, but they have no idea what kind of promise they're making, of what's being called for. No one tells you until later that breaking your word amounts to treason. No one tells you until later that you can't take it back. I was having my own treasonous thoughts as I drove. They were half formed, but went a little like this: asking something like that from someone ought not to be allowed.

Arthur, I'll stop here. I should have stopped several hundred words back. You'll do some cursing of your own, when you see how long this fucking e-mail is, but you'll read it all anyway. I said it once: *I know you.* I'm pretty sure that it's still true, in spite of everything.

Yours,
Jess

From: Jess Frobisher <jfrobisher@umich.edu>
Sent: Sunday, April 13, 2014 1:38 am
To: Arthur Danielson <danielsav@umich.edu>
Cc:
Bcc:
Subject: Re: wheeze, wheeze, gasp, gasp

Hmm. Arthur + beard. Arthur minus 20 lbs. I'm having a hard time picturing this new . . . What did you call it? Wasted shadow of the man you used to be?

Seriously, though: good for you. Scruffy is back in—at least that's what I've inferred from my time in the Meijer checkout line, staring (mindlessly, I swear) at *People*'s Sexiest Men Alive. And all that sweating will make you live longer, at least according to know-it-all scientists like us. That is what you want, isn't it, Arthur? There have been a few times when I wondered. But we don't have to talk about it. You don't have to tell me. *We're not talking about me right now, we're talking about you.* I told Paula once how we used to say that all the time, how it was a punch line to all our kidding around. It was just an aside, related to some story I was telling about work, but as soon as I said it, I knew I'd said it a little too casually and that I'd just given something away. Paula was staring at me, and then she did a little whistle. "Hooo brother," she said. "What?" I demanded. "You know what," she said. "Whatever you do, don't order the chocolate cake here. It looks good, but it's like chewing on a mouthful of potting soil."

I digress. After my run-in with Kramer on Tuesday morning, I meant to go to the lab to start getting ready for a batch of *Prasophyllum petilum* I'm supposed to be getting in next week. Instead, I went to my office and started googling "Norell Ops." I was scrolling down the list of results—I hadn't had a chance to find out anything beyond the fact that Norell Ops is indeed a company that does indeed have a website—when my cell went off at full volume like a doomsday alarm, making me jump out of my chair. Two days ago Jack changed my ringtone to the Imperial March from *Star Wars*, and I haven't been able to figure out how to change it back yet. He thinks it's hilarious. I find the doom and gloom rather apropos.

It was Paula. "Are you near a TV?"

"Happily, no," I said.

"Well, find one. You're going to want to see this."

"I'm not sure I do." I glanced over at my laptop, at the steely blue and gray lettering on the screen. "This wouldn't by any chance have anything to do with a company called Norell Ops, would it?"

"With what?" Paula said. "Turn it to CNN. They're just getting started—are you going to watch or what?"

I threw open the door and started walking briskly down the hall, as close as I could to running without actually breaking stride, hoping not to draw attention to myself. I'm trying to stay under the radar these days, Arthur. The reason why I hardly mentioned Liam's job, the reason why I didn't tell anyone except you when Liam went up into space last April—it wasn't that I was trying to keep it a big secret. It's because the whole thing always felt like something I was making up. Like if you told people you were married to a lion tamer or a bounty hunter. What I mean is: it's just not something many people *do*. People raise their eyebrows and lean in with another twenty follow-up questions. I got sick of it, that's all.

And guess what? My painstaking cover has now been blown. The *Michigan Daily*, never so quick on the uptake, finally made the connection between Spaceco and UM's associate botany professor "Jessica Fobisher." Some student gumshoe posted the story online Thursday morning, and when I walked into the faculty meeting that afternoon everyone sitting at the table got quiet and turned around to size me up, with the exception of Thom, who shuffled his papers and cleared his throat uncomfortably. All I could do was take a seat and participate in the discussions that followed to the point of obnoxiousness, voting down the lab reassignments and bitching about the new purchase requisition forms for all I was worth. My hand was clenched around my phone in my pocket, and I was thumbing one furious, rapid-fire imaginary text to Liam after another.

That ancient POS TV is still in the staff lounge where someone stashed it. I didn't know whether it could get any stations, but I closed the door and turned it on.

"Are you there?" Paula said.

"Just a second." With a staticky whoosh the TV came to life, and through the jumping lines, I could barely make out two blond heads. "I'm looking at a TV that's circa 1985. The crawl's completely cut off. Except for . . . wait—did scientists finally discover a way to clone Suzanne Somers?"

"They're talking about Kelly Kahn," Paula said. "Shh. I want to hear this."

"*Again, if you're just joining us,*" said one of the announcers, "*we're talking about a new development in the* Titan *disaster story. The mother of Kelly Kahn—Kelly Kahn, you'll remember was one of the four passengers killed in last month's Spaceco accident—*"

The words were on a time lag, a two-second delay. I could hear them coming through the phone, crisply and clearly, then echoing again through the crackling speakers in front of me. All the reverb made them hard to understand. I had to pull the phone away from my ear.

"—*Has confirmed that her daughter was eight weeks pregnant at the time of the launch. The news has taken everyone by surprise. Not even Kelly's father, the Australian TV tycoon Robert Kahn, apparently had any idea. Now we can't say anything for sure, but there's speculation that Kelly was keeping the pregnancy secret until after the launch. A representative has put out a statement saying that, of course, they had no knowledge of this. I'm quoting here—'all Spaceco passengers are required to complete a physical exam before spaceflight . . . pregnancy is one of many medical conditions that precludes us from allowing a passenger to travel with us.' Now, Caitlyn*"—she turned to the woman sitting next to her—"*tell me a little about the impact that this revelation might have on the investigation and on Spaceco's situation in general.*"

Caitlyn was sucking in her breath to answer, but I beat her to the punch. "Not good," I said. I reached out and clicked off the TV, plunging myself into merciful silence. "I didn't know she was married."

"She isn't," Paula said. "That's the thing. No one knew. The news broke about an hour ago, and there's already all this speculation about who the father is and whether he's going to come forward."

No doubt Paula had more details she could tell me, but suddenly I didn't want to talk about it with her anymore. I turned around and glanced at the conference room door. "I have to go."

"Jess," said Paula. "Come on."

"I'm serious. Thanks for the update."

"I just thought you should know."

"I appreciate it."

"Jess, they're right. You know that, don't you? If she didn't tell them, then it's on her. *She* made the call. *She* took the risk. *She—*"

"Hanging up now."

On that note, I have to stop. Try to go easy on the Bengay. The bears will smell you coming from a mile away.

J

From: Jessica Frobisher <jfrobisher@umich.edu>
Sent: Monday, April 14, 2014 2:12 pm
To: Arthur Danielson <danielsav@umich.edu>
Cc:
Bcc:
Subject: Re: whiling the download away

I know she's right. I know you're right. Is that supposed to be some sort of consolation? Because, if so, it fails.

That's not what I'm looking for anyway. I don't know what I'm looking for. I think what I want, Arthur, childishly, is for this story to make some sort of sense. I keep latching on to the stupidest pieces of information and brooding about them. Like this morning, for example. I was outside wandering around in the greenhouse-to-be, trying to figure out where I'm going to install the electric outlets, trying to plan ahead for once in my life. Instead I got distracted by thinking about the name Kelly Kahn. Kelly Kahn—what the hell kind of name is that? You think *Kelly Kahn,* and you get a woman in Minnesota baking snickerdoodles, or a seventeen-year-old varsity cheerleader, or a soccer mom with an SUV and two Labrador retrievers. A sweet, banal name like Kelly Kahn seems like it should have been a gift, doesn't it? Like an alliterative charm to ward off Fate with a capital F? Instead, what it got her was pregnant by a secret lover and death by exploding spaceship.

But I said I didn't want to talk about it, didn't I?

I'm glad you have me to while the time away during your data uploads. At a rate of 40 kb/sec you're going to have time to read everything I write twice. Lucky you.

Jess

From: Jessica Frobisher <jfrobisher@umich.edu>
Sent: Tuesday, April 15, 2014 12:22 pm
To: Arthur Danielson <danielsav@umich.edu>
Cc:
Bcc:
Subject: Re: <--Fine, I'm changing it

Thank you.

I had a meeting on Monday with the contractor who was supposed to do the dig for the greenhouse trench and pour the knee wall. The guy seemed like he was on the up-and-up but unfortunately the figure he quoted me for a four-foot trench was . . . let's just say it would have involved Jack and Corinne and a game of rock-paper-scissors to decide who would go to the state school of his/her choice.

Honestly, the money wasn't the real problem, especially since Liam wasn't here to veto the expenditure. The contractor was planning on bringing a backhoe up here, and if "Lie low" and "Don't draw attention to yourself" are the orders you're supposed to be following, then you probably shouldn't be taking on a serious home-improvement project with a bunch of preemptively pissed-off neighbors, several of whom might be more than happy to take a break from their praying to pass on tidbits to any "journalists" who are still poking around. (That's what Liam calls them. With air quotes like that.)

The thing is, though, I've started on this undertaking, and I'll be damned if I'm going to stop now. I spent this evening after dinner staking out the corners and setting up the batter boards. I've decided I'm just going to dig the trench myself. Earlier this morning I ran to Home Depot for a new shovel with a handle that is ergonomically designed, according to the label, to make my backbreaking labor more enjoyable. (I also scored several lavender plants, on sale for cheaper than the dirt they were planted in. Now that it's getting warmer, I've started stashing a few greenhouse acquisitions in the backyard.) If Pa Ingalls can build a house out on the prairie, how hard can it be? And it'll be a workout to put your whole hiking-in-the woods regimen to shame, no?

Rolling up my sleeves,
Jess

From: Jessica Frobisher <jfrobisher@umich.edu>
Sent: Wednesday, April 16, 2014 6:41 am
To: Arthur Danielson < danielsav@umich.edu >
Cc:
Bcc:
Subject: Re: digging to China

I know. Four feet seemed deep to me too. But that's what the
contractor told me I'd need to get below the frost line. Anything
shallower than that, and any hard freezes we might get could
cause the foundation to shift and drift. *Shift and drift.* That's
exactly what he said.

"Four feet?" I said. I was struck by the man's unintentionally poetic
turn of phrase, distracted for a moment into envisioning the
greenhouse peeling away slowly from the house and wafting off
across the lawn, like some sort of glass ark full of orchids and
heirloom tomatoes. I could see it all so clearly: me inside, Liam and
the kids waving reproachfully at me from the dining room window . . .

Then I snapped out of it. "Are you sure that's necessary?" I said.
"Wouldn't we be OK with three? I mean, what with all the global
warming going on, pretty soon there won't *be* any more freezes.
It'll be like Florida up here, only with more unions and less
shuffleboard."

He—his name was Bernard—gave me a long, hard look. You should
have seen this man, Arthur. He was about six foot two, with
stooped shoulders and a brown beard weathering toward silver.
He had this taciturn, stoic composure. You could imagine him
stepping out of a tent on the battlefield of Shiloh. Whatever
disdain he harbored, he was going to keep to himself. I liked him,
even if he didn't like me—a tree-hugger academic with a liberal
agenda who was wearing men's shoes.

"Ma'am, you can do three feet," he said. "If you don't care whether your addition meets code. If that's the case, though, then you're going to have to find yourself a contractor who doesn't mind cutting corners. I am not that man."

"No, no." I said. "Absolutely no cutting corners. We don't believe in that." I told him I would call him, and I feel bad that I didn't. My back feels even worse.

Breakfast rush starts soon, and I have a toaster to reassemble.

Hope you're at base camp sleeping well, and have a good morning,

j

From: Jessica Frobisher <jfrobisher@umich.edu>
Sent: Friday April 18, 2014 10:10 pm
To: Arthur Danielson <danielsav@umich.edu>
Cc:
Bcc:
Subject: Re: Herculean efforts

_____

Arthur,

Yes. Still digging away. It's taking a little while to build up my endurance, but I'm now able to put in an hour stint at a time. The day I first broke ground, on a whim—no, scratch that, in the interest of science—I went rummaging around in Liam's shed and found one of his scales. I cut out one foot by one foot by one foot of soil and I shoveled it onto the scale. One cubic foot of our earth weighs 125.32 pounds. It's clayey, so that's on the heavy side. The knee wall trench needs to be one foot wide. Its dimensions are fifteen by twenty feet, and four feet deep. So that adds up to—you do the math. I am certifiably brain-dead today.

Our soil's pH also clocks in at an acidic 5.2 and is chock-full of nematodes. I know this because not long after Liam and I moved in, I brought a handful of it in to work, took a look at it under the electron microscope, and ran a few tests. I wanted to know exactly what we had gotten ourselves into, to arm myself with information. You were teasing me once, and you said something that I'm sure you don't remember. You said that in my heart of hearts I was more an aesthete than a scientist. Maybe there's some truth to that, but I've been trained in dispassionate inquiry just like you. I believe even laymen have a term for this. They call it "facing the facts."

I'm sorry to hear about your dream. I've been having some doozies myself.

I'll be careful, I promise. I'll look both ways before I cross the street. I'll check the sky for lightning. I don't know what else to tell you. I'm OK. We're OK.

I'm off in search of some Ibuprofen now.

Jess

From: Jessica Frobisher <jfrobisher@umich.edu>
Sent: Monday, April 21, 2014 4:12 pm
To: Arthur Danielson <danielsav@umich.edu>
Cc:
Bcc:
Subject: Re: some things, say the unwise ones

Glad you got it.

Mary Oliver makes me think of the first time I saw you, you know.
I'm sure you don't remember it. It was my second day on campus.
I was putting my stuff in my office. I had my door open and I
could hear you out in the hallway talking to a doctoral candidate
from Portugal. The one with the unreal waist-length jet-black
hair. She used to plait it up around her head in that disheveled yet
demure *Tess of the d'Urbervilles* way. You were quoting one of
Oliver's poems to her. I thought I'd never heard someone so full of
himself. Reciting poetry out loud like that, in public—seriously,
Arthur, there should be a law against it.

Anyways, I had just hung up that bulletin board above my desk.
I had been vengefully stapling papers to it, but I had paused
mid-staple to listen to you, to confirm just how full of shit you
were, when, out of nowhere, you appeared in the doorway
behind me. I nearly jumped out of my skin and then proceeded
to drive the stapler straight into my thumb. All the blood
started running down, soaking into the cork and the photo of
me and Liam and Jack I had been tacking up. All that gore
made things look way worse than they felt, is what I kept
insisting to you. And now I can't remember it hurting at all,
only how annoyed I was that you kept hanging around, that you
wouldn't leave me alone to bleed in peace. That picture of Liam
and Jack was ruined beyond saving—the whole thing
bloodstained and gouged with the jagged staple holes I had

punched straight through Liam's chest. Which was too bad, because it was one of my favorites. Some stranger took it for us when we were at Lake Michigan years ago. In it, the water was shining like it was being mysteriously lit from underneath its numinous surface, and Liam and I both looked like younger, less annoyed versions of ourselves. I can't describe it any better than that. Maybe I'm just at the age now where all the past is becoming poignant, where it aches the way so-called bygone, allegedly healed-up fractures ache when it rains. I always told myself that sentimentality wouldn't happen to me, but I'm starting to think it's one of those traps you just can't escape, one of those fates all of us are consigned to—like dying, like denial, or like sullying the things we want more than anything to save. You keep talking about global warming and the evidence of plunging rates of coniferous reproduction, Arthur, but I keep thinking about the crumpled Coors Light can you found nestled down in the roots of that pine tree, that jarring, inexplicable eyesore out in the wilderness, miles from anything, far from where any person had any right to be. When you described it, you made that single piece of litter sound like a harbinger of impending doom, and that frightened me more than anything has so far. If you, my beloved, my indefatigable optimist, are throwing up your hands, if you have given yourself over to doom-saying, I don't know what that means, except that we are really in trouble.

"What are you going to do?" you asked me. It was yet more of your prodding disguised (badly) as a question. Well, I don't know, Arthur. There have been more developments here, ones that you're sure to disapprove of, but I don't have time to regale you with them right now. Paula left on Friday, having used up all her family-in-the-national-headlines leave. That's what she told me, anyway, although maybe she didn't phrase it quite like that. I think the truth is that she's just tired of the crazy people she can't help, and wants to get back to the people she can. That means I'm on the hook to pick up Jack from tae kwon do in . . . shit, ten minutes ago.

So start your preemptive headshaking now. Or don't. I don't give a rat's ass.

~jpf

From: Jessica Frobisher <jfrobisher@umich.edu>
Sent: Tuesday, April 22, 2014 5:37 am
To: Arthur Danielson <danielsav@umich.edu>
Cc:
Bcc:
Subject: Re: the sound of one head shaking

Stop twisting my words around. I never said I hate Mary Oliver.

I just think poetry is something people should keep to themselves. It's a little embarrassing, like being caught with a bodice ripper. I press the covers against the bus seat in front of me, or shield the pages behind my grande latte cup. Or I read it in the bathroom. That's what I started doing after Liam and I got married. He was only teasing about Jessica Plath, or *po'try* (like that, two syllables), but it got old. Not long after the kids were born, I started doing my reading in there, just so I could have some peace and quiet. Everyone thinks I'm suffering from last night's fish tacos, and instead I'm sitting cross-legged in the bathtub reading back issues of *Plant Biology*. I turn the hot and cold taps on all the way so I can't hear the plaintive wailing on the other side of the door. I'm guessing that's a problem you've never had—not being able to hear yourself think—and Arthur, you don't know how bad it can be.

Speaking of reading, Corinne and I are reading *Little House on the Prairie*. I haven't read Laura Ingalls Wilder in years, and I've forgotten a lot of things about those books. Like how harrowing they are, for one. Wolves, poison gas in the wells, malaria. I was a little taken aback. For all the childish simplicity of the stories, the stakes are deadly high, and it's not Laura I find myself wondering about, but Ma—Ma, the stoic, going along with all her husband's gambles, but thinking God only knows what. We never find out either.

Corinne seems unfazed by any of it. She breathes with her mouth open in a dreamy, blissed-out sort of way while she's being read to, but once I reach the end of the chapter, when I clap the floppy old paperback shut for the night, she doesn't seem to give any of these extraordinary near misses a second thought. I don't think I did either when I was her age. Desperate times, desperate measures. To quote a certain *New York Times* reporter.

We were stretched out hip-to-hip on Corinne's tulip bedspread, reading, when Liam came home late last week. A prairie fire was menacing the Ingallses' cabin, and Corinne and I were so intent on finding out what would happen that I failed to hear Tristan's car pull into the driveway. I failed to hear Liam open the front door or come down the hall. I didn't know he'd arrived until I looked up and saw him standing there in the doorway, and he lifted his right hand, his damaged thumb, and pressed it to his lips, a signal telling me—I took it as such—to carry on. I kept on reading, determined to give nothing away, but at the sight of the gesture, the words on the page trembled strangely and went swimming away. Corinne's eyes were half closed; she was lost in her trance. She didn't lift her head from my chest, but she stirred at the tremor and sighed in that guttural, troubled way dreaming people do.

He had grown a beard in the time he'd been away. He was windburned and raggedy. He looked like an agate-eyed stranger as he stood there studying us. I feel like I'm expected to hew to a narrative cliché here, to remark on how the past few terrible weeks have aged my husband in some appreciable way. But that isn't true, so I'll spare you. If anything, it is the opposite. It would be more accurate to say that some youthful remnant of Liam has resurfaced, one dating back to the time we first met, back in the days when he was zealous and unshaven and arrogant. He has on that old embattled expression of his I had almost forgotten. He used to wear it out the door every morning. It came from having something to prove. You could see it in everything he did, no matter how offhand—in the way he signed his name at the top of his engineering papers, carving a groove with every flourish. Our old dining room table, a hulky pressed-wood monstrosity, was covered in "Liam Callahan" engravings, and by the time we stopped being poor and threw it away, you could run your hands across the surface and feel them all—it felt like topography, like the map of a world he was fearlessly making his impression upon. It was that absolute certainty that drew me in. Back in those days, I could spend five minutes standing in front of the rutabagas at the supermarket, turning them all over in my hands, weighing the merits of each one. OK, yes—I still do this on certain days, when I am running my errands alone, and time seems bent on getting away from me. And—as you have kindly pointed out—this indecision is a kind of cowardice, a kind of shrinking away, or faltering disguised as caution. But you, you of all people, should understand that it isn't that simple.

The sight of Liam after a trip always affects the kids like a sugar high: a giddy rush, followed by an inevitable crash. This time, though, they were even more ecstatic to see him than usual, especially Jack. He wrapped his arms around Liam, burrowing his flushed face against his chest and talking in a punctuationless rush. Liam couldn't get a word in, not even in the breaths between paragraphs. All he could do was nod and say *uh huh uh huh* over and over while he got down on one knee and began pulling off Jack's shoes. The tenderness of this gesture, the careful meticulousness with which he picked out the knots in the laces and laid the sneakers side by side next to the radiator—it made me absolutely certain, for a moment, that whatever insinuations I had heard from our own personal bearer of bad tidings, they didn't matter. Because they were wrong. I felt so sure, Arthur, as I stood there in the hallway, looking on, with my arms crossed like a one-woman judge and jury waiting to pronounce a verdict.

Our chance to actually talk didn't come until almost two hours later. We were sitting downstairs at the kitchen table, both of us propped up on our elbows. Liam was nursing a glass of Glenlivet from his carefully guarded stash. The blinds were open, and you could see out into the backyard. Even in the dark, you could make out my handiwork of the past few weeks—the mangled saplings, the overturned birdbath, my eclectic collection of newly acquired plants, the churned-up dirt where I have started digging. If you didn't know better, Arthur, you might think that we had been hit by a storm, a microburst, one of those freaks of the atmosphere that concentrates all its punishing force into a single point and leaves everything else around unscathed.

"You've been busy," Liam said finally, and I thought I detected a hint of bitterness in the words. I understood then that he thought I'd been home playing Gertie the Gardener while he'd been thousands of miles away wandering through the desert, ankle deep in smoking spaceship wreckage. It made me remember a picture I had seen on the *Times* site a few days ago. In it, several Spaceco guys are crouching down in the sand, looking at some twisted piece of metal. The wind must be up—they all have their faces wrapped, like a bunch of mujahideen, and their dress shirts are ghostly with dust. I knew Liam was there in the crowd, and I kept looking and looking, but I couldn't for the life of me pick him out.

"You have no idea." I reached out for his glass and took a careful sip. I actually can't stand scotch, you know. I don't care how much you and Liam love it. But I dabble in it anyway—just every now and then when Liam is away, something compels me to measure out one of his precious, golden rations and drink it down, to feel its sickening burn smoldering in the back of my throat. "What with dodging the paparazzi on the grocery runs, and getting the stink eye at faculty meetings, and teaching Corinne how to spell the word *explosion,* and attempting to explain to our neighbors that we're not terrible people—"

"Did you?" Liam said. "Did you explain it? That's good to hear. I wish I could have been there. I'm sure it was a rousing defense." He stood up from the table and began jerking his tie loose. It was his bloodred silk one. His litigator tie, he calls it. He bought it a few years ago when he and his fellow wannabe spacemen started making their pitch to investors. It was a tie to win hearts and minds, and it worked. He'd clearly been at a board meeting earlier that day. I've always known, Arthur, that whatever gets discussed behind those closed doors is something so technically and intellectually rarefied that it is completely out of my reach, that I would never understand it. It was a fact that I took a kind of vain, vicarious pride in—even if you were the only one I ever admitted that to. Sitting there, at that moment, I was thinking again how these bragging rights now seem stupid, or worse, downright sinister.

I was momentarily diverted from these thoughts by Liam's long, profoundly weary sigh. "Look, Jess," he said. "I get it. I threw you to the wolves. These people, they're fucking relentless. Hunter was telling me about this guy from *Vanity Fair*—"

"Just a second." I held up my hand. I was thinking that it was important that he not distract me. "I have something else I need to ask you. Does the name Norell Ops mean anything to you?"

I watched him slowly put his scotch glass down. "What?"

"Norell Ops," I said. "It's a contractor based out of Dayton. They make aeronautical—"

"I know what they make," Liam said. His face had suddenly flushed, Arthur. It was startling to see him looking so caught off guard, because you never see Liam looking disconcerted. "How the hell did *you* hear about them?"

"I had a nice little chat with a reporter from the *New York Times*," I said. "We woke up the other morning to find her lurking at the bottom of the driveway. I'm sure you would have found her a little hipper-than-thou, but she had some interesting things to say." I had to force myself to let go of the kitchen table, which I was clutching, for some reason, in a death grip. "It was actually one of the most informative conversations I've had in weeks."

"I'll bet it was," Liam said. He had been wandering around the kitchen while I was talking with an aimlessness that was frightening. "Fuck," he said. "*Fuck.*"

I could feel my dread ratcheting up with every step. "Please, Liam," I said. "Tell me it isn't true."

"For God's sake, Jess," Liam said. "We haven't even finished the preliminary report yet. Do you know how many moving parts there were on that rocket? Over two million. The debris field has a radius of over eight kilometers. There are pieces of shuttle that we're never going to find. They're going to turn into these little, like—" He was sputtering, Arthur. "These little titanium geological artifacts that hitchhikers are going to be finding on the side of I-8 decades from now. And now you're telling me that some girl Friday at the *Times* has done two fucking hours of research, and she thinks she's got it all figured out. That's great. That's just—"

We realized simultaneously that he was shouting, and both of us glanced up toward the ceiling where Corinne was sleeping, eight feet directly above our heads. Or at least I prayed that she was sleeping, that she was dead to the world and dreaming of pioneer girls in calico sunbonnets, fearless little girls who were flourishing in the face of adversity. "That's just fantastic," he finished more quietly.

"But a defective control panel is one of the possibilities," I said. "You haven't ruled it out."

His jaw was clenching and unclenching. "We haven't ruled anything out," he said.

I got up and went to the window. I pressed my forehead against the cool, slightly sticky glass. Through the steam of my breath on the pane, I could just make out Liam's shed. It's a sleek little conical outbuilding that Liam built with his own hands. When he has time, he goes out there and tinkers around with his inventions—a zero-gravity hinge, special patches and seals, contraptions that supposedly can keep a person from dying if he's out in space and something tears apart or springs a leak, something that damn well shouldn't. They may not be useful to the average Joe Schmo, but they are ingenious, perfect in their own way.

It—by which I mean the shed—is down past the loop of our driveway, and in the spring it's hidden behind the lilac trees. I don't know if you saw it—the one and only time you were here, that afternoon you dropped me off. Two years ago, it must have been. I remember the timing because it was a few weeks after I had my miscarriage. Liam was in Arizona, and it was the only time in my life I've ever had a migraine. Up until that point, I'd only believed in migraines in a theoretical sort of way. But then I felt it—and nothing has ever been more unbearable or more real. I remember slumping down in your car, leaning my head on your shoulder, and you put up your hand to anchor it there—your fingers on my temple, your thumb pressed carefully along my jaw—to keep it from being jarred by the potholes. When I opened my eyes, the jagged chinks of sky between the tree leaves were burning fiery trails across the windshield, so I had to close them again.

We haven't ruled anything out, Arthur. Do you hear me?

jess

From: Jessica Frobisher <jfrobisher@umich.edu>
Sent: Thursday, April 24, 2014 10:23 pm
To: Arthur Danielson <danielsav@umich.edu>
Cc:
Bcc:
Subject: Re: Fool's errand (n): a task or activity that has no hope of success. See also . . .

I hate, hate, hate it when you call me Jessica. Nobody calls me by my so-called Christian name except for my dead mother, who still shows up regularly in my dreams to tell me that she can't understand how on earth I didn't see X, or Y, or Z coming from a mile away. "Tell her to fuck off," says Paula. But I can't. That's the problem with the dead. You can't tell them to fuck themselves. You can't tell them anything. They always win.

You, on the other hand, are still among the living, if only barely, subsisting on some subarctic periphery, so here it is: go fuck yourself, Arthur. You're the one who relishes that stupid quote, "Insinuations are for cowards." If you have something to say, then say it. Otherwise

piss off,
Jess

From: Jessica Frobisher <jfrobisher@umich.edu>
Sent: Saturday, April 26, 2014 1:01 am
To: Arthur Danielson <danielsav@umich.edu>
Cc:
Bcc:
Subject: speaking of my mother

I know I must have told you that story about her will. How she bequeathed to me those ridiculous chandelier earrings. Two grand on each ear—to a woman who once accidentally dropped a ruby-cluster engagement ring down a storm drain. The only other thing she specifically willed me was her ancient edition of *Emily Post's Etiquette*. All her gifts came with a reproach, even after death. The book is a tome—I accidentally just typed *tomb*, whoops—more than 700 pages long, and I read it straight through from Formalities to Funerals in the week after her death, looking for something. A note in the margin, a sticky spot of jam, a grocery store receipt for orange juice and toilet paper. I found nothing. I didn't realize until weeks later that I had memorized it—not the entire book, but whole passages. I would be out in the garden early in the morning pulling up radishes all bitter and gone to seed—when it was still too dark to see—and I would bend over to tie my shoe and these lines would pop unbidden into my head, word-for-word correct, as though I'd just read them straight off the page:

"How are you?" is a widely-used phrase. Since it is not usually accompanied by sincere interest in an answer, the best response is either "Fine, thank you," or "Very well, thank you."

It was a neat little trick, and it's one I've never been able to pull off since.

I've wandered OT, but I'm getting to something that seems apropos to me: there's a whole section on how to say you're sorry. When you look up "apologies" in the index, it takes you to a section titled "Letters That Shouldn't Be Written." The book's upstairs, so I'm paraphrasing here, but it goes something like this:

> The Unwise Letter
> Every day mailmen deliver letters whose fallout would be disastrous if they fell into the wrong hands. Letters that should never have been written are frequently produced as evidence in courtrooms, and most of them cannot, in any way, be excused. Do not forget: Written words have the power to endure, and thoughts carelessly set upon paper can exist for hundreds of years.

You get the gist.

Always unwise, sometimes repentant,
j

From: Jessica Frobisher <jfrobisher@umich.edu>
Sent: Sunday, April 27, 2014 1:29 am
To: Arthur Danielson <danielsav@umich.edu>
Cc:
Bcc:
Subject: Re: bygones and caveats

Thanks. I'm OK leaving it their if you are.

By the way, I saw you and your team mentioned on *Nature*'s news site. They did a short piece on a multidiscipline expedition based out of McGill University that was investigating the effects of global warming on at-risk subarctic ecosystems. There was a picture, but you weren't in it, just two grouchy-looking Norwegian scientists tagging a tern. I was a little disappointed. I miss seeing your face.

Hell, I miss seeing all of you.

Yours,
Jess

From: Jessica Frobisher <jfrobisher@umich.edu>
Sent: Sunday, April 27, 2014 1:31 am
To: Arthur Danielson <danielsav@umich.edu>
Cc:
Bcc:
Subject: Re: bygones and caveats

Whoops, I meant *there*.

From: Jessica Frobisher <jfrobisher@umich.edu>
Sent: Wednesday, April 30, 2014 12:19 am
To: Arthur Danielson <danielsav@umich.edu>
Cc:
Bcc:
Subject: Re: dismal doughnuts and other Godforsakenland
hardships

Favorite colleague, I have two points if you'll allow me:

1. If you and your team members put in as much time counting
   pinecones as you did inventing place names, you'd probably
   have that study all wrapped up by now.

2. You'd better stop using topo maps for drinking-game
   dartboards. If you don't, you'll never find your way out of the
   forest.

For the record, I like Tim Hortons. And yes, I'm rather fond of
Canadians. You may be right about them. (What did you call it?
Their "leery politeness"?) But Arthur, be fair—can you blame
them? After all, we're Americans. I would be leery too, if I wasn't
one of us, if I couldn't understand why we think what we think.
Don't get me wrong. I'm not saying that I condone our perverse
American logic, that certain aspects of it don't make me heartsick
or gnash my teeth. Only that our philosophies do make sense to
me, even as I am helpless to explain them to those on the outside
looking in, that there is, in fact, an order to it—that mess of
crisscrossed, contrarian tripwires that separate our devout loyalty
from our passionate hate.

God, do I miss all our hell-in-a-handbasketing. I miss it more than
ever now that it's gone. What you don't realize until later is that
all that fulminating, it's a luxury, exactly what our undergrads

sneer at as "first-world problems." It all recedes once the real, grade-A trouble begins. Rage, indignation, grief—it turns out that they're all finite resources, just like everything else on this planet. A person only has so much to burn through.

It's hard to describe what things have been like here since Liam's been back. Jack and Corinne and I have all turned into strangers in our own house. There are goings-on, but we're no longer privy to them. It forces the question: Were we ever? Our dining room door to nowhere has started to feel like an escape hatch. Every night, after I put the kids to bed, I open it and jump out. When I come back in, there's Liam sitting on the couch, with his headphones on, frowning at his computer screen. He's usually so focused that he doesn't seem to hear me clapping the dirt off my shoes. I did glance over his shoulder the other night, and it took me a second to recognize what he was so absorbed in: a video of the accident. He was clicking through it frame by frame. I didn't stick around to watch. I went straight back outside and tried to decide where to plant the fingerling potatoes. I haven't been able to make up my mind and so the spuds have been languishing in our fridge for days. Their eyes have started to sprout, and they're freaking Corinne out, so I need to get them in the ground.

I've spent the past one and a half hours digging. I would kill right now for one of those scorned Tim Hortons doughnuts, you elitist, but it's bedtime now, it was bedtime hours ago.

Jess

From: Jessica Frobisher <jfrobisher@umich.edu>
Sent: Tuesday, May 6, 2014 11:12 pm
To: Arthur Danielson <danielsav@umich.edu>
Cc:
Bcc:
Subject: Seeking: UM botany professor, dead or alive

Yeah, I'm still here. Sorry. The past couple of days have been
crazy. No more time for reading in the bathtub. No time for
digging my greenhouse fortifications. (Although I did manage to
get the fingerling potatoes cut up and planted with the carrots in a
little patch along the south side of the greenhouse footprint.
Fastest planting ever. I was practically flinging handfuls of dirt
onto those creepy, sprouting eyes, burying them as fast as
possible.) No time for thinking. Whether that's a good thing is
debatable, but I haven't had time for that either lately.

I *have* been finding time every morning to get up early and check
the nytimes site while Liam is out for his run—I have to get to my
laptop before someone else commandeers it.

So far nothing from our friend Melissa Kramer. There are
moments when I'm sure that this is a good sign, that maybe the
story was nothing more than a provocative lead gone dead. Then
there are times when I think, no, we're just waiting for the other
shoe, faulty control panel switch, whatever, to drop.

Meanwhile, Thom Erickson has roped me into teaching a
last-minute summer class. Maureen's toddler was just diagnosed
with autism, so that trumps all my tawdry problems. Though I'm
not sure Thom knows all the particulars. When he knocked on
my door last Tuesday and asked apologetically if he could have a
minute of my time—you know that's how he does everything—he
paused only briefly to eye the Pepto-Bismol bottle on the desk

before he referred to my "family concerns," and then he went briskly on again with his request. He seemed genuinely clueless, and I don't think it's an act, Arthur. I think he's the one person here who really doesn't pay attention to gossip, instead of just pretending to be in the dark. He had a coffee stain on his shirt the shape of Brazil. His absentminded professor shtick brings out even my maternal urges. I want to straighten his collar, to spit on my thumb and start trying to slick down that blond cowlick of his. You know the one I mean. I'm pretty sure it was you who said he that he looks like a Swedish Dagwood Bumstead.

I agreed, of course. Even someone as clueless about tactical planning as I am realizes how important it is to be obliging right now. Everyone is thinking the worst. Goodwill is in short supply, and we have to ration it out, like canteen dregs in a desert.

Drip . . . drip . . . drip . . .
~j

From: Jessica Frobisher <jfrobisher@umich.edu>
Sent: Thursday, May 8, 2014 2:16 am
To: Arthur Danielson <danielsav@umich.edu>
Cc:
Bcc:
Subject: Re: guillotines falling

Not to change the subject again, but we got a batch of *Prasophyllum* in from Australia this morning. Total expense to the grudging taxpayers of state of Michigan: $5,600. I told Thom that it's a bargain—less than what it would cost to get one laptop with all the bells and whistles for a faculty member in the computer science department. Good old Thom. He took out his pen and signed right on the dotted line. Still, I had to jump through a lot of sticky red-tape hoops to get the request through Purchasing, including an epic number of customs forms.

Prasophyllum are endangered, as you may or may not know. They can only be exported for research purposes. In order to get them here the Australia's Natural Resource Management Department gives a permit to some scrappy Aussie who hikes out into the bush and is gone for days, sometimes for weeks, with the snakes and the bugs. I picture him (it's always a him) living in a trailer, making his coffee on one of those little portable stoves while he watches the sun rise extravagantly over the grassland. He has to know exactly what he's looking for, because unlike your ubiquitous pine trees, my friend, orchids are like phantoms.

And yes, that's one of the things I love about them—that they're finicky, that they're secretive, that they're sly, that they subsist only in the narrowest of ecological niches. Think of the epiphytes, living their ethereal lives way up in the tree canopy, snatching their food from the air. I know it would be smarter to set my heart on something else. I don't have to be where you are, collecting the data, to know what's coming. We should all turn our affection to hardier things. We should all cultivate our love for cockroaches and crabgrass, or be like Liam, and be ravished by the stars. These things will outlast us and our human doom. When I'm at my most despairing or my most bitter—they're cut from the same cloth, I suppose—I think, well, thank God, we all have such good cameras. We can all take pictures of the *Prasophyllum* and the cheetahs, and Jack and Corinne can show them to their children, and they'll remember us as the people who lovingly, painstakingly documented our way of life into a myth.

I'm sorry this is so depressing. I just wanted to say that I understand that feeling of being so far away. I hope you can find your way back.

Stay with me,
Jess

From: Jessica Frobisher <jfrobisher@umich.edu>
Sent: Friday, May 9, 2014 9:20 am
To: Arthur Danielson <danielsav@umich.edu>
Cc:
Bcc:
Subject: (no subject)

---

http://www.nytimes.com/2014/5/09/us/contractor-with-history-of-problems-linked-to-spaceco-accident.html?ref=us

From: Jessica Frobisher <jfrobisher@umich.edu>
Sent: Sunday, May 11, 2014 1:11 am
To: Arthur Danielson <danielsav@umich.edu>
Cc:
Bcc:
Subject: Re: fallen blades

Actually, no. If the ax that's been hanging over you finally falls and it hits you square in the back of the head, you don't say, "What a relief it's finally over," do you? You do not. Thanks for trying, but Arthur, let's face it: sometimes things are *exactly* as bad as they look. Or even worse.

I guess I don't need to tell you that the article landed like a bombshell here. I was the one who read it first. It was a little after five in the morning. No one was awake but me. I was sitting there in my bathrobe at the kitchen table in front of my laptop, and as soon as I opened the *Times* site and read the headline, I was covered in sweat. My armpits were soaking. I had to get the robe off before I died, and so I read the rest of the article in my T-shirt and underwear. Read or something that resembled reading—it took me at least four times through before I could begin to comprehend what was right in front of my face. The only thing more surreal than the descriptions of our house (a "tastefully weathered Victorian"? a lawn "gone to seed"?) was reading my own name. Yes, I'm absentminded about some things, but I remember every word of that conversation with Kramer, and Arthur, I swear, never once did I say "No comment." You and everyone else in the world know how that sounds—it sounds like I know things, all sorts of things that I'm not telling. When in fact whatever I thought I knew, I know less. The irony could almost make you laugh, if it weren't so exquisitely sickening.

I shut the laptop. I left the bathrobe in a puddle on the kitchen tile. Still half naked, I walked through the living room and up to the bedroom.

Liam was still in bed. Asleep, maybe, or maybe two-thirds awake. Sleeping in fractions is about the best either one of us does these days. I felt my way around the bed in the dark, and then I bent over him and stared down into his face. I waited for my eyes to adjust so I could make it out, but they didn't.

"Li," I said finally.

He must have been sleeping, because he reached out to me. He took my hand and pressed his cheek against my palm. A thoughtless affectionate gesture, the kind he once performed all the time, past tense, before such tiny things became so fraught, such miniature devastations. My heart was still pounding, and all the hair on the back of my neck lifted, but that was the last thing I could stand—to be undone—and so I took a step back, carefully, to keep from falling on something I couldn't see.

He let my hand drop. "You feel warm," he murmured.

"Li," I said. "You have to get up." I reached out and shook his shoulder—harder than I meant to, I guess, because he lurched upright, like I'd just given him a shot of Adrenalin to the chest. Just like that, he was wide awake and in full crisis mode. "What is it?" he said.

"It's happened," was all I could say. Never mind how cryptic this doomsday declaration sounded. He knew.

"Shit," he said. He reached out and began fumbling on his nightstand, where his laptop usually spends the night, but it wasn't there. "Shit, shit, shit."

"Mine's downstairs in the kitchen," I said. "I pulled the story up. It says—"

But he had already pushed past me and was barreling down the stairs, taking them two at a time. All I could do was chase after him. Running seemed perfectly logical at the moment—although of course it was ridiculous. We might as well have sauntered, brought our coffee up, and sipped it leisurely in bed, for all the difference it would have made. The damage, as they say, was done.

Downstairs in the kitchen, he sank into my chair. It was less like he was reading than he was devouring what was on the screen in front of him, zipping the scrollbar down so fast that the words were practically flying past him. Somewhere in the dark behind me, a phone began ringing, but Liam didn't seem to notice.

"If you go down to the fifth or sixth paragraph," I said, "there's a quote from Kelly Kahn's business associate calling her—what did he say?—'notoriously secretive.' At least it makes clear that you guys didn't have a clue about . . ."

I could hear myself trailing off lamely. I was trying desperately, Arthur, to find a bright side, to think that the article didn't make things sound as bad as I thought they did, like we had just become the villains in this saga. It should have been clear from looking at Liam's stricken face that there wasn't going to be any consolation. In fact, he didn't even seem to hear me. When he finally turned his head and looked up at me, his eyes were unexpectedly hard.

"Well, at least they got a quote in here from *you*," he said. "The senior engineer's wife. Let's talk to Jessica Frobisher. She's *obviously* the person most familiar with the ins and outs of this story. She's *obviously* the resident expert. She's *obviously* the most logical source, right?" He picked up my mug, looked into it, and slammed it down again as though the sight of the coffee dregs at the bottom had just confirmed his worst suspicions. "No wonder the *Times* is the gold standard for journalism in this country. No wonder we're all so well-informed. Thank God these stewards of truth walk among us." He lifted the mug, toasted, and took a slug. "Pulitzers for everyone! Why wait? Let's bring them out now."

"Wait a second," I said. "You think this is *my* fault?" The phone had stopped ringing and started again.

"Of course not." But he was smiling at me a little sardonically. I jerked the coffee cup out of his hand.

"I'm glad to see that you're finding the humor in this situation," I said. "No, I wouldn't call myself an expert. I wouldn't presume to do such a thing. But I'd say I'm well versed in the ins and the outs of things. They were living at the end of the driveway, remember? They were pumping the neighbors for gossip. This—" I was going to say, *This stupid company is the story of our lives*, but the phone had started ringing again, rising to an infuriating crescendo. "Will you *please* answer that?"

"Gladly," he said. "I think we're done here." Off he stomped, leaving me staring at the glowing screen. All that scrolling had landed on a picture of Kelly Kahn. She was dressed in a business suit and smiling like a corporate Mona Lisa, secretively.

Now it's my turn to leave you staring at a screen, Arthur. I wish so much—oh, never mind.

Jess

From: Jessica Frobisher <jfrobisher@umich.edu>
Sent: Monday, May 12, 2014 1:31 pm
To: Arthur Danielson <danielsav@umich.edu>
Cc:
Bcc:
Subject: boarding house hell

So Corinne lost her first tooth yesterday morning. The one on the bottom row, just right of center. It's been hanging on by a thread for the past week. Unlike Jack, who was tight-lipped about this milestone, ignoring both pleas and bribes to open his mouth and let us take a peek, Corinne turned her sweet rite of passage into one nonstop grossfest, commanding us all to *Look! Look!* while she twirled her tiny white fang at stomach-turning angles. Even tightwad Jack broke down and offered her a dollar if she would let him yank it out and put us all out of our misery once and for all. (She declined.)

When the big moment came, though, it was surprisingly anticlimactic. She came marching into the kitchen in her ballet getup and tugged on the back of my shirt. When I turned around, she dropped the tooth into my hand without a word. She looked a little bereft. "Sweetie, there'll be plenty more where that came from," I said, but she just stood there, pulling at a loose thread on her leotard and looking forlorn. It makes me afraid that the sadness in our house is contagious. I believed Corinne could escape it, but now I'm not sure.

So I made a bigger deal of the occasion than probably I should have. Mostly because I didn't want this milestone to get lost in all our stupid drama. The tooth fairy left a record-breaking $5 under Corinne's pillow Sunday night. It turns out, Arthur, that fairies are afflicted with the same problems we mortals suffer from. Inflation, for one. And guilt.

Spaceco is planning a press conference next week, as soon as they've finished their preliminary report. All those reporters who had lost interest, gone on to bigger tragedies—they're back. We even have our own protesters—a small band of students in raggedy jeans, wielding signs. They've been schlepping out to the office in Livonia to walk around in circles in the parking lot and chant slogans about the evils of the 1 percent. I saw a clip of them on the news. Except for the footwear—the boys were wearing deck shoes and the girls were wearing ballet flats, there wasn't a Birkenstock to be seen—the whole scene could have been lifted from the summer of 1968. It made me think again how you were right—Ann Arborites' motto really should be "The More Things Change . . ."

Tristan attempted to look on the murky bright side by saying the fact that we have our own personal rabble-rousers means we've now officially made it. You're no one, he says, until you have people who are vehemently against everything you stand for, until those people are willing to stand out in the rain and shout themselves hoarse at you.

But they're willing to do more than that. Someone put a brick through the window of one of the cars parked in the Spaceco office lot. It wasn't a Spaceco employee car. It was a Chevy that belonged to some luckless minimum-wage slave working at the Paper-B-Gone next door. After an eight-hour shift with an industrial shredder, the poor guy came out to find his driver's seat skewered with a bunch of broken glass shivs. Not surprisingly, he lost his shit.

The upshot of all this is that the Spaceco men have been camping out here the past few days. It seems to be the centermost location, and everyone can park their cars up close to the house, the better to keep their Goodyears from getting slashed. (Liam's also installed the mother of all motion-detector lights on both the front and the back of the house. At least once a night, they'll blaze on without warning, transforming the dark into a garish noonday. If I happen to be sleeping, I wake up with my heart in my mouth, thinking that I've slept through my alarm and God only knows what has happened while I've been dead to the world.)

So for the moment we're a hostel for Spaceco employees. Or a war room where they're holed up to plan their defense. There's Tristan, who's taking a break from his wife, but there are others too, people I'm pretty sure I've never met before: a silver-haired man who wears his silk ties in half-undone lassos around his neck, some boys in flip-flops who look barely old enough to shave, carrying iPhones and laptops. Someone gave them the keypad code to the side door, and so they wander in and out at all hours of the day and night. I'm pretty sure one or two of them are sleeping here, but it's hard to confirm who's working what shift. I walked into the bathroom yesterday morning thinking the man in the shower was Liam, but when I said, "We're out of toothpaste," talking to myself, as I have begun to do, no longer expecting an answer, a complete stranger's voice, sotto voce, said, "Check under the sink."

So this is what I've been doing: washing extra towels and turning this into a game. It's not as hard as you'd think, Arthur. Jack and Corinne and I compete to see who can build the highest tower with the plastic takeout containers piled up in the kitchen. Jack always wins. (For all his ditziness, he's got Liam's uncanny engineering gift, an intuition about how to make things stay together and how to take them apart.) We've named Liam's study the Situation Room. That's where all the meetings are held. Every single chair in the house has been commandeered and moved there, and it's a pain to reclaim them, so Jack and Corinne and I have taken to eating our dinners while sitting cross-legged in a circle on the kitchen floor. I make pancakes, and the three of us pass around the half gallon of milk, swigging straight from the jug, pretending we're cowhands out on the range. We were sprawled across the linoleum when one of the younger guys came in to nuke a burrito in the microwave, and he visibly jumped when he saw us there. No one had told him about the squatters in the house. "I'm sorry," he said, flushing a little, as though he had walked in on us doing something we shouldn't, to which Corinne responded, and I quote: "No worries, bro." She was wearing an old cowboy hat Jack got from the rodeo a few years ago, and is now too cool to wear, and she didn't even look up from the maple syrup she was attempting to lick off her elbow. My five-year-old has become blasé around strangers.

Most of these men (and they are all men, there's not a single woman among them) don't do any more than nod at me when they pass me in the hallway, but a few of them treat me with a strange deference, smiling at me almost apologetically. It makes me far more nervous than anything else, Arthur. It's like they know something I don't.

On that note . . .

More later,
Jess.

From: Jessica Frobisher <jfrobisher@umich.edu>
Sent: Tuesday, May 13, 2014 3:07 am
To: Arthur Danielson <danielsav@umich.edu>
Cc:
Bcc:
Subject: Re: quick question

Sure. "Just curious." If you want someone to answer that question, Arthur, you'd be better off asking one of the guys crashing on our sofa, one of the men who spent a week of his life at a Marriott in Arizona, where the Spaceco employees locked themselves into a conference room and stormed their brains out coming up with a mission statement and a list of company principles. An inordinate amount of time and effort went into that document—you would have thought they were a constitutional delegation. They took such painstaking care. They agonized. They finessed their phrases down to the Oxford commas, taking them out and then putting them in again. I know, because I saw one of the drafts lying on Liam's laptop bag. You know, I didn't even read it. I just remember staring at all the arrows crisscrossing it, all the dense, intricate loops of red ink in the margins, a record of all their second-guessing.

So, no, I can't tell you what Spaceco stands for. No, scratch that, I *won't*. I know a lose-lose question when I hear it, or when I see it glowing out on a screen in front of me late at night. And anyway, spokeswoman is never a role I've been comfortable with. It doesn't matter how much I believe or think I do—I always feel like I'm lying. I always feel like everyone can tell. It never ends up working out. As we've just seen.

It's not like I don't get that those students have a point. The timing is pretty terrible. The country's coming out of its worst recession in years. There are people out there who can't afford $60 for the blood pressure medicine that will keep them alive, old people who are getting liens on their houses because they can't pay a measly $100 in property taxes. And here are our nation's best and brightest dropping a couple hundred grand to play astronaut for a day. You don't have to be an idealistic twenty-year-old naïf, or some bourgeois hipster taste-testing the social justice flavor of the week, to be troubled by the profound unfairness of this situation.

But you know what—I don't want to talk about this anymore. It's so fucking late. I was supposed to complete my quest to find my single strand of pearls, which I'm pretty sure Paula put away for safekeeping. (I'm betting that wherever they are, they're so safe that I'll never find them.) Instead I spent the evening digging up some stones out of the greenhouse trench and then writing you, and now I have nothing to show for myself.

Arthur, I hope you sleep tight, don't let the bedbugs bite, etc.

Jess

From: Jessica Frobisher <jfrobisher@umich.edu>
Sent: Thursday, May 15, 2014 11:33 pm
To: Arthur Danielson <danielsav@umich.edu>
Cc:
Bcc:
Subject: Re:

That's not how I meant it. I just meant that there are only so many hours in a night. And no matter how hard you grind them out, there's never enough. You know that. You've worked (and/or caroused?) your way through a few wee hours yourself, if I recall.

And no, I'm not sitting around "polishing my jewels." (Which sounds vaguely obscene, btw.) The pearls are for the press conference. Normally you'd never catch me dead in that kind of getup—you know that perfectly well—but I've been ordered to wear them. I'm simply doing what I'm told.

I have to go to bed now and try to actually sleep sans medication. The Ambien's been some seriously bad juju the past few nights, so I'm going cold turkey.

Wish me luck,
Jess

From: Jessica Frobisher <jfrobisher@umich.edu>
Sent: Friday, May 16, 2014 2:29 pm
To: Arthur Danielson <danielsav@umich.edu>
Cc:
Bcc:
Subject: Re: pearls before swine

Yes, Paul Bunyan. I know it's hard for you to imagine because right now you're probably sitting around in the same flannel shirt you've been wearing for days. I'm imagining your cuffs practically fossilized with tree sap. (I remember you said once that tree sap was one of your favorite smells in the world, that it smelled like resilience. *One* of your favorite smells, you repeated, looking at me and waiting for me to ask the obvious question. I heard you, Arthur. I was still playing dumb at that point. I still didn't want to hear the answer.)

Anyway, if I'm imagining this correctly, then take a tip from someone who's spent her fair share of time doing triage in front of the laundry hamper with a tube of Resolve Stain Stick—you might as well bury those clothes when you're done with them. You're never going to get that stuff out.

My presence, along with that of all the other Spaceco wives, has been formally requested by Spaceco's PR team. Or, more specifically, by Lynsey, the crisis consultant they've hired. You should see this woman, Arthur. She can't be much more than thirty. She's got three phones on her at all times and all the schmoozy charm of a SWAT team leader. She walks into a room, and all the men stand up. Wardrobe is just one of her jurisdictions, I guess. One of the first things she did was put me and the other conference attendees on an e-mail list and then start sending out her commando-style updates. They're all sentence fragments, the definition of terse.

Example:

>>Ladies! Opt for skirts and heels. Soft colors (i.e. pastels) preferable. >Stick with minimal jewelry.

Yesterday morning she showed up at the house to do a quick wardrobe checkup. Liam made the appointment (he claimed) and then forgot to tell me about it. With barely so much as a how-do-you-do, she marched upstairs and straight into the walk-in closet, bulldozed her way through the piles of my dirty digging jeans and old, unraveling afghans (Paula's crochet phase, circa 1998), and then proceeded to flick through the hangers, sighing at everything she saw. While she flicked and sighed, she subjected me to a rapid-fire list of what she called her "on-camera no-nos." No nail-biting. No foot-jiggling. No slouching. Nothing that might make me look shady. In other words, I'm screwed.

She finally settled on the least objectionable outfit she could find, that green silk suit I wear once a year when I'm presenting at a conference, the one you said makes me look like a woman playing a politician in a miniseries. "You should get this dry-cleaned," she said. "And get some pearls to wear with it. If you don't already have some." Her voice implied that she thought this was likely the case. She herself looked impeccable, perfectly equipped in a pair of tight rolled-up blue jeans, heels, and blazer. It made me think about the platitude I keep feeding Jack and Corinne, Corinne especially—the one about appearances not mattering. It made me think that I might as well give that one up. Even a five-year-old knows what a crock of shit that is. Appearances absolutely matter. They mean damn near everything.

Just so you know, I saw that Jackie O joke coming from a mile away.

Your not-amused,
Jess

From: Jessica Frobisher <jfrobisher@umich.edu>
Sent: Friday, May 16, 2014 10:39 pm
To: Arthur Danielson <danielsav@umich.edu>
Cc:
Bcc:
Subject: Re: re: pearls before swine

Seriously, Arthur, it's not funny. Can you please drop it?

From: Jessica Frobisher <jesspfrobisher@yahoo.com>
Sent: Monday, May 19, 2014 2:03 am
To: Arthur Danielson <art.danielson2010@gmail.com>
Cc:
Bcc:
Subject: ok, ok

I'm not sulking, you know. It's just . . . I'm not sure where to begin.

The preliminary accident report was finished up on Wednesday
evening. I can't remember—did I already tell you that? Everyone
and their brother was here working on it round the clock, and
they didn't leave until almost ten. I'd been upstairs, reading to
Corinne, and after that I came down to start rounding up stray
coffee mugs. (The Spaceconauts consume prodigious amounts of
caffeine.) When I walked into the study, there was Liam, sitting in
the dark. I almost didn't see him. He was in his desk chair, leaning
back, his legs stretched out in front of him. He had my old UM hat
covering his face, as though he were dozing, although I knew he
wasn't. Liam has never napped in his life. It's against his
nonreligion.

In fact, it was so odd to see him that way that I didn't turn around. I just stood there for a minute, the mugs in my hand, watching him and waiting. Finally he pulled the hat down onto his chest and looked at me.

"Yes?" he said.

"All finished?" I said.

"More or less." He rubbed his eyes and reached over to wake up his laptop.

No more details seemed to be forthcoming. "So?" I said. I could hear an accusatory edge to my own voice. It seems to be there all the time now. When did that become a habit? And why can't I stop myself? I tried again, more gently. "What's the verdict?"

He was clicking with one hand in a half-assed sort of way at the keyboard, not looking at me. "That's a good word."

"What?"

"*Verdict*. Decree. Judgment. " He slammed the computer shut. "What other ones am I forgetting? What else smacks of guilt?"

"It doesn't smack of anything, Li." I was still trying to speak as mildly as I could. "If I'm remembering correctly, the word *verdict* comes from a phrase—'true saying.' Or something like that."

"Well, I'll defer to you," he said. "You're the one who took all that Latin. I always liked that. It was like you knew this secret code. The way you could rattle off the scientific names for all those shrubs outside my apartment. You were how old when we met? Twenty-seven? It made you seem so fucking cute and, I don't know, wise."

The aimlessness of the conversation was starting to disturb me. "Liam," I said.

"You want to know the verdict, Jess?" He pushed the chair back and stood up. "The verdict is that Kramer got lucky on her hunch. Everything in the postmortem analysis points to a faulty switch in the control panel we got from Norell Ops. So there it is in a nutshell. There you have it."

It was the answer I'd been fearfully imagining for weeks, but it still felt like a punch in the stomach. "And you're sure?" I said.

"Like 95 percent," Liam said. "That's as sure as you get. At least when you're trying to reconstruct something that's been blown into a million half-vaporized pieces."

He picked up my hat and began beating it against his leg. "So that's what we're going to say on Friday. We're going to point out that the switch we were using was a whole different model than the one NASA recorded problems with. We're going to point out that we use an entirely different shuttle model than they do, so any comparisons between the two situations are pretty much apples and oranges. We're going to say that the simulations we ran were flawless. That's how we're going to spin it."

I stepped into the dark. I was trying to read his face, Arthur. "What exactly do you mean, 'spin it'?"

"I mean, 'flawless' is a little bit of a stretch." He sighed. "I'm sorry. I've already hashed through this at least fifty times tonight. I don't think I have the stamina for another round. Can we please finish this discussion later?"

"We can't." I stretched out my arms, blocking the doorway. "I'm going to that press conference too, Li. I'm going to be sitting there, nodding along on cue. I have a right to know—" I was going to finish: *the truth.* But something about the way he was looking at me, beating the hat against his leg, made me trail off.

After a second, he went on: "There were anomalies in the feedback we recorded. Only a few. Do you get that? A few very small ones. There was some disagreement about what exactly that indicated. Some of the techs felt very strongly that they were statistically insignificant. Some didn't. We argued about it, and then we made a call, Jess. In hindsight, it's obvious we made the wrong one."

I was suddenly aware that the coffee mugs were rattling in my hand, and I bent over and put them carefully on the floor.

He was still talking, faster now. "Jess, you have to realize that Norell Ops was bidding for us aggressively. I voted against the procurement. But I was overruled. The board decided—"

I remember putting my hands over my mouth, turning around and walking a few steps, then turning back around. "Liam, oh my God."

"Jess, my vote was just an overabundance of caution. I honestly believed that. *I* rode on the *Titan*, remember? That's how practically nonexistent my doubts were. That shuttle ran without so much as a single tiny glitch for over a year—"

"For God's sake, Li. *I* know that. You know that." I was rubbing my temples hard enough to hurt, as though that would somehow help me think. "But think how it's going to sound to everyone out there." I waved my arm toward the window. "Or out there." I flicked his laptop. "How much money are you guys paying that PR consultant? Do you think there's any way that it's going to be enough to keep this story from taking on a damning—"

"You don't understand," Liam said. "The stats in the risk analysis we ran said that switch could have been in use for another decade, and the rate-of-failure threshold would still be—"

"No one cares, Liam!" I was practically yelling. "That's what I'm saying. It doesn't matter anymore."

Is that enough, Arthur? It doesn't matter, because this is where I'm stopping.

You'll notice that I switched accounts—so I hope you're checking this one. It occurred to me at around 2:00 a.m. yesterday morning, completely out of the blue, that I really shouldn't be using my university e-mail to document all our collective malfeasance. It's not the NSA I'm worried about these days, it's pretty much everybody else.

Jess

I know, but it gets worse.

I had a million little administrative bullshit fires I was supposed to be putting out on campus today. Instead I had to spend the day running errands: picking up my suit from the dry cleaners, getting a haircut, hunting down that damn pearl necklace. When I finally broke down and called Paula to find out where it was, she informed me that she had put it in a shoebox in the master bedroom closet. It was clear that she thought my call was a flimsy pretense for something darker and more nefarious, and the more I tried to get off the phone, the harder she tried to grill me. "I know something's going on," she said. "What is it? You can tell me."

"Maybe later," I said. I couldn't think of a simple way to tell my sister that I was getting ready to go watch my husband lie on national television, or to explain, exactly, what I was about to be a party to. I keep thinking that we just need to get through the end of the week. I can practically hear the clock ticking. Forty-seven hours and forty-two minutes to go.

"Jess," she said.

There's a little mirror hanging over my dresser, and I stopped pacing for a minute to inspect myself. It suddenly occurred to me that I hadn't looked at myself—really looked—in weeks. It's like every time I lean in toward my reflection, there are a thousand other things flashing in front of me, and I stop being able to see what's right there in front of my face. There was a woman in a pilling fisherman's sweater and a silky, unfamiliar haircut, holding a phone and staring back at me with a deer-in-the-headlights expression. The stylist had convinced me that the pixie hairdo made me look chic. At the moment, the adjective sounded promising—like it could describe a woman who had her shit together—but standing there in my bedroom, all I could think was, How the hell did I get here? Dr. Paula told me once that she used to have patients ask her that question all the time, and that, honestly, it's a pretty stupid one. "I just want to tell people: think back," she said. "No, think harder. You know the answer. You always do."

"Someone's at the door," I said.

"I know that's a lie, Jess," she said. But I hung up.

What Paula failed to mention, though, was *which* box. We have a huge collection of antique shoeboxes, Arthur, and most of them don't even have shoes. They're these dioramas Jack made. He went through this phase last year where dioramas were his art project of choice. He spent hours detailing them—drawing treads on a racecar's tires, cutting tiny curlicues for shoelaces, making aluminum foil buttons for the control panel of a spaceship. I ended up saving most of them. Their obsessive, meticulous attention to detail filled me with this feeling of dubious awe. I can't remember if I ever told you this, but I used to think up allegorical names for the various people I know. It was a game I'd sometimes play, if I was bored and trying to pass the time—while I was scrubbing the grout in the bathroom, say, or sitting through a sexual harassment seminar. Thom was always Tact. Moira was Stridency. Corinne was Pragmatism. Liam was Brilliance. Or Fanaticism. It depended on the day. For Jack, I usually settled on Discernment, although occasionally it would be something closer to Harebrainedness. Or Melodrama.

Anyway, for a moment I got distracted from my search by looking at these boxes. I began picking up one after another, holding them up toward the lightbulb dangling above me and peering through the jagged little peepholes at these fanciful, intricate construction-paper scenes. There was a boy fighting a dragon, and a jungle filled with birds and some sort of bizarre, blue-faced apes, and one that looked like pilots in a cockpit flying their plane through the yellow zigzags of a thunderstorm. Arthur, I know I'm biased—and that it's in poor taste to brag about one's children—but they were really beautiful.

Finally, I came to the last one in the pile. As soon as I looked it, I knew it was one I hadn't seen before. In it, there was an astronaut hanging from the lid of the box, which was covered in orange crayon stars. He was waving down at a house that looked like ours—same droopy gutters, same tire swing tied to a tree in the front yard. There were a few people standing out on the driveway, and they were looking up and waving back. All except one—a woman who's staring dead ahead at the peephole. Her little red mouth is turned upside down in what appears to be a frown.

I remember what you wrote me: "When someone's in dire straits, every little thing seems like a sign. Resist that urge, Jess." This is so sensible, Arthur, and it's so hard to do.

Just then, the doorbell rang. Some knee-jerk superstition or premonition made me jerk open the closet door and holler out, "Don't answer it!" But it was too late, and no one heard me. Jack was thumping down the hall, and a second later I could feel the suck and shudder in the walls that you can feel anywhere in our house when the door is pulled open and someone comes in or goes out. A second later he was calling for Liam.

But here's where it all leads. The person at the door was a process server. Robert Kahn—that would be Kelly Kahn's father—is suing Spaceco. Liam has been named as a defendant in the suit.

I have to leave off now. Class is in 10 . . . 9 . . . 8 . . . 7 . . .

Jess

From: Jessica Frobisher <jesspfrobisher@yahoo.com>
Sent: Thursday, May 22, 2014 2:12 am
To: Arthur Danielson <art.danielson2010@gmail.com>
Cc:
Bcc:
Subject: Re: allegories

You were Kindness. Or Gregariousness. Or Savoir Faire. Or Disarming Charm, maybe. Or Empathy. Or Common Decency. I don't know, Arthur. Do you see now how the game is harder than you'd think? How you could spend a lifetime playing it?

As to your second question: I never chose for myself. At first it seemed too hard, and then later it became too easy. I'd be Guilt, I suppose, or maybe Deceit. I'm not interested in having you refute this. I'm telling you that it doesn't matter if you think you agree (grudgingly) with Liam. I'm not wise. I'm not anywhere close. I gave up that aspiration a long time ago.

I don't know any more details about the suit right now. Everyone aboard the *Titan* signed releases, and Legal is still telling us that they're ironclad, but with the Norell Ops allegations, all bets are off.

I had another bad dream last night. The Ambien makes them practically apocalyptic. This one was about Kelly Kahn. The two of us were sitting in the clearing of a pine forest, and there was lightning off in the distance. You could smell the electricity in the air. I remember that she was smoking a cigarette very casually, never mind that she must have been seven months pregnant. She was wearing a Spaceco space suit, just like the one she died in, and holding one of those bubble astronaut helmets on her stomach, even though no one who goes up in the Spaceco shuttle actually wears one of those things. Something about her aura was much more salt-of-the-earth than you would have guessed from her polished corporate photos, and I liked her for that. She had freckles. I had the feeling that we understood one another perfectly, that intense camaraderie you have in dreams that's so pure and intense that it's like a stronger version of love, and something that isn't possible to experience in real life.

Something was bothering me, though, making me more and more anxious. I thought it was the cigarette. I started trying to tell her that the smoking was a bad idea, pregnant as she was, but I was doing a terrible job explaining, and she wasn't listening to me anyway. She was patting a golden retriever and watching the lightning move toward us across the trees (which I suddenly noticed were dying, were brown and exploding with millions of tinder-dry needles) and smiling a sly, wise smile. "You should worry about yourself," she said in a way that sounded profound, and then she put her lit cigarette down to the pine needles, and everything went up into flames . . .

And then I snapped awake. It was a little after one, and I could hear Liam downstairs, practicing his speech for the conference tomorrow.

T-12 hours.

Jess

From: Jessica Frobisher <jesspfrobisher@yahoo.com>
Sent: Saturday, May 24, 2014 12:15 pm
To: Arthur Danielson <art.danielson2010@gmail.com>
Cc:
Bcc:
Subject: in transit

The Town & Country is in the shop right now, so I'm riding the bus home to meet the electrician. The greenhouse construction has slowed to a crawl during the past week, although that hasn't stopped me from buying another batch of plants to put inside its imaginary four walls. To Li's great annoyance.

You may or may not have noticed. This is my first attempt at e-mailing on the run. I think it will be my last. Liam gave me this iPhone for my birthday (note the product placement signature at the bottom, I can't get it to go away). He's so smitten with his handheld technology that he can't even imagine anyone not feeling the same way. It's true that this phone is better than I am at everything. It knows it. I know it. We don't even need to argue the point.

So maybe Li is right, and technology will save us all. I have my doubts—but maybe this tech marvel is just making me insecure and aware of my deficiencies. My sturdy proletariat fingers may have been a benefit to my potato-picking Irish ancestors, but soon they're going to be a liability. It was 11:42 when I started writing this e-mail. That was 5 miles ago and my stop is coming up, so

adios -Jesss

Sent from my iPhone

From: Jessica Frobisher <jesspfrobisher@yahoo.com>
Sent: Saturday, May 24, 2014 11:06 pm
To: Arthur Danielson <art.danielson2010@gmail.com>
Cc:
Bcc:
Subject: Re: modern "conveniences"

I know, right? But Liam keeps telling me I can't fall into that trap. Pretty soon, he said, hating technology will mean hating every single thing about modern life: how we eat, how we sleep, how we talk to other people, how we drive, how we read, how we write. How we carry out our dalliances. How we construct our lies. OK, I added those last ones. And Liam and I haven't discussed anything in a long time. He's hardly been doing much talking to me at all, except for responding to questions of the "Can you pick up Corinne after ballet?" variety and his *don't worry about it, don't worry about it, don't worry about it,* which neither one of us believes.

Re: greenhouse additions: snapdragons and tiger lilies. Or dragon and tiger flowers, as Corinne and I call them. I saw some giant sequoia seeds for sale online, but I resisted the urge.

Later, you.
~j

From: Jessica Frobisher <jesspfrobisher@yahoo.com>
Sent: Sunday, May 25, 2014 9:11 pm
To: Arthur Danielson <art.danielson2010@gmail.com>
Cc:
Bcc:
Subject: Re: bloodsuckers

Jesus.

I've only seen mosquitoes like that once before. It was the summer after Corinne was born and we'd had all that rain— remember that? One evening I put her in the sling and took her outside with me to pull some weeds. We were out there for about five minutes, and I came running back inside. I'd thrown down the trowel and was shielding her with both arms. They were devouring us alive. There were dozens of them nestled in her blond baby hair, and I kept crushing them against her head with my thumbs as gently as I could, trying to restrain myself, trying not to slap.

I may or may not have been a little hysterical—it was the postpartum hormones. And I made the mistake of telling Liam about the bugpocalypse. And he went out the next night and mowed down the whole back lot, then soaked it down with DEET. I tried to stop him. I'd calmed down by then and come back to my senses, but he wouldn't listen to me. "Be sensible, Jess," he said. "We have a baby, and mosquitoes carry West Nile. We can't just cross our fingers. We have to do something." He slung the pesticide container over his shoulder and went outside, and I stood up in the bedroom and watched him. Even in the dusk you could see the swarms billowing up from the grass, like a force field that had been disturbed, thousands of them, smelling death. Some superstition made me put my hand over Corinne's eyes, and eventually I put down the blinds and walked away.

I'm not ignoring your question, Arthur. I just haven't felt like writing about it.

Do take care of yourself.

Jess

From: Jessica Frobisher <jesspfrobisher@yahoo.com>
Sent: Monday, May 26, 2014 6:30 am
To: Arthur Danielson <art.danielson2010@gmail.com>
Cc:
Bcc:
Subject: Re: seriously though

I guess that would depend on who you ask. "It's all relative," Jack says. It's his latest catchphrase, and he has no idea just how fitting it is.

Here's how it went down:

We left late. I drove. Liam and I didn't speak the entire way. The drive seemed to take a long time. We hit every single red light. Liam had a stack of accident reports in his lap, hard copies for the reporters. He kept drumming his fingers impatiently against them and staring up at the sun strobe-lighting through the afternoon clouds, dark, light, dark, light. Like a switch being thrown. The blouse I had bought was too small. The sleeves were chafing my wrists every time I went to make a turn.

When we got to the office, I couldn't even turn into the lot, there were so many vans clogging up the entrance. Cars were crisscrossed across the parking spaces, all regard for rules gone to hell. The Spaceco office shares the lot with a sketchy document-shredding company called Paper-B-Gone—wait, I already told you that, didn't I? The point is that it's not an establishment that's doing a bang-up business. It was never intended to hold a three-ring circus's worth of people.

We followed the directions of a kid in a polo shirt who was directing traffic into the field across the street, ignoring the No Trespassing Violators Will Be Prosecuted to the Full Extent of the Law signs haranguing us every ten feet. Nope, Arthur, unrepentant violators that we were, we parked and stepped out into the tangled grass. I was in my Lynsey-mandated heels, and I had to practically run to keep up with Liam, risking a broken ankle with every step.

There was a swarm of people waiting at the door to be buzzed in. Over their heads was the sign with the now-famous Spaceco logo. They took such pains designing it, trying to make something that would be memorable. And now there's nothing to say, Arthur, except: well, mission accomplished.

As soon as we crossed the street into the parking lot, we were engulfed. And here's where it gets a little confused. People were jostling us, talking to us, and around us, and over our heads, and then the door opened, and we were all sucked into a cinder-block hallway, like cattle into a chute. I was less walking than being carried along by the crush of people. Someone was grabbing my arm, clamping down almost to the point of pain, trying to keep me from being swept away, and maybe it was Liam or maybe it was Lynsey, who was calling to us above the crowd in a surprisingly loud, hoarse voice, like she was a platoon leader. Someone was talking into my ear in a low voice, a man saying *steady steady steady* in a consoling voice that, in the confusion of the moment, reminded me of yours. At first I thought it was Liam, and then I realized I was imagining it, because Liam had been pulled ahead of me. All I could see was the back of his head, and there were so many people talking around us that even if he had decided to turn around and say something to me, I couldn't possibly have heard it.

Then just like that, everything was orderly again. We were sitting in the conference room, although it took me a second to recognize it. I was only there once, two years ago, right after the office opened and Liam, proud papa that he was, wanted to show it off. It had changed. Gone was the gargantuan polished table that used to dominate the room. I don't know how they'd gotten the thing back out through the doorway. They must have had to carry it out in pieces. It had been replaced by a sea of folding chairs. Every single one of them held a person; those who hadn't been fast enough to claim one were loitering in the back, drinking from water bottles and tapping on their phones. I wouldn't say that there was a festive air—everyone looked too serious—but there was a sense of anticipation that made my stomach cramp.

I was about to make a beeline for the back so I could mill anonymously, out of the range of the cameras, but Lynsey grabbed me before I had a chance and directed me to sit against the wall near the front of the room, along with three other women. They were all married to someone at Spaceco, and I must have met at least one or two of them at social gatherings, but I didn't recognize anyone except Helen, Tristan's soon-to-be-ex-wife. Her hair was twisted back into its usual sleek chignon, and the lapels of her jacket were perfectly arranged. She looked, as always, impeccable. She looked, as always, positively brittle with barely sublimated rage. Our eyes met, just once, when I sat down beside her, and then we both looked away without a word. There was nothing to say. Later it occurred to me to wonder how Tristan had talked her into coming, and who had used what leverage, and why, but at the moment I didn't have time to contemplate the mysteries of Tristan's marriage, because Lynsey was standing up and clapping her hands. "OK, folks, let's get started," she said, and

Liam got up from the table, smoothed his tie, and walked to the rented podium.

"Thanks, everyone, for coming," he said.

I was so nervous that for a second I blanked out. It was all I could do not to start gnawing on my cuticles—but nail-biting was one of Lynsey's on-camera prohibitions. Instead, I focused on the "Earthrise" picture behind Liam's head. It was about the only thing that hadn't been removed from the room, the single flashy touch someone had left behind. It's a photograph someone blew up into a mural, somewhere in the vicinity of eight by twenty feet. Running along the bottom is a gritty gray lunar surface, and above that nothing but the flawless black of space. And then there's Earth, swimming toward you. Some trick of the light makes our planet luminous, Arthur, like it's not simply reflecting the light of the sun, but actually radiating its own. Those remote, beckoning blues and browns, those ethereal swirls of cloud, are so ravishing that you can practically feel yourself swooning toward them with a feeling like lust. It's a million-dollar picture, meant to seduce. *See what you could have*, it whispers. It was Liam's idea to hang it there, and it was a good one. Looking at it, even an avowed Earthlubber like me feels conflicted, filled with awe so strong that it turns to longing.

It must have been right about then that I got distracted by a man with a camcorder who was standing against the wall on the other side of the room. I'm not sure what made him catch my eye, Arthur. Maybe it was his hair, which made him look like he'd just been struck by lightning—shockingly white and standing on end. Maybe it was the fact that he was wearing three pairs of glasses— one on his face and two pushed up into that electric force field of a haircut. It was like Corinne's favorite old *Sesame Street* song, "One of These Things Is Not Like the Others." While everyone was leaning forward in their folding chairs, focused intently on

Liam as they manned their enormous TV cameras or furiously tweeted updates (we have a brand new hashtag, did you know that? #spacecofail), this guy looked completely blasé. His camcorder was trained on Liam, but his eyes were wandering around the room, panning the crowd, as though he were searching for more entertaining prospects. All that drama, which was riveting everyone else in the room, clearly wasn't doing a thing for him. Just then we made eye contact, and he smiled at me, a big bright alligator smile that showed all of his coffee-stained teeth. I realized that I was chewing on my thumbnail, and I forced myself to put my hands back in my lap.

I tried to focus back in on Liam's voice. Liam's a decent speaker, Arthur. Almost as good as you, but not quite. He's always been hampered by this tendency to stare at a point above the crowd, a bit loftily, and to pause and reach for the most precise, technical word at his disposal. It's nervousness that makes him do this, not some sort of nerd elitism, but it doesn't always come across very well. It seems like he's trying to speak, literally, above the heads of his audience.

But something was different this time. He was holding onto the podium with both hands, leaning forward, staring fearlessly into the crowd while he reviewed the investigation's findings, bullet point by bullet point. He didn't look down once. He'd committed them all to heart. Whatever coaching Lynsey had given him, it was working its magic. He was intelligent. He was articulate. He was gravely thoughtful. Everything about him said *Here is a conscientious man, here is a man who would do the right thing*. I used to imagine that if Liam had lived hundreds of years ago, back in one of the New England villages of his Puritan ancestors, that his fellow citizens would have made him an elder. All his neighbors (Goody Blake, Reverend Procter—I gave them all names straight out of a Nathaniel Hawthorne novel) would have put their stern Calvinist faith in my husband's sound judgment.

Watching Liam up there at the podium, I was thinking that Spaceco's potential clients probably felt the same way. They all listened to Liam's knowledgeable explanations about the mind-bending physics of low-earth orbit over a dinner at the Chop House, never dreaming that he was playing the odds. If he had any tiny, nagging doubts, he never let on. I know now that this is how it happened, Arthur.

When I finally tuned back in, he was at last getting into the crux of things. He was telling us that a malfunctioning switch in the control panel had caused an auxiliary booster rocket to fire prematurely. The control panel had been purchased, as earlier news reports had extensively covered, from Dayton-based contractor Norell Ops.

For a second, just a second, Arthur, he paused. For the first time, he looked directly at me. He seemed to be warning me against something. *Don't,* said the look. But I didn't know what. *Don't move? Don't say anything?* I started to shrug at him, but out of the corner of my eye, I could see the rogue, camera-wielding stranger. He had turned his camcorder away from the front of the room and appeared to be pointing it in my direction. He seemed to be zooming in, as though maybe he had found something interesting at last. I remember thinking right at that moment that he was either the most ADD person in the room, or the only one who had a clue where the action really was. Then he smiled at me again, that same knowing smile, as though the two of us were in on a private joke, and I knew what the answer was. You remember, Arthur, how you used to drop your voice into a faux baritone and say to me, "Jessica Frobisher, you are trouble with a capital T?" (It was just one of what I later came to think of as your "non-jokes.") Well, that was exactly what popped into my head right then. *Camcorder Man, you are trouble with a capital T.*

Liam had found his momentum again. He went on: "We ran extensive tests on the Norell Ops equipment. Testing included over 125 simulations. These simulations worked flawlessly, and the results were overwhelmingly conclusive. Spaceco engineers found absolutely no evidence to suggest—"

Someone from the back yelled out, "So Spaceco engineers were unaware that NASA had experienced problems with Norell equipment?"

"And what about the new shuttle that you guys just finished construction on?" someone else called out. "What's it called? The *Goddard*? I heard you guys contracted out to Norell Ops on that one too—do I have that right?"

"As a matter of fact—," Liam said.

But Lynsey had jumped to her feet. "We'll be opening up the floor to a Q&A in just a few minutes," she said. "If you can just hold your questions until after we get through the statement—"

"We were aware of the problems NASA reported," Liam said. "Spaceco does due diligence on all its contractors and suppliers. We take that part of the process extremely seriously. But you have to realize that the drastically different specs between—"

"So you're saying there were no indications of any problems during your simulations?" someone else called out. The voice was familiar, and before I even looked, I knew who it was: Melissa Kramer. She'd swapped out her sociology professor look for a pencil skirt and lipstick, but she was slouching back tomboyishly in her folding chair, her lanky runner's legs stretched out, her heels hooked on the chair legs in front of her. Her expression was the same one she'd been wearing back on that icy day in April, one of excessive interest, as though she were deeply concerned that she might be missing the point. I can see how it would work for her, Arthur, how it would goad people into answering questions, how it would make them want to keep talking, while she simply let out the coils of rope and let them hang themselves. "Because according to Bill Freed over at NASA, there was—"

"I believe I just said that our simulations were flawless," said Liam. The amount of background murmuring had started to swell, and he had to raise his voice over it, but he was still speaking in a level tone. Except for a faint, hectored flush creeping up into his cheeks, you wouldn't have guessed that he was getting pissed. "I think that statement is more or less unequivocal, but if that's not the case, then let me clarify: there was nothing in the tests we ran that indicated any problems." You could see Lynsey, on the sidelines, shooting him a death-ray look, trying her best to signal him to shut up, but he kept barreling on ahead. "I'm not acquainted with Mr. Freed, and while I'm not questioning his expertise or the stellar reporting of the *New York Times*, I would like to say that there seem to have been a lot of people playing fast and loose with their speculations, people who aren't involved in the investigation and don't have all the facts at their disposal—"

"Oh, here we go," said Helen under her breath, but there was a trace of admiration to it. All the people in the front rows had turned around and were craning their necks to look back at Kramer. The rest of the room had their hands raised and were trying to yell over one another. I could hear Liam still talking into the microphone, saying something like "Look, I'm not disputing the *Times'* right to cover the story, I'm just saying it's a little strange that this story fell into the purview of someone whose previous work has focused on, what—coverage of the EPA and environmental law?" Then someone cut the mike, either on purpose or accidentally. The room had exploded into chaos. Everyone had jumped from their seats. Everyone was yelling— questions or accusations, it was impossible to tell which. A couple of the other Spaceco execs were standing up from behind their card table and holding out their hands like choir directors, but it was too late. Any pretense at restraint was gone, and the air was practically electric with hostility. It seemed like folding chairs might start flying at any minute. Some self-preserving instinct made me stand up, reach for my purse, and start looking for the exit. Several years ago, Arthur, I got caught in a mob outside the In-N-Out. It was right after an MSU game. I'd stayed late at the lab, and I was walking down the sidewalk with my headphones on, not paying attention. The next thing I knew, there were people everywhere, yelling and shoving up against me, absolutely churning with rage. They sucked me up, and for a few adrenaline-filled seconds I was dragged along with them until I was able to bail out into some bushes outside of East Quad. The headphone cord had gotten tangled around my neck and was practically strangling me, but Alison Krauss was still singing away in my ears, with her usual spooky sweetness, about death, death and mercy, as though nothing had happened, nothing at all.

The point is, I wanted to get a head start if things were going to get ugly. The press conference was over.

That's how it went down, Arthur.

More or less.

Jess

From: Jessica Frobisher <jesspfrobisher@yahoo.com>
Sent: Friday, May 30, 2014 12:37 am
To: Arthur Danielson <art.danielson2010@gmail.com>
Cc:
Bcc:
Subject: a little more

I did too.

While we were in the press conference, it rained. Hard. We never saw a drop, but when we came out everything looked like aftermath. The pavement had a dark, soaked look. All the bright new leaves on the trees looked battered. All the shimmering dust hanging above the parking lot, churned up from the gravel by spinning tires, had vanished. I know you've been practically living in a monsoon up there, but down here in civilization we've barely seen rain for weeks. All the meteorologists checking their overflowing rain gauges would later say "Thank goodness" and "It's about time," all of them would say we so desperately needed the relief.

The field was a sodden mess. It took us twenty minutes to get out, to propel ourselves out of the muck, and we only escaped thanks to Liam's fancy footwork with the clutch, and his willingness to torque the tires at breakneck speeds until we could smell the engine burning and chunks of earth were flying sky-high.

He had to concentrate, and neither of us could talk. This was a good thing. The silence allowed me to inspect my hands, my digging calluses, the faint gray traces of greenhouse dirt trapped in the half-moons of my fingernails. (Our soil seems to have these magical, soap-proof, detergent-proof properties. It's unscrubbable. Whatever it stains, it stains.)

When we had finally rocked our way out of the rut, it was Liam who broke the silence first.

"Well," he said. "That could have gone better."

"No, no," I said. "You handle a battle-ax beautifully." I dropped my hands into my lap, pressed my face against the window, and closed my eyes, surrendering briefly to the cold clarity of the glass. "Christ, Liam."

"I didn't say anything that wasn't true." He must have seen me opening my mouth, because he added: "About *her*. About *her*. Jess, those people weren't there to get the facts. They were there to crucify us. They're pretending they're on some sort of noble quest—that they're bringing some sort of painful truth to light— but they're not. They don't know even the first thing about it."

"Let's please have the debate about journalistic integrity later," I said. "You guys do realize that that's the least of your worries right now, don't you? Although that was a nice touch, by the way, going after the *Times*. Liam, *you lied*. You stood up there in front of all those people, and *you lied*. And you made me a party to it. I got all dressed up in this stupid suit, and I—" I had to raise my voice to be heard over Liam's phone, which was sitting on the console between us. It had been angrily buzzing nonstop since we'd gotten in the car.

"First of all," said Liam. "I didn't *make* you anything," Liam said. "Second of all, if I was you I'd think long and hard when I was picking which high horse to climb up on. Honesty? Is that the one you want to go with?"

"What are you talking about?" I said. But I could feel myself shrinking back a little into my seat.

"We don't need to talk about this now. There's no rush." Liam jerked us into second gear and gestured impatiently at the line of muddy cars that were bottlenecking in front of us. "Seriously. Every single person here is making a left turn? You've got to be fucking kidding me."

You'll want to know what I said next, of course, Arthur. Well, here's your answer: a big fat nothing. I didn't even open my mouth. Not because I was afraid to—although I know that's what you're thinking.

No, it was because right then, I spotted a man in my rearview mirror. He was a ways back, but jogging steadily up the line of cars, and he appeared to be making a beeline toward us. He had both arms above his head and was waving them—clearly he was trying to flag someone down, and as soon as I saw who it was, I knew that someone was us. Do you know who it was, Arthur? I'll give you one guess and only one, because I'm sure that's all you'll need. You've always been better at guessing than a person should be. A person can be too astute for his own good, you know. My mother told me once that all gifts are double-edged swords. They cut both ways, she said. So watch out.

Time's up, Arthur. Do you know the answer?

That's right. It was my new friend, the eccentric cameraman from the press conference. The sight of him gaining on us distracted me from the pressing question at hand and made me let out an involuntary groan.

"What's the matter?" Liam said.

"Nothing," I said. "Can we drive faster?"

"Does it look like I can drive faster?" Liam said. "If no one up there is willing to actually use the gas pedal, we're going to be here until we rot."

But it was too late. The man had caught up to us and was knocking on Liam's window. Liam hit the open button with his thumb for about half a second, giving the guy no more than an inch gap. "Yes?"

"Liam Callahan?" said the man.

"Yes?" Liam said again. He hadn't stopped the car, Arthur. We were still bumping along slowly across the ruts, and it was forcing the guy into an awkward sideways trot, but he didn't seem discouraged.

"Theo Lacroix. I'm a documentary filmmaker. I'd like to talk to you about a possible project—"

Much to my relief, Liam cut him off. "Sorry. I'm under instructions not to speak off-record to the press."

"I'm not the press," the guy said. Liam was attempting to roll up the window, but the man had managed to wedge his fingers inside the frame. "I've already spoken with one of your board members. Vince Fay. He told me he was going to speak to you." Keep in mind, Arthur, that this intrepid filmmaker was still jogging right alongside us. His steps were a little lead-footed, the strides of someone with knees on the fritz—the guy must have been in his mid-sixties at least—but he wasn't the slightest bit out of breath. He was giving off the impression that he might be able to keep up with us for the next several miles.

"Well, he didn't," Liam said. We were finally coming up to the shoulder of the road, and I could feel him stepping on the gas. One

114

of the cars behind us had started honking. "So I'd appreciate it if you would let go of my vehicle."

"Just let me give you my card." Somehow Lacroix had managed to reach into the pocket of his blue jeans, extract his card with his free hand, and shove it in the slot above the window.

"I don't want your card," Liam said. "I want you to stop accosting us. I want you to—"

"Liam, for God's sake. Just take it." I reached over and snatched the card. "There. There." I waggled it at our unwanted hitchhiker. "See?"

At that, he finally let go. When he waved at me, I noticed that he was still wearing all three pairs of glasses.

I think that about sums things up. Are these details gory enough for you? I know the nights are long up there, and you don't have TV, and you have more than enough time to kill. (Seriously. *War and Peace* and *Moby-Dick*? You're just showing off.)

More later.

Jess.

From: Jessica Frobisher <jesspfrobisher@yahoo.com>
Sent: Sunday, June 1, 2014 10:59 pm
To: Arthur Danielson <art.danielson2010@gmail.com>
Cc:
Bcc:
Subject: Re:

Arthur, there's nothing else to tell. The conversation ended there. I had plenty of good reasons for not pushing it. I sure as hell am not going to spell them all out for you.

He could have been referring to any number of things, you know. We have no shortage of skeletons in our marital closets—the predictable collection of festering specimens, the things that go bump in the night, etc. Honestly, I don't think he even knows you exist—besides meeting you that one time at that dreadful party at Thom's.

But let's change the subject. How about you send me a good poem from that Mary Oliver I sent you? I never got a chance to finish reading it before I mailed it.

I'm going out to dig.

j

From: Jessica Frobisher <jesspfrobisher@yahoo.com>
Sent: Tuesday, June 3, 2014 11:12 pm
To: Arthur Danielson <art.danielson2010@gmail.com>
Cc:
Bcc:
Subject: Re:

I'm sorry. I didn't mean it like that. I'm not even sure it's true. He might know something. Or part of something.

You remember that night you invited me over for dinner at your place so we could talk about that BioSys metadata problem? This is such a small thing, but when I walked in the door that night and was standing by the coatrack shucking off my jacket, Liam glanced up briefly from his laptop, tapped his chin, and said to me in a very offhanded way: "Your lipstick is smudged." It was such an anomalous comment coming from him. He barely knows what lipstick is, and it took him three days to notice the last time I drastically cut all my hair off.

I paused, and—I remember this—I looked at the clock above the couch. It was 9:53, and that made me relieved for some reason. It seemed like such a sensible, prudent time. Liam was already reabsorbed in his work. That night was the first time, and at that point, Arthur, I stupidly believed that I had strayed over the foul line just once, and that I could sneak back across and go back to playing by the rules, and no damage had been done.

I was ruminating endlessly about all this last night while I was out digging. I keep turning up odd objects with my shovel. A grimy pink calico sunbonnet of Corinne's. Five Scrabble letters. A wineglass with a shattered stem. A tennis bracelet crusted with mud and what appears—to my inexpert eye—to be real diamonds. Last night it was an empty turtle shell. It belonged, I'm afraid, to

Jack's turtle Spike, who went AWOL last summer and never came back. When I get done shoveling, I gather my finds and put them in a box on the shelf in the garage. If this lawsuit goes to trial and we lose (the "highly unlikely worst-case scenario," according to the lawyers) we will at least have these artifacts to remember our old life by.

Be safe.

Your morbid,
Jess

From: Jessica Frobisher <jesspfrobisher@yahoo.com>
Sent: Wednesday, June 4, 2014 2:42 pm
To: Arthur Danielson <art.danielson2010@gmail.com>
Cc:
Bcc:
Subject: Re: the digging hour

I know. Late is the best time to do it, though. Everyone's sleeping, or pretending to, behind their cozy blackout curtains. I can turn on all the motion-detector lights and plow through a few cubic feet of topsoil without any interruptions.

It's true that my new hobby requires me to take GI-bleed amounts of Ibuprofen. I don't even bother with the water anymore. I just crunch up the pills with my teeth and swallow the bitter grit, relishing the slow burn as they go down. But you should see me. I've gotten this digging thing down to a science. It's like I've turned into a one-woman machine, a human backhoe. There's something Zen-like about the rhythm of heaving dirt. Once I get started, I have a hard time stopping. It's like it's myself I'm carving away at—the carelessness, the regret, the useless longing. The explosion in the desert sky. You half a continent away. No wonder so many religions and spiritual gurus link physical suffering to enlightenment—because yes, Arthur, there are moments when I feel as though I'm coming close to something, to Truth with a capital T, the stuff of metaphysicians or your beloved poets.

Just for a moment, though. Then I stop and snap back to myself. My shoulders and back are on fire, and I know it's a lie. I'm getting too old for this.

Liam has taken to pointedly stuffing up his ear canals with Jack's swimming earplugs when he's getting ready for bed. Or, if he's up late working, he puts them in and paces around the house like some sort of deaf-mute. He hates the sound of the shoveling. He claims it's like being lulled to sleep by the sound of a chain gang. Which has tempted me to start belting out a rendition of "Sixteen Tons" while I'm out there flinging dirt around. But there's Jack and Corinne to think of—subjecting them to my singing would be tantamount to child abuse. And there's also the fact that I don't want to up the ante in our passive-aggressive standoff. I'm not sure what it would lead to, only that it wouldn't be good.

There's also been another interesting development, but I don't have time to talk about it now. I'm out the door—there's someone coming from MSU who wants to see (by which I mean drool over) the *Prasophyllum*, and she's supposed to be here any second now.

Off to sell my soul to the company store.

Jess

From: Jessica Frobisher <jesspfrobisher@yahoo.com>
Sent: Friday, May 31, 2014 6:06 am
To: Arthur Danielson <art.danielson2010@gmail.com>
Cc:
Bcc:
Subject: Re: the plot thickens

Yeah, those numbers are screwy all right. Either you guys have hit the jackpot or your postdoc is asleep at the wheel. That's what Rick Ellison would say. Back when I was working with him at BU and we would get some sort of freakily aberrant result on an assay, he would say, "Either we have just made a radical scientific breakthrough, or Frobisher's been logging some serious head-in-ass time." He was dying of cancer by then, you know. He had it for three years and he didn't tell a single soul, not even the man he was practically married to. I'd been here for about a week when Karen e-mailed me to tell me. He was at work and he just went over face-first into a rack of glassware and centrifuge trays. The people down the hall thought something in the chem lab had blown.

Personally, I'm rooting for the inept postdoc theory.

We've had our own, unexpected plot twist here this week. Remember Theo Lacroix? The cameraman-cum-hitchhiker at the press conference? It turns out that he's not just a delightful eccentric. He's a bona fide filmmaker. Or more precisely—he's half of a documentarian duo. His wife, Elle, is a heart-stoppingly beautiful Afrikaner heiress he took on as an apprentice and taught his craft—"the secret of hefting and wielding the camera like a weapon." I lifted that last part out of this review. I'd never heard of either one of them (neither have you, I'd imagine), and nothing on the list of obscure Cannes films that Liam rattled off from his flawless memory rang even the faintest bell. I think I would remember if I'd heard of that kind of hefting and wielding or the "transformation of every gesture, no matter how unremarkable or how brutal, into a lyrical meditation on the experience of being alive in the world." I attached a picture of the woman, and I mean, look at her, for God's sake. That's the kind of arresting, over-the-top beauty that probably stops charging rhinos and rock-hurling crowds of protestors dead in their tracks. No wonder time slows down and the world parts around the path of her lens. She probably doesn't even know things work any other way.

Anyway, it turns out that she and Lacroix have been on Spaceco's waiting list for over a year. They were originally scheduled to go up in June 2015. They signed up back at the beginning of last year, and that was the earliest slot they could get. Ravishing beauty and critical acclaim notwithstanding, the Lacroixs were low men on the Spaceco totem pole. Liam thinks—correction: Liam *thought*—it was funny to be cagey about how the Spaceco list worked. "We here at Spaceco believe firmly in the democratic principles upon which our fine country was founded," he would say. (He was usually gesturing grandly with something here, a screwdriver or a fork.) "First come, first served. All men are created equal." He would pause for a beat and then add: "Of course, some men are created more equal than others." And then he'd lift his free hand and rub his thumb and fingers together.

It was a joke, Arthur. So don't go raising your eyebrows in that meaningful way you do. It's extremely unattractive. You think no one sees it, but they do. I did, and I swear to God, it makes me want to clock you right in the teeth. I'm just not tall enough to draw a good bead on you. Liam never had anything to do with Spaceco politics or the calling in of favors, and not because he couldn't have. So there.

At any rate, it doesn't matter now. There are no longer any favors being called in. People aren't exactly queuing up for a ride in Spaceco's new *Goddard* shuttle. Hardly anybody wants anything from Spaceco these days—except their nonrefundable deposits back. The Lacroixs have suddenly found themselves catapulted to the top of the list, but the fact that they are the last bidders standing in a deal everyone else has bailed on doesn't seem to faze them. Nope. It turns out that this is now an extremely advantageous position for them. Because, get this: Lacroix has decided that he wants to make a documentary about Spaceco.

"Really?" I said. This was at dinner the other night, and we were all sitting around the table. We've managed to get everybody to the table for the past seven straight evenings in a row, a feat we haven't been able to pull off in I don't know how long. But it doesn't feel like an accomplishment. Every single one of us except for Corinne sits like our ankles have been manacled to our chair legs, tensely chewing our undercooked peas like it's an act of will. It's like we're putting on a charade for some unseen audience, a jury of our peers, that's sitting just offstage in the shadows and taking notes, scratching rows of implacable tallies on their legal pads.

"Yes, *really*," Liam said. When I didn't say anything else, he added impatiently, "Go ahead and say it. I can see you're dying to."

"Say what?" I said. All through dinner I'd been concentrating on my greenhouse plans, arranging and rearranging the layout in my head, subtracting and adding up the square footage like a mental math trick. I was trying to figure out whether it would be possible to squeeze in another strawberry planter. (Forget apples, Arthur. I think strawberries should have been the forbidden fruit. They're so small and harmless-looking. You could see Eve thinking, What the hell, just one, only to realize later her devastating mistake— that the fruit's gritty, seedy sweetness has overpowered her, made her insatiable against will.) The point is that, for once, I wasn't thinking about Spaceco. I'm sick of thinking about Spaceco. They can do what they want.

"Say you think it's a terrible idea," said Liam. He was wearing his old Space Cadets T-shirt. For those not in the know, the Cadets are an obscure electronica band. Their music consists of these hair-raising (i.e. "cerebral") plinks and plunks and long quavery notes. The shirt has an equation emblazoned across the chest that's supposedly some sort of inside math joke. Liam has explained it to me three or four times, but I still don't get it.

"All right, then. I think it's a terrible idea." I took an enormous, unladylike bite out of my roll and stared at him. "I think you guys are well on your way to making yourselves the exception to the whole no-such-thing-as-bad-publicity rule. Plus—" I'd bitten off more than I could chew and it was hard to swallow without wincing, but I managed. When I finished, I said, "You saw that guy. You don't think he came across as a little, um . . ." I drummed my fingers on the tabletop, trying to come up with the right word. "Deranged?"

"Oh, there it is." Liam tossed his napkin onto his plate. "Can't we please for once have a discussion without all this hyperbolic—"

But Corinne interrupted him. "Someone's coming to make a movie of us?" she said. I've been forgetting lately, Arthur, that she's at that unreliable age. The best way I can think of to describe it is to say that she's like the foreigner in our house. She doesn't seem to comprehend half of what's said around her, and then suddenly, when you least expect it, she clicks in with disturbing acuity.

"Yes," said Liam at the same time I said, "No, sweetie."

"No one's doing anything yet," I said, glancing at Jack. He appeared to be studiously ignoring us. There was the faintest greeny-gray shadow under his left eye. Yesterday, Arthur, he came home with the sleeve of his windbreaker torn halfway off. He couldn't/wouldn't tell me how it happened, or how he came by a mysterious set of scratches on the knuckles of his right hand. I have (deliberately) failed to mention either of these playground phenomena to Liam. Partly because the explanation they point toward seems so ludicrous: it's almost impossible to imagine Jack having the presence of mind to haul off and deck somebody. And partly because I just don't want to listen to Liam's inevitable boys-will-be-boys response. I'm guessing this may be one of the few points on which you'd actually agree with my husband. And so I'm sorry about how this comes across—like I'm some kind of aggrieved women's studies major with an ax collection to grind— but that expression, Arthur, it fills me with a feeling of doom. Because I know: boys will be boys, and then boys will be men. And I have to confess that I have moments when I think, if I could, yes, I would do anything I could to stop my son from crossing over, · from joining you and Liam over there on the dark side.

"We may not have a choice," Liam said. He was gently patting Corinne's hand while giving me his best to-be-continued look.

Speaking of which, it looks like I have a free hour, so I'm going to go churn up some dirt. Send more details about those census numbers whenever you get a chance.

JF

From: Jessica Frobisher <jesspfrobisher@yahoo.com>
Sent: Sunday, June 8, 2014 1:39 pm
To: Arthur Danielson <art.danielson2010@gmail.com>
Cc:
Bcc:
Subject: Re: greetings from the dark side

Well, I'm glad you found it amusing. I knew as soon as I hit the send button that I should have deleted that last part. That was exactly the kind of remark I used to be able to make to Paula, and I knew she understood what I was talking about even if she wouldn't admit it. These days when I use phrases like "the dark side," all I get is one of her long, solemn, shrinky-dink pauses, and then she asks me if I've given any more consideration to her suggestion about finding a therapist—*just someone to talk to during this stressful time*. She doesn't seem to realize that talking is the last thing I should be doing these days. What I should be doing is keeping my mouth shut.

Anyway, to answer your question: damned if I know what the documentary would be about. Crazy people who want to go into space? The crazy people who send them there? I'll say one thing for Monsieur Lacroix—if this documentary actually comes to fruition, he'll have no end of material. Details are being discussed, deals are being wheeled, and I'm privy to pretty much zero percent of it, so I can't give you any more details. Honestly, it's a fucking relief.

Favorite colleague, if those results you're getting really are valid, then you might be actually onto something terrible and huge up there. Are you more exhilarated or depressed?

I'm off to pick some carrots, so adios.

Your misandrist,

Jess

From: Jessica Frobisher <jesspfrobisher@yahoo.com>
Sent: Tuesday, June 10, 2014 11:14 pm
To: Arthur Danielson <art.danielson2010@gmail.com>
Cc:
Bcc:
Subject: Re: on [not] being elated

No, no, no. I would never want to deny you first authorship on a *Science* paper that's going to get picked up by the AP and spread the illustrious name of Dr. Arthur Danielson far and wide. It would be well deserved.

OK, I would be a little jealous.

OK, I would be a lot jealous. But I'd be envious quietly. I'd make sure to close my office door before the tooth-gnashing started. You'd never hear a sound.

In all seriousness, Arthur, reading those propagation estimates you sent made all the hair on the back of my neck stand up. I was thinking about it again yesterday while Jack and I were thinning out the carrots. The soil's warmer than it was five years ago, the last time I did this, and the seeds grew way faster than I expected. The whole patch next to the southwest corner of the house is teeming with feathery green fronds. We can't pull them out fast enough.

The soil is also, apparently, rockier than it used to be. The ground's been pushing up some heavy-duty stones. Half the carrots we pulled up were deformed. They looked like formaldehyde specimens. They had three or four ends apiece, or these strange tumorous bulges, or they were zigzagged like lightning—the result of their slow-motion collisions with all those stones down there in the dark. "Frankencarrots" is what I called them to Jack. I was trying to lighten our mutual glumness, but he was having none of it. "These things are just *wrong*," he said, and I couldn't help but silently agree. It made me think, Arthur—you're up there counting pinecones, and we're down here staring at carrots. It feels like every single thing is another letter in a sinister message, but one we're not qualified to read.

I meant what I said about the Spaceco project, Arthur. Sometimes ignorance really is bliss. I know we're scientists, but don't tell me that this heretical thought hasn't crossed your mind from time. If those trees have stopped propagating at replacement level, if things appear, in fact, to be slowing to a stop up there in that remote pinewood, if it's beyond our power to save, don't you ever wonder what good it is to know?

I have to go, Arthur. Good luck packing those samples.

Jess

From: Jessica Frobisher <jesspfrobisher@yahoo.com>
Sent: Saturday, June 14, 2014 7:29 am
To: Arthur Danielson <art.danielson2010@gmail.com>
Cc:
Bcc:
Subject: Re: Fwd: The Truth Teller

Sorry. I wasn't ignoring you. Things have just been a little hectic.
It never rains, but it pours like hell.

The film project hasn't gone away. In fact it seems more imminent
than ever, although right now it's being held up by some sort of
schism among the Spaceco employees. There are a group of board
members who see Lacroix and his film as PR repair, a chance to
show off the sexy prowess of the new shuttle, which was finished
just before the *Titan* exploded. It hasn't even been on its virgin
voyage yet, and what better way to celebrate the occasion than to
have a filmmaker with serious street cred capture it on film? Then
there's the group of people—most of Spaceco's rank and file and
the legal department—who think it's a terrible idea, the people
who haven't been blown away by Lacroix's charm offensive. They
think the company should be focused on trying to woo back the
clients who haven't completely bolted yet. I guess I don't have to
tell you which side Liam is on.

So the two sides have been going back and forth, each one nailing
proclamations on the other side's church door. So to speak. That's
how I found out about it a few days ago—when I ran into Tristan
while I was out digging in the backyard. He was walking around
with his laptop under his arm, on the hunt for Liam.

When he saw me, the first thing he said was: "Are you guys getting
ready for your big film debut?"

I put down my shovel and said, "I beg your pardon?"

Immediately he grimaced like he should have known better. Maybe he did. I have no idea how much Liam confides in him about what goes on behind our closed doors.

Long story short, the details above are the ones I managed to extract from Tristan. I guess I've probably told you I've known Tristan for almost twenty years. He may be heading hard toward fifty, but he has that bullshitty charm women go for even if they know better, and I certainly do. Watching him work a room, you would never peg him for the masochistic workaholic he is. Back in his MIT days, he would pull a twenty-hour stint in the lab, then load up his pickup with a barrel full of "borrowed" benzene and drive out to this abandoned quarry where he would torch things and watch them burn to a crisp. Not much has changed since then—except his pickup, since he totaled the old one years ago. And the arson habit, which he eventually kicked, in painful fits and starts, the way other people quit smoking.

By the time we got done talking, it was almost dark and about to rain, and the lilacs were practically overpowering us with their mawkish scent. We should have moved upwind. I have no idea why we didn't. Somewhere during the conversation, he had taken the shovel from me, and he was using the tip of the blade with surgical precision to pick apart an anthill.

I remember putting my hand on his knuckles. "Stop that," I said.

"You do realize that Lacroix is offering to pay us double the going rate for an Earth-spin if we'll cooperate with him to make the film," he said. "That's not nothing. It'll help us stay solvent, pay the lawyers, until we can get a few more people on board and get in the clear."

I shook my head. "I don't get it. Why the hell is he paying you guys for the privilege of making a piece of corporate propaganda? I didn't think that kind of thing was really part of his, you know . . . *oeuvre*." My attempt at being snide fell flat when I mangled the French. "I got the impression he was all about sticking it to the Man. You know, truth to power. That kind of thing."

"Maybe back in the 1970s it was," Tristan said. "What the guy is *all about*, Jess, is making money. Just like the 7 billion other people who live on this planet. Besides." He had started picking at the anthill again. "He'd probably object strongly to your use of the term *propaganda*. He and his wife are going to retain editorial control of the project. That would be part of the deal. Or so I'm told. This is all thirdhand. Or fourth or fifth."

"Well, that's very reassuring," I said. "It sounds as if you guys have got yourself one hell of a plan." I reached out and made a grab for the shovel, but he tossed it out of my reach and took hold of my face. The expression on his face was affectionate or it was rueful, or it was some blend of the two. It startled me. Tristan hasn't touched me in years—not since before Liam and I got married, when he thought it was funny to grab Liam's stuck-up girlfriend and give her noogies until she begged for mercy.

Here's another Tristan story for you: He grew up in South Carolina. His grandfather was a Baptist minister, the old-school fire-and-brimstone kind. At the baptisms, he'd sweet-talk his congregants down to the river's edge and then he'd grab them and hold their heads underwater until they damn near drowned. Tristan will do impressions of him, but only when he's blasted. He thinks they're hilarious. No one else does, but Liam has always made a point of laughing at them, either out of sympathy or protective solidarity, I suppose.

"You know I shouldn't be the one debriefing you on all this, Frobsie," he said. "You need to lay off the home-improvement projects, or whatever all *this* is." He gestured around toward the greenhouse trench. "And fucking talk to Liam. Get your shit together. You know—unified front, and all that garbage."

Speaking of getting my shit together, I have to run, Arthur.

More later.

jess

From: Jessica Frobisher <jesspfrobisher@yahoo.com>
Sent: Sunday, June 15, 2014 11:49 pm
To: Arthur Danielson <art.danielson2010@gmail.com>
Cc:
Bcc:
Subject: Hail Marys

No, Liam's on the pro-Lacroix side. He was originally opposed to the project, but Tristan gave him a come-to-Jesus moment. Which makes sense when you think about it. Who would understand the power, the deep visceral allure, of spectacle better than an ex-pyromaniac?

That puts him and Tris in the same camp as the PR people and four of the board members. It was originally a 50/50 split but they're starting to pull other people over to their side now. Mainly because no one else has any better ideas about how to solve the immediate cash flow problem.

Anyway, what I left out is that—I know I'm jumping around here—yes, there's a chance that Lacroix would be coming here to do some filming. That's what Tristan was talking about. The idea is that the film would be about one or two of the Spaceco guys themselves—a sort of "day in the life of a spaceman." That's how Lacroix's pitching it, and apparently the PR people are eating it up. They love what they're calling the "human element" of it: on Monday morning the Spaceco man goes off to work at a spaceship station, on Friday night he comes home to drive his kids to soccer in the family minivan.

I guess they're figuring that they can use all the humanizing they can get, since this little gem from the press conference is still making the rounds: http://www.youtube.com/watch?v=KiMIrO3kAI9.

And not that this matters, but you know who else is on the pro-Lacroix side now? Paula. Only what won her over was that *New Yorker* profile. (The same one you forwarded to me. Whatever happened to your Internet-free lifestyle, btw?) It wasn't so much what the article said, per se, as the mere fact that our French filmmaker is important enough to be written about in the *New Yorker*, period. She takes this to mean that Lacroix's made it, that he's a respected, legitimate artist, and therefore he can't be a complete whack job.

But where is it written that those two things are mutually exclusive? That profile certainly wasn't one of the more enlightening pieces the *NYer* has ever done. The only thing that jumped out at me was that quote they used as a caption under the photograph of Lacroix. I'm too lazy to look it up, but it went something like: "Theo Lacroix's films are as unsettling as they are ravishing; they often have the feel of parables with ambiguous or perverse lessons. 'All I do is follow people around with a camera,' he says. 'I wait for them to take me to the heart of the story. The troubled heart.'"

Did I pull that off with the appropriate amount of *New Yorker*-esque finesse?

In all seriousness, Arthur, what does this *mean*? I read the article right after you sent it to me, and I sat down to write you some sort of smartass reply, something to the effect of: "Troubled heart? I usually just take Pepcid for that sort of problem." But the harder I tried, the more I realized that I didn't sound funny at all. And then I clicked back again to that pretentious photo of Lacroix in his windbreaker staring spookily straight into the camera, and I felt so uneasy that I just deleted the whole e-mail without sending it.

Arthur, that's all I can fit into this particular dispatch from Crazytown, so I'm sending it off now to the heart of Godforsakenland and hoping you read it soon.

Any chance that I can get you to write and tell me when you're coming back?

Jess

From: Jessica Frobisher <jesspfrobisher@yahoo.com>
Sent: Monday, June 16, 2014 12:12 am
To: Arthur Danielson <art.danielson2010@gmail.com>
Cc:
Bcc:
Subject: Re: trick shots

I know, exactly. That cameraman didn't actually get punched. It only looks like that because of the angle of the shot. (You can see what really happened <u>here</u>.) No journalists were injured during the making of Spaceco's press conference. But you see how bad it looks.

I didn't say that Lacroix was coming here for sure. Although it's looking more and more like it could happen, Arthur. Spaceco thinks we'd make "good ambassadors for the brand." (Again, I ask you, what does this *mean?* This corporate space jargon is even worse than what you like to call "the froth of academia.") We have two kids and one-point-five hermit crabs. We drive an honest-to-God minivan. Liam, when he gets around to his shave-and-a-haircut, can pull off a photogenic, clean-cut Everyman. When I scrub the dirt out from under my fingernails and trade in the galoshes for a pair of flats, I can pass for a dutiful wife. Or something like that.

As sad as this is to say, we're more camera-ready than several of the other Spaceco employees. They don't want, for example, Tristan, who's been living out of a suitcase over in some rat-shit hotel in Ypsi since he and Helen split up. And the PR people don't want Lacroix to go anywhere near several of the board members and their Bloomfield mansions. He wouldn't even need to set foot inside one of those palaces. The landscaping alone screams out 1 percent.

134

In other news, my summer class has been going like shit. The dud students are even duddier than usual. I wish you were here to remind me again why you like these kids. When you tell me there's hope for them, I actually believe you. A little, anyway.

Nighty-night.

Jess

From: Jessica Frobisher <jesspfrobisher@yahoo.com>
Sent: Thursday, June 19, 2014 10:46 am
To: Arthur Danielson <art.danielson2010@gmail.com>
Cc:
Bcc:
Subject: The SBD stench of disapproval in the air

Radio silence. Does this mean you're already working on your paper? That would be a little hard to believe. I've never known you to once sit down and start cracking on a grant proposal with more than ninety-six hours between you and a deadline. Since it seems I'm going to be the first one to take a crack at the airing of grievances, I'd just like to say that I always found your procrastinating to be show-offy and a downright pain in the ass. Why should the wicked prosper? Why should they rake in all the NSF money?

There. I took the first shot. Now write me back and say whatever it is you want to say. I know you're dying to.

Jess

From: Jessica Frobisher <jesspfrobisher@yahoo.com>
Sent: Saturday, June 21, 2014 10:55 pm
To: Arthur Danielson <art.danielson2010@gmail.com>
Cc:
Bcc:
Subject: crickets chirping

Ok, fine, I get it.

It's probably for the best. Your productivity has probably gone up
200 percent since you've stopped writing me. I know mine has.
Today I vacuumed the entire house *and* patched up all the holes
in the screen door (a defensive play after our recent bee
infestation) *and* scrubbed the kitchen floor (more like an
archaeological excavation than housework). It was easier than I
thought. All I had to do was get started and then, voilà, physics
took over. Bodies in motion, etc.

I know none of these accomplishments are as dramatic as your
recent biplane trip or gathering data on the coming arboreal zero
hour, but they are—it turns out—necessary. On Thursday Spaceco
finalized a deal with the Lacroixs that will allow them to film,
starting as soon as next week. Some of that filming will be taking
place here, and the PR people keep reminding us that
"appearances will be of the utmost importance." As though we're
idiots. One of them even called to ask me if I wanted them to send
over someone from Merry Maids, but I told them no, I was
perfectly capable of operating a vacuum cleaner, that it's like
riding a bicycle—no matter how long you go between doing it, you
don't forget. Also that they had probably other things they needed
to spend the two hundred bucks on. Like rocket fuel, perhaps. Or
legal counsel. With that kind of money we can buy another fifteen
minutes of advice and a couple of Xeroxes.

Actually, I didn't say any of that. I'm trying out the whole unified-front routine, practicing for the camera. No, I politely said, no thank you, and then I hung up the phone and got to work cleaning our "artfully disheveled" house. (Thank you, Melissa Kramer, for saddling us with that fucking adjective. It stuck like glue to everything yesterday while I played Holly the Happy Housekeeper, and formed a damning mantra: Windexing the "artfully disheveled" windows, Pledging the "artfully disheveled" newel post. And so on and so forth.)

We did, however, get wrangled into hiring a gardening service to tend to our artfully disheveled lawn. Those Lawn Pro men came this morning, and they took such drastic measures that it was like the foliage equivalent of a police academy haircut. I opened the front door after they left, and I actually gasped out loud. We now look just like our neighbors in Eden Estates. The Queen Anne's lace foaming down in the ditch by the birches, the tender beginnings of the dandelions, the lovely-but-technically-an-invasive-species clover: gone, gone, gone.

That's all I have time for now, Arthur. It's time to go slather on some more elbow grease.

If you feel the urge to end the silent treatment, don't, you know, resist it.

Jess;

From: Jessica Frobisher <jesspfrobisher@yahoo.com>
Sent: Monday, June 23, 2014 3:13 pm
To: Arthur Danielson <art.danielson2010@gmail.com>
Cc:
Bcc:
Subject: Re: black hawk server down

You're right—I should have guessed. How ridiculous of me to assume that you were giving me the silent treatment, especially since there's no precedent whatsoever of you having done any such thing in the past . . .

Oh, wait.

OK, I'm sorry. I was projecting about your being pissed off. But a projecting clock is still right twice a day, and you have to concede that this is one of those times, no?

Arthur, before you say that I'm not listening to you, I want to say, *I am*. I read your e-mail last night while I was milling around in the flower lot at Home Depot. I abandoned my cart and plopped down onto a stack of discounted Adirondack chairs, and I read every single word. Then I read them all again . . . and then a harried-looking man in an orange apron went rushing by and said, "Ma'am, you can't sit there."

Now you have to listen to me. There are certain times when principles are luxuries. Now is one of those times. We're in this, Arthur. We're in it up to our necks. Don't you understand? I'm tenured now, and we could (probably) keep our heads above water on the mortgage, even if Spaceco folded. But there are other pieces of our lives in play here. There's still the Kahn lawsuit, which is sitting out there like a huge wild card. Even if no evidence of Spaceco negligence comes out, our lawyers are still worried about what will happen if it goes to trial. They're worried ("seriously concerned" is the phrase, I believe) about jurors that don't even exist yet. They're "seriously concerned" about those hypothetical jurors' hypothetical sympathies. (Which they claim to be able to predict—never mind how impossible that seems. Shouldn't any one person's sympathies—made up of all those churning, complicated, and infinitely varied factors—shouldn't they be as difficult to forecast as that climate modeling your resident "expert" seems to keep fucking up, or one of those out-of-the-blue heart attacks? But that's their job, I suppose.) They say those jurors will think, *grieving father.* They'll think, *pregnant woman.* They'll think, *dead baby.*

And they're probably right. That's what I would think, even though I don't admit it. Because like I said, Arthur, we're practicing for the cameras here. Whether you approve or not.

I've got exams to grade, so I'm signing off at our end. Good luck with all your technical problems. If it happens again, you might try engineer Liam's tried-and-true method of slapping around the hardware a few times. We've gotten results using that tactic in the past. Though not always desirable ones.

J

From: Jessica Frobisher <jesspfrobisher@yahoo.com>
Sent: Tuesday, June 24, 2014 2:25 am
To: Arthur Danielson <art.danielson2010@gmail.com>
Cc:
Bcc:
Subject: the unexpected guest

Um, OK. I didn't realize that you were so offended by the use of
the first-person plural. If that's the case, then you must hate the
recent spate of department "mission statement" e-mails that have
been spawning in your in-box with a passion. (I know you're
getting them; I looked for your e-mail in the cc list, and there it
was.) Yes, Arthur. To answer your stupid-on-purpose question:
yes. Yes, I am perfectly capable of speaking in the singular. So
don't be an ass—you know that one-letter pronoun is a luxury as
well as a curse. I'm sure you're happy singing the song of yourself
up there in the pine forests of the wild north, go ahead and yawp
away, but remember that being one of a tribe isn't a weakness. I
know you think so.

But all of these arguments are moot since Lacroix's here now. As
in here at our house, Arthur. He materialized in the middle of our
backyard yesterday—or more specifically in the middle of our
carrot patch.

If this strikes you as sooner than expected, you're not alone.
Lacroix wasn't supposed to show up until Thursday. No one was
expecting him, and to say he caught us off guard would be an
understatement. Liam was upstairs, and I was out back, trying to
get in what I thought would be the last of the digging before I had
to go in to campus for a meeting. I've finished two sides of the
knee wall trench, and I'm almost done with the third—there's just
one small gap left until the foundation.

In order to get the full effect of this scene, you have to picture it. The weather is piss-poor—fog, drizzle, a temp in the mid-fifties, and I'm out there in a sweaty, shrunken Spaceco T-shirt of Liam's. I'm up to my knees, heaving and flinging, flinging and heaving, and thinking, mercifully, of nothing, when suddenly, right behind me, a man clears his throat.

It happens at the worst possible moment—right on the upswing—and I'm so startled that I completely let go of the shovel. It goes flying, dirt and all, like a javelin, surprisingly high and far. All this digging has made me stronger without my even realizing it, Arthur. The other night, in the Home Depot parking lot, was the first time I noticed. I was standing there, unlocking the car door with a forty-pound bag of fertilizer on each shoulder, when it dawned on me. I'd been so busy composing my response to you that I had hoisted them up and carried them out of the store without even being aware of what I was doing.

But to continue:

The throat-clearer has to duck to avoid the flying projectile, which he does with impressive agility. It's almost like this is the way he's always greeted—with people throwing objects at his head.

Then he straightens up and smiles at me. And just like that, I recognize him. It's Theo Lacroix, our deus ex machina in the flesh. Except now there are dirt clods resting in his hair and the shoulders of his sweater, which looks like it was, once upon a time, expensive. The only thing I can think is—all that time spent perfecting appearances, all that trying to scrub the grub off the newel posts and pasting up the wilting wallpaper corners—good-bye to all that. It's just been ruined in one fell swoop.

He speaks first. "Jessica Callahan," he says. "We officially meet at last. I am so sorry to have startled you. I should have made my presence known."

He really does talk like that, Arthur, with that kind of formal, borderline grandiose cadence. Maybe it's because English isn't his native tongue, although he doesn't sound quite French either. His accent is some sort of unidentifiable West European patois.

He went on: "I was reluctant to disturb you. You were so focused on your task. Which appears to be—" He jabbed at the edge of my trench with his toe, and looked around at what has become, Arthur, my rather spectacular plant collection. "Some of the most ruthless gardening I believe I have ever seen."

First things first. "My name is Jessica Frobisher," I said. "My husband and I have different last names." I don't know why there was an edge to my voice. Maybe I was disconcerted by the fact that I had no idea how long he had been standing there watching me. Maybe it was the fact that I had to crane my neck to look up at him; I had dug myself down about three feet. Something about the way he was looking down at me, a little too intently, made me reluctant to scramble up. I was wearing Jack's galoshes and there was no way I was going to make it to ground level with my dignity intact.

Whatever the reason—as soon as I said it, I could have kicked myself. I've never given a shit what people called me. I didn't hang on to my name because I was hewing to any lofty second-wave feminist principle. I just never got around to going to the DMV; I was never in the mood for waiting in line. It's only really been since the accident that I've started correcting people. The elementary school secretary. The reporters who called after the story broke. I actually stayed on the line to correct one or two of them. *Frobisher. Frobisher. Frobisher. Are you familiar with Google?*

Do you need me to spell it for you? I've become the worst kind of pedant—which was always Liam's specialty, not mine.

But he didn't seem offended. "Ah," he said. "A woman after my own heart. I wouldn't allow any of my wives to take my name. 'Get your own,' I said." He bent down, picked up my ergonomic shovel, and inspected it. "Besides, you never know when you might have to change it back. And then there will be all that bureaucratic nonsense and—" He waved his hand dismissively. "It is all very tiresome. When it comes to marriage, most people are very . . . What is the correct word? Unrealistic. It is better to be prepared."

It was impossible to tell, Arthur, whether he was bullshitting me or not. "That's a great philosophy," I said. "I bet all your wives really loved it."

"They understood. Some of them sooner than others." Lacroix flicked a piece of dirt from the sleeve of his sweater. "They were smart women," he said. "And beautiful." He sighed with a touch of what I assumed was nostalgia. "And tough. They would be doing what you are doing, I believe."

I looked down at the mud slicks on my blue jeans. "And what is that, exactly?"

"I'm not sure," he said. He stared down at me with those faded and faintly menacing blue eyes and smiled at me again. "How would you like to tell me?"

"I don't think so," I said. One quick scramble, and I was up and out of my rut. "Will you excuse me for a minute?"

I had to hunt for Liam. I found him in the bedroom, his phone against his ear. He jumped a little when he saw me. I made my *hang up* gesture at him—a thumb-and-pinkie receiver followed by a throat slash.

"Can I call you back?" he said. He hung up and took in the continent-size sweat stains on my T-shirt. "That's a good look for you."

"Thanks," I said. "Lacroix's here."

"What?" Liam said. He actually put the phone down—all the way down—on the nightstand and detached his hand. "As in *here* here? That's not possible."

"OK," I said. "But he's standing in the backyard right now."

Liam got up off the bed and walked toward the balcony window, but I reached out and slapped the curtain flat to the glass. "Don't. He'll see us looking."

He did what I said. He stepped back and picked up the phone, running his thumb back and forth across the screen. The harried look he'd been wearing was gone, replaced by an expression of alert concentration. You could practically hear the gears turning. "I'm going to call Tristan," he said. "You know what this is, don't you? Him showing up early like this? It's a power play. I'd bet you anything. He's trying to throw us off. He thinks it's going to give him the upper hand."

"Well, mission accomplished." Against my own advice, I peeled back the edge of the curtain and peered down into the backyard. "You guys picked a real doozy, Li. Have you talked to him? I think he might actually be crazy."

Out on the lawn, Lacroix had taken out his phone and was pacing carefully around the greenhouse trench, holding it out in front of him, filming things: the eaves of the house, the purple-prose lilac trees, Liam's shed, Corinne's abandoned Barbie doll moldering in its ball gown in the grass, like a corpse. Then he turned his laser-like attention to the roses. I remember wishing that you were there to see it, Arthur. He had bent down and was fingering the petals, turning all the buds this way and that to inspect them. No one looks at flowers like that unless they're doing some kind of scientific study on them, or searching for signs of blight. I should know. All of these details in and of themselves were nothing, but it occurred to me that, captured together on his tiny screen, they might add up to something else, like tiny troubling clues. I said, "Did you hear me?"

But Liam already had his phone back up to his ear. He shook his head at me.

"I know, I know," he was saying. "That's what Legal will say, but he's not there, is he? He's standing in the middle of my backyard right now. What am I supposed to do? Chase the guy off with a baseball bat?" He opened the closet and jerked a dress shirt off its hanger. "I don't want to be caught on camera telling him to piss off, whatever the reason. It'll look hostile, or like we've got something to hide." He rolled his eyes at me. "You know what I think— Listen. I think we should show him that two can play this— Fine, fine, fine. I can't have a heart-to-heart about this right now, Tris. Call Jeff and put him in the loop. I have to go deal with this guy."

He hung up the phone, walked over to the mirror, and began buttoning up his shirt. He was staring at his reflection, but clearly not seeing a thing. It was the exact same expression of rapt concentration he wears when he's working, when he's staring at a computer screen, watching a simulation unfold, working his way through a chain of cause and effect. There are moments when I'm afraid, Arthur, that there's some part of him that thrives on this. The crisis, I mean.

When he finished, he turned to me. "Are you coming?"

An image of Lacroix's smile flashed in front of me. "I think I'm going to shower."

"All right." Liam turned to the door. "I have no idea what his plans are, but I told Tristan we'd welcome him with open arms. Kill him with kindness. Resort to any and all clichés that will be required. We may need dinner tonight. Can you take care of that?"

"Sure thing," I said. To his already-disappearing back.

That's all I have time for now, but more later.

Jess

From: Jessica Frobisher <jesspfrobisher@yahoo.com>
Sent: Thursday, June 26, 2014 4:58 pm
To: Arthur Danielson <art.danielson2010@gmail.com>
Cc:
Bcc:
Subject: Re: life on the movie set

It's been . . . interesting. Theo's wife, Elle, came up yesterday. She appeared promptly at 2:00 p.m. at the Livonia office, thus proving that at least one Lacroix knows how to stick to an itinerary. The woman is clearly Theo's better half. Or at least his younger one. That picture I sent you was taken more recently than I thought— she can't possibly be much older than thirty. She arrived in a camper, tailed by two friends in a van—Nigerian guys, I think. Amidst all the chaos, no one bothered to introduce us, but I did manage to catch their names: Abah and Ikenna (sp?). They both had musical accents and a Protestant work ethic like you've never seen before. They spent the better part of this morning doing nonstop laps up and down the driveway, transferring the contents of the van into our house. Floodlights filled with intricate filaments. Clamps and stands and sound equipment. Stacks of duct tape. Miles of extension cords. At least three MacBooks. A thirty-six-inch monitor. Those were just the things I could identify. They worked well past lunchtime, and then they declined the deli sandwiches Liam offered them, choosing instead to sit on the hood of the van and smoke and confer with one another and study the house with carefully neutral expressions.

As far as Elle goes, well . . . She dresses in tastefully faded T-shirts and cargo pants and some kind of designer track shoes, but it doesn't matter. She still looks like Rapunzel, right down to the spun-gold braid and the periwinkle eyes. Corinne's head over heels for her, and so are most of the Spaceco swains. We had gotten the house back to ourselves, but Elle's been here for just a few hours and they're back en masse. (What is the proper plural for nerds anyway? A gaggle? A flock? A herd?) Even the barely divorced Tristan showed up on our doorstep, claiming that he wanted to "just check things out."

"Right," I said. "Things." But I stepped out of the doorway and let him inside. "Last I saw her, she was out in the back," I said. "Why are you even ringing the doorbell? Nobody else bothers to."

"Atta girl, Jess," he said. He picked up Corinne, gave her his best suave look, and hoisted her expertly up into the air while she practically swooned. Six years old, and even she's susceptible to his charms.

I have to go now. More exciting updates to come.

Jess

From: Jessica Frobisher <jesspfrobisher@yahoo.com>
Sent: Friday, June 27, 2014 7:18 am
To: Arthur Danielson <art.danielson2010@gmail.com>
Cc:
Bcc:
Subject: snooping, sleuthing

Arthur,

Today officially ends day four of the Tour de Lacroix. So far, not
much to report. Elle and Lacroix seem to be following a pretty
grueling schedule, which goes more or less like this: Leave a little
after seven with Liam. Arrive at the Spaceco office before eight.
Spend the day filming, asking a slew of questions, taking notes,
and hashing out the details of the upcoming launch. Come back to
the camper parked in our driveway sometime after nine. Hole up
there for a few hours. Lights out around twelve. All that sweeping
and dusting and bee-spraying and screen-repairing, and so far
they haven't done much more than duck in through the front
door, sling a coil of extension cord over their shoulder, and then
duck back out.

Lacroix acts as though we've never had a conversation. He just
hurries past me on the porch, loaded down with a camera on one
of his shoulders—or sometimes one on each—and gives me a
perfunctory, professional nod.

I did catch him at something once, just once. I'm not exactly sure
what it was. I had terrible insomnia on Wednesday night, and
sometime around one in the morning, I decided to get up and
write you. I was coming downstairs when a noise made me freeze
on the landing. I looked over the railing, and there was Lacroix,
standing in the living room. He was standing in front of our
defunct fireplace and studying our collection of family

148

photographs. It's a pretty meager display compared to what most people have nowadays, mostly school portraits of Jack and Corinne. There's just one photograph of Liam and me, the one snapshot we got from our wedding. It's not terribly flattering. In it, I'm wearing a pair of blue jeans, and my ridiculously long hair is blowing in the wind. I have on this crown of flowers, the only bride-like detail I insisted on. We both look a little drunk, although we're not. We're stone-cold sober.

That was the picture that seemed to have caught his eye. As I stood there watching him, he picked it up off the mantel and held it up to a stray beam of light, turning it from side to side as though he was trying to commit the details to memory.

When I cleared my throat, he jumped.

"Looking for something?" I said.

"No, no." He picked up a laptop from the chair next to him and waved it at me. "Just picking up the computer. I was going to get some editing done." It was too dark to make out his face, to see if he looked embarrassed at being caught in the middle of his flagrant snooping. All I could see was the shrug of his shoulders. "To burn a little of the midnight oil. You know how it is."

"I'm not sure I do," I said. Or started to, but something stopped me. Suddenly I remembered that I had left my shorts upstairs—all I had on was on a T-shirt that barely covered me. It was so dark that I doubted he could see me, but I took a step back from the railing anyway. "Lock the door behind you, please," I said.

"Of course," he said. I could see him waving his hand as he pushed open the screen. "Good night, Jessica."

I'm not wrong in finding that whole scene a bit creepy, am I, Arthur? Gone was the elaborate e-mail to you that I had been composing in my head for the past hour. (My sleepless epiphanies about possible greenhouse flooring. You should count yourself lucky.) Instead I turned around and snuck back upstairs. I was hoping to crawl back into bed next to Liam, like I'd never left, but I could tell as soon as I opened the door, by the sound of his breathing, that he was awake.

"What's going on?" he said.

"It's Lacroix," I said. "He was down there in the dark, staring at our pictures. When I caught him, he claimed he was coming in for his computer. Didn't you lock the door?"

Liam rolled over and looked at his phone. "I told him I'd leave it unlocked in case he needed anything."

"Well, apparently what he needed was time to do reconnaissance on all our knickknacks," I said. "While skulking around at one in the morning."

"Well, that makes two of you then." He rolled back and lifted the phone over his head, so that we were both cast in its spooky spotlight. "You seem to be doing an awful lot of prowling yourself these days. Are you still taking that Ambien?"

"It gives me hellacious dreams." I pushed away the phone. I didn't want to change the subject. "This seriously doesn't bother you, Li? You don't think he's, I don't know, a little off?"

"Of course he's a little off," Liam said. "He runs around sticking a camera in people's faces for a living. What normal person does that? Look." He put the phone down. "The film is supposed to have—what did he call it? A personal side. He's probably just trying to, I don't know, get a feel for things. He came in and got distracted."

I'm not convinced, Arthur. But my opinions about our French filmmakers-in-residence aren't the ones that matter. I think Liam's being seduced. Not by the exquisite Mrs. Lacroix (or whatever the hell her last name is) but by Theo. All those questions Theo's been asking? Liam keeps telling me how good they are. Not just good questions. Great ones. Industry-insider questions. The kind laymen don't even know enough to ask. Questions about the angle of the thrusters, about fuel weight and payload, about the new alloy in the *Goddard*'s reusable booster rockets. Hell, he even knew the *Goddard* reference—and was able to rattle off the man's contributions on three-axis control. Liam tells me that he retains every single detail you tell him. This is extremely fortunate for Lacroix, because it just so happens that there is no better way to win the hearts and minds of Spaceco men than to listen to them rhapsodize about rockets, all that ferocious technological power at their disposal.

"What do *you* think of him?" I asked Corinne last night. She was taking a bath, and I was sitting on the floor next to our old claw-foot tub, basking in her soothing presence. She doesn't really need me there anymore, handing her the soap and shampoo; soon she'll be booting me out. That's probably why I want to stay. She was wearing a tiara of soapsuds, but she just lost another tooth, and you can see already how it's changing her face, clues to its adult architecture.

She wrinkled her nose. "I think he's *weird*." She rearranged the neckline on her bubble bodice and reconsidered. "But I guess that's OK if he helps us to be famous."

So there you have it, straight from the mouth of babes.

-jf

151

From: Jessica Frobisher <jesspfrobisher@yahoo.com>
Sent: Saturday, June 28, 2014 10:49 pm
To: Arthur Danielson <art.danielson2010@gmail.com>
Cc:
Bcc:
Subject: Re: space, lies, & videotape

OK. Not *seduce* seduce. But Arthur, you should see it. I came downstairs this morning to find Liam and Lacroix sitting next to one another at the breakfast table. They were hunched over their respective laptops and eating cereal in companionable silence.

"Good morning, Li," I said. "And Theo." It was like I'd accidentally wandered onto the set of *The Odd Couple*.

"Morning," said Li, looking up and smiling at me for the first time in I don't know how long.

"Good morning, Jessica," said Lacroix. "Can I get you something? Coffee, perhaps?" He pushed his chair back from the table. "I noticed some eggs in the refrigerator that looked like they should perhaps be used sooner rather than later. Maybe I can make you an omelet?"

"Sounds good," said Liam.

"No, thank you," I said. I yanked the tie on my bathrobe tighter and frowned. It seems that in our newest family drama, I've been cast in the role of suspicious hausfrau, and Arthur, I am acting the hell out of it.

Re: the flooring: Thanks for your suggestion, but I've decided on slate. Maybe it's less practical, but you should see the tiles I've picked out. They're stunning.

jf

From: Jessica Frobisher <jesspfrobisher@yahoo.com>
Sent: Sunday, June 29, 2014 11:22 pm
To: Arthur Danielson <art.danielson2010@gmail.com>
Cc:
Bcc:
Subject: Re: rocks

Yeah, I just ordered all the gravel and slate online. The color's called rustic gold, and it's beautiful. Blue with these brown and golden swirls. It looks like coastlines and oceans. The Internet is amazing. Are you sure you don't miss it?

Jesseeeca

From: Jessica Frobisher <jesspfrobisher@yahoo.com>
Sent: Monday, June 30, 2014 10:49 pm
To: Arthur Danielson <art.danielson2010@gmail.com>
Cc:
Bcc:
Subject: Re: rocking it, sort of

That's what Lacroix calls me. I've told him at least five times that
no one calls me that (with the exception of you, darling colleague,
when you are trying to deliberately piss me off), but he won't stop,
and I've given up. There is something about his accent, the soft S,
the long wistful E, that makes it almost sexy—but sexy with a
whiff of sophistication, not in the trashy soap opera blond way
that I've always loathed.

It still doesn't make him any less annoying, Arthur. Nor does it
help that he's been hanging around the house more and more
these past few days. He's starting to become ubiquitous.
Everywhere you turn, there he is: smoking out on the stoop in
front of the camper, or pacing around the yard at sunset with a
cigarette in one hand and a book in the other, even when it's too
dark to read. When I was out there last night, making
measurements for the flooring, he wandered by in a ghostly cloud
without noticing, lost, I presume, in some sort of cinematographic
rumination. It looked like his head was smoldering.

It wouldn't be so bad if I could laugh at his pretensions. Like
when I come home and find him lying out in the grass under the
tire swing and shooting the thunderclouds through the branches
of the birch trees, say. Or when I look out the kitchen window and
see him prowling around through the greenhouse plants. But I
can't . . . quite. It's the *way* he films, Arthur, the way he looks. He
hunches into his camera, and his head tilts with this almost
canine acuity, like he's tuned in to something out of the normal

human sensory range, like he's seeing something that other people can't.

I don't know why watching him do this makes me so uneasy. There was even one time after he had finished in the greenhouse space—I probably shouldn't admit to this—I went to see if I could tell what he had been staring at so raptly for the past ten minutes. I unlocked the deadbolts on the dining room door and pulled it open and stood looking down into my veritable jungle. There was the new batch of roses I haven't had a chance to de-pot yet. The planters of lettuce. The impatiens. The teacups of basil and dill and cilantro. The twin gardenia trees. (I'd only meant to buy the one, but there was a sale.) And that's just to name a few things on the list. It was a small leafy fortune, staring back at me, and I think that's when the exorbitance of my little project truly hit me, Arthur. I slammed the door shut and leaned against it and tried to catch my breath. That was it. From now on, I'm going cold turkey on Home Depot.

Now Lacroix's asking Liam for what he calls some "domestic scenes." He's asked if he can come in and film a few shots of us at dinner one night. Of course, Lacroix being Lacroix, he did his best to make his request sound much more high-flown than that. What he said was something along the lines of "I would love some footage of the spaceman at the dinner table. With the wife. With the children. You know, home from a day in space." (Imagine a grand arm wave here, Arthur.) "Home from a day of crafting spaceships." They were out on the porch talking, and this is what I overheard as I was hauling a lazy man's load of grocery bags up the steps. I would have rolled my eyes, but I didn't want to risk losing my balance.

So I finished Lacroix's sentence for him: "'The sweat dripping off his heroic brow into his plateful of steak and potatoes.'"

They both turned and saw me then.

"Ah, Jessica," said Lacroix.

I shook my head at Liam. "Absolutely not, Li," I said. "Do you hear me? Absolutely not."

"We'll think about it," said Liam.

Famous last words.

Gotta go.

Jess.

From: Jessica Frobisher <jesspfrobisher@yahoo.com>
Sent: Wednesday, July 2, 2014 1:08 am
To: Arthur Danielson <art.danielson2010@gmail.com>
Cc:
Bcc:
Subject: Re: lead with your left side

Yes, well, in case you were wondering who won that one: our dinner with Theo is now scheduled for next week.

Arthur, I'm losing ground every single day to that man's charm offensive. After Liam, Corinne was the next one to succumb. Trying to keep her away from the camera is almost a full-time job. I have resorted to carrying around an old lab timer. If it dings after five minutes, and she's not in the room, then I get up and go find her. I've managed (I think) to make it clear that Lacroix doesn't want endless footage of her dance routines, so she is now resorting to stealthier tactics. She hangs out for a while in her bedroom, and then when she knows I'm distracted, she swaps out her T-shirt and shorts for her Sleeping Beauty ball gown or the purple tutu from her last dance recital, and then she goes to find Lacroix. She sidles into his frame by pretending to be distracted by some other innocuous activity—fiddling with the blinds, say, or restacking the books on the coffee table, or flicking her hair, like a movie extra gone rogue—and someone has to go grab her. *What?* she protests. *What?* This cunning side of her is new, and I'm not sure whether to be impressed or disturbed by it, Arthur.

Jack looked as though he was going to be a holdout, but Lacroix won him over by showing him how to fasten a tiny fish-eye camera into the elbow of the dining room chandelier with a handful of bread-bag twist ties. When I came downstairs the other day, the two of them were standing on chairs, making faces into the lens—Jack pulling open his nostrils as far as he could with his fingers, and Lacroix baring his teeth like fangs.

"Jack," I said. "I walked by the hermit crab tank, and they're sniffing each other hungrily. Would you mind feeding them, please, before they resort to cannibalism?"

He heaved a long, extravagant sigh—that's at least one way he takes after me—and jumped down from the chair with a crash. When he left the room, I turned back to Lacroix, who was adjusting the twist ties, twirling the ends around one another with a surprising delicacy. You wouldn't think someone with fingers like rolls of quarters would be able to pull off something so finicky.

"Don't you have some spacemen to film?" I said.

He pushed his glasses up into his hair and peered appraisingly down at me. "Of course," he said. He let go of the chandelier and started to make a heavy-footed descent, but I tapped his knee and pointed up to the camera, which was spinning above our heads in plumes of disturbed chandelier-dust.

"Don't forget to take that with you," I said.

I suppose it's paranoid to think that Lacroix would accidentally-on-purpose leave cameras up without announcing their presence. After all, he made a point of telling Liam three times that he was putting one up in the library where the occasional Spaceco confab is still being held. But Lacroix has taken over the living room, clearing Jack's Erector set off the coffee table so he can fit his mega-trillion-pixel monitor on it. Half of the nights now, he's in there, sitting in the armchair with his headphones on, watching the brilliant history of the day flicker past in some kind of trance. Which means the dining room is *mine*. Last night I was sitting in there, writing to you, and when I looked up, he was standing there in the dark doorway—no warning, just boom. He should have been accompanied by one of those forte horror-movie piano chords. I was so startled that I fumbled a keystroke and somehow hit the delete button. And—*poof*—my e-mail vanished into the ether.

Most of whatever I was writing you doesn't matter now anyway, but I did want to thank you for the words of encouragement. I know they didn't come easily. I know how hard it is to talk/type something when one is biting one's tongue, metaphorically speaking.

I'd forgotten about your appearance on that PBS special. You don't need to pretend that there's any chance in hell that I'm ever going to come close to rivaling your performance, Arthur. It's not a matter of "relaxing" or "being yourself." Honestly, being myself is the last thing I want to do. Not everyone has that gift, that shine, that fearless sincerity, that whatever-it-is. You do, Arthur. You have it to burn. Here's another thing I shouldn't confess to:

sometimes watching you in your element, at your most golden moments—it made me a little sick. I wasn't envious although maybe I should have been. I think the feeling was something even more pernicious. I think it was fear.

That's the reason why, the day after the special aired, I didn't say anything about it. I was standing in the hall when you came in that morning—I don't know if you even remember this—and Moira went running toward you in full-blown screech mode, flapping her hands and squealing: *ArTHUR, ArTHUR, you were aMAzing!!!* And I just turned around and went into my office and closed the door.

Not long after that you knocked. (Actually, I'm pretty sure you just barged right in. Knocking has never been your style, has it?)

"Well?" you said.

"Not bad," I said.

You took it perfectly in stride. You accused me of being constitutionally incapable of giving credit where credit was due. Arthur, tell me you were joking.

Well, too little too late, here it is: I DVR'd that damn special. I hung on to it for over two years. Then this past summer I erased it in a moment of resolve. Actually it was a fit of pique disguised as some sort of self-help Buddhist tenet, the one that advises you against clinging to what is lost.

Anyway, you haven't seen my face in a while, so perhaps you don't recall that my right side's definitely my best one. I'm going to do my damnedest to keep Lacroix on that side, but I don't know if it will work. He is one wily bastard.

You, on the other hand, look just charming from whatever angle. I absolutely remember that.

Jess

From: Jessica Frobisher <jesspfrobisher@yahoo.com>
Sent: Thursday, July 3, 2014 10:59 pm
To: Arthur Danielson <art.danielson2010@gmail.com>
Cc:
Bcc:
Subject: Re: recriminations

Oh, please. Moira's always had a thing for you. Don't tell me you didn't know. Even your lousy man-radar should have been able to pick up those signals. They were about as subtle as one of those air-raid warnings.

Yes, Elle's around. I do like how even you, btw, from a distance of a thousand miles, are interested in that woman's whereabouts. Goldilocks has been involved in the filming over at the Livonia office, but my impression is that she's much more hands-off than her husband. "A free spirit" is what Lacroix calls her, with what is, as far as I can tell, Arthur, wholehearted admiration. "An ice queen" is what the Spaceco guys say, with obvious envy. There are entire days when she takes Abah, hijacks the Lacroixs' van, and disappears. Someone told me that she's hanging out in Detroit, filming all those grand imploding train stations and movie theaters and courtyards gone to seed, the ones with trees growing out from between the paving stones and wild pheasants roosting in the fountains.

I'm pretty sure that she's more intrigued by American urban blight, our rack and ruin, than she is by Spaceco's existential crisis. (This makes me like her, gratefully, despite the fact that she can hardly be bothered to speak two words to me.) It's hard to say for certain, because the Lacroixs converse almost entirely in French. No one from our party can understand it, although thanks to two semesters in college, I can catch a few words like fly balls out of the air. Just enough for wild speculation.

One more thing before I sign off again. You still haven't told me your ETA for coming stateside. Are you thinking about what classes you're going to be teaching this fall? I think Thom said there's still an unclaimed 265 section. I know I sure as hell don't want it.

Have a good night, Professor Danielson.

Jess

From: Jessica Frobisher <jesspfrobisher@yahoo.com>
Sent: Monday, July 7, 2014 5:16 am
To: Arthur Danielson <art.danielson2010@gmail.com>
Cc:
Bcc:
Subject: eavesdropping

Well, think about it. Three undergrad sections is about all I can take.

I just got back from taking out the trash. I normally try to get the cans down to the bottom of the hill before dusk, when the raccoons come out. It's always been a little dicey with them, and this year it's been worse than usual. Maybe the mild winter caused a population spike—something has made them meaner and more territorial. More than once I've come out to find them pulling off the lids, working away at the airtight latches with their canny, prehensile little fingers. When you startle them, they sit up on their haunches and hiss at you like harpies in lumpy gray bathrobes and smudged eyeliner, clutching their rotten apple-core treasure and showing their fangs. There's a warning there, I think, about the potential for malevolence, even in small things. I still think of that story Moira told about being up in the U.P. with her BB gun boyfriend and his beagle and those raccoons . . . and I still shiver every single time I do.

I told you that Lacroix and Elle have parked out in our driveway, haven't I? Well, they have. A friend in Ohio lent them some sort of camper. (*Not* a Winnebago. Lacroix corrected me—the word seemed to offend some Euro-sensibility of his.) Its wheel wells are trimmed in rusty lace and the weather has left oddly evocative patterns in the aluminum siding, but it has a functional bathroom and a dinged-up cooking range. Elle has hung out a clothesline (upon which she unabashedly hangs her exotic unmentionables) and arranged around the steps pots full of mysterious herbs that I can't for the life of me identify. (Some sort of African hallucinogenic? Some sort of homeopathic aphrodisiac?) It looks like a Space Age homestead.

The point is, the thing takes up pretty much the entire driveway. I couldn't even squeeze the trash cans past it. I had to maneuver them into the grass, and that's what I was doing when I heard a noise. All the lights were off in the trailer, so it took me a second to realize where it was coming from. It was the sound of Elle laughing from inside, a giddy, delighted sound that crackled subtly in the quiet air, like lightning does when it's forming, when it's still electrons racing from the clouds to the clods, the charges rushing to meet each other in the air before the entire sky lights

162

up. As soon as I heard it, I knew I should go, should pick up my trash cans and get the hell out of there. It's a sin to eavesdrop on others. It's like theft, like taking away something that isn't yours to take. I have always believed that, Arthur. Even if I laughed when you used to slow down exaggeratedly outside other people's closed office doors or slide that shot glass along your wall with your ear pressed against it. I never believed anything that you claimed to hear; I honestly believed you were making it up. Tell me that's true. Think what they were saying about us.

Still. I couldn't go. It was like something was holding me there by the scruff of my neck, pinning me to the grass against my will. All I could do was stand there, my bare feet soaking with dew, my palms slick against the trash can handles, riveted, and listen to them in their passionate fervor. When it's not you, in the throes, you can hear how it sounds differently outside the storm, that it sounds like sobbing, and a little like grief. My heart was pounding like a sledgehammer in my chest. I felt like someone dying of thirst, Arthur—listening to rain in the distance.

So there it is, my most shameful confession yet. You know that this is something that I wouldn't tell anyone, don't you? There has got to be a way of breaking myself of this habit.

But in the meantime, it's morning here, and there are stale cornflakes and toast to burn.

Yours,
Jess

From: Jessica Frobisher <jesspfrobisher@yahoo.com>
Sent: Tuesday, July 8, 2014 2:07 am
To: Arthur Danielson <art.danielson2010@gmail.com>
Cc:
Bcc:
Subject: rooftop encounters

Arthur,

So I'd managed to avoid Lacroix for a solid four days. My streak was broken yesterday when I came home at lunch, thinking no one would be here, only to find our filmmaker friend wandering around on the roof.

The first thing I spotted when I pulled in the driveway was Lacroix's van. The second was the ladder propped against the side of the porch. That ladder came with the house; it's practically an antique. I think the model stopped being sold years ago—maybe because of the locking mechanism, which is temperamental, or maybe because some genius in the marketing/design department decided to call it the Lightning Rod, and have orange and yellow zigzags painted down the sides. The thing is a fifteen-foot telescoping aluminum death trap. I don't allow anyone to set foot on it, except me, because I'm the only one who's fully mastered its quirks.

You can guess, then, why seeing it there made me . . . unhappy. What I wanted to do was walk straight into the house and slam the door behind me. But I didn't. There's some infernal maternal instinct that kicks in when you have children, Arthur—no one warns you about this—that makes it hard to turn around and walk away, that compels you to save nitwits from themselves.

Sighing heavily, I got out of the car and slogged across the lawn. I grabbed the ladder and rattled it. "Theo!" I yelled. "Theo, I know you're up there."

Silence.

There was nothing to do but go up after him. I grabbed the fourth step of the ladder and jerked it up and down, racking the thing sort of like a shotgun, until I heard a telltale click. Hearing it confirmed what I'd thought: he'd climbed the whole way up with the latch undone, nothing but dumb luck keeping him in the air.

He'd also pitched the ladder at a near vertical, considerately, to avoid crushing my rosebushes, but I wasn't afraid. Thanks to all that tree-climbing as a kid, I'm not afraid of heights. It's one way I'm fearless that Liam's not, which is why I clean the gutters every fall, while Liam—if he's around—sticks firmly to the ground and rakes the leaves. "Stop that, Jess," he says when I moonwalk in my sneakers all the way to the edge, just far enough that my heels are hanging over the edge, nothing but two stories of windy, empty air under them. "I'm not kidding. Stop it right now." It's a stupid stunt, yes, but it's a long way from what he calls it: "cheating death." A funny accusation for a man who once strapped himself into a seat perched on half a ton of rocket fuel and then let someone else ignite it. Such a thing to have done—I knew it even then. Such a reckless extravagance—setting all your luck on fire, as though you have an infinite supply to burn through—that it's amazing it took so long for this to end in tragedy. It's this blasphemous thought that hits me with such force that there are times when it stops me in my tracks.

When I got to the top, I had to wander around for a minute before I spotted Lacroix. (I'm a little in love with the geography of our roof, with its little mossy peaks and valleys and its smoldering vents, but visibility is poor up there.) He was standing on the gable above our master bedroom window with his camcorder out, and he was filming the beautiful leafy altitude, the sun going in and out of the clouds.

Theo, I was about to say, but then I stopped. I said it quietly, Arthur, because there was a kind of uncanny intensity to his demeanor that made me reluctant to break it. When I took a step closer, I could hear him talking to himself in an odd froggy voice. It seemed to be this peculiar narrative that went something like this: *Space as seen from the roof of rocket scientist Liam Callahan. Tantalizing. Mysterious. Most of us are content to admire this view from here. For some though, this is a view synonymous with desire. What if one could escape our planet's clutches, catch a glimpse of the universe? What if one could come back with a tale of what you had witnessed, a story that the rest of billions of stranded earthbound could only imagine and envy? The CEO of Spaceco perhaps put it best. "It's seeing Earth like God," he said. This is the dream that he and the men of Spaceco are selling.*

I waited to see if he would continue, and when he didn't, I cleared my throat. Carefully. Because he was awfully close to the edge, Arthur, and front-loaded with that heavy camera. How he hauled it up the ladder, all by himself, I haven't the faintest idea. I said, "For a price."

"Ah, Jessica." I could tell by the way he said it that he'd known I was there the whole time. Still holding the camera, he turned around, step by step, until he was facing me. "Come here. I want to show you something."

"Theo," I said. "You can't be up here. "

"And yet here you are." He was still holding out his hand, beckoning me closer, while he fiddled with a tiny foldout screen on the side of his camera. "The intrepid botanista." He was clearly not listening to me. "Come, come, come."

"No." I crossed my arms over my chest. "Not until you step back from the edge," I said. "We've had an unlucky streak lately, remember? We don't want to push it. We can't afford to lose anyone else. Think how it would look."

It was the first time either one of us had alluded to the accident. Liam and I, Arthur, are under strict instructions from the Spaceco legal department not to discuss this matter with Lacroix. "Not on the pain of death" was the phrase Liam used, employing a rare bit of hyperbole.

"I would think it looked very clumsy of me." He sat down, hoisted the camera up on his knees, and patted the shingles next to him. "Sit. Don't sigh, Jessica. It's very unbecoming."

When I had slithered down next to him, he pointed to the screen. "I was admiring your particular sliver of sky. Look at this marvelous shot I got. No, you have to get closer."

The screen couldn't have been more than 3x5. I had to lean sideways and squint to pull the image into focus. At first it was nothing but an electric green flickering, but then it resolved into leaves, then into rippling treetops, a whole sea of them. The wind was traveling through them in odd gasping heaves. So steady-handed was Lacroix's shot that it took a second to realize that he was panning out. Then a rooftop appeared, like a drab, lonely island, then another, a small archipelago of them gathering together. Far off in the distance you could see the highway, as clear as the boundary line on a map, glittering with distant speeding cars. The farther back he pulled, the more the clouds towered, until they seemed a kind of atmospheric tour de force. The whole thing couldn't have lasted more than ninety seconds, tops, before Lacroix snapped the screen closed with a click.

"Beautiful," he said. "If I was going to die while seeing with my own eyes all of this from up there—" He gestured with his free hand toward the sky. "I would say, well, that it would not be the most terrible way to go." He scratched his chin thoughtfully. "How many of us human beings are allowed to witness something truly awesome? I do not mean *awesome* in the American sense of the word, you understand. I mean a glimpse of something that feels as though it was intended to stay hidden from our view."

I jerked up, pulling away my cheek, which had almost come to settle against his knee, without my being aware. It was like I'd been in some sort of trance, Arthur, for just a few brief seconds, but then I snapped to. "What did you say?"

"It was a quick death," he said. "Very quick. That's more than most people get."

"That's easy for you to say," I said. "You weren't on that shuttle." Something about his equanimity was infuriating. It goaded me to add: "Or Elle."

"I am not afraid of dying." He was fiddling with his camera, making adjustments with one of its myriad buttons, but he was still looking at me. "There are worse things, you know."

"Right." I realized I was running my hands through my hair, and I had to start smoothing it all down again. "I suppose you know all about that."

"Not all. Some. I've seen a few things. I've gotten around."

He had lifted up the camera again, this time toward me. I could see the green light was on. "Stop that, Theo," I said.

"Stop what?"

"You know what." I said. "We had a responsibility to those people. To keep them safe. To bring them back. You and Elle, you have this boho lifestyle—"

He frowned. "I am not familiar with that expression."

"'Free spirit,'" I said. "But some of us have obligations—"

"We most certainly do," Lacroix said. He had dropped the charming shtick. I had never seen him look so serious. "To be witnesses to one another, to think about how we exist in this world. To try to squeeze out a little bit of the fucking truth. It is very difficult."

"That wasn't what I was going to say. But OK," I said. He still had his camera running, Arthur, and I sighed and turned away—my unsightly left side to the camera—to look studiously out across my haphazard garden with its torn-up turf and its profusion of lavish flowers. "I was told you weren't an idealist, Theo. I was told you were a money-grubbing opportunist."

"Who told you that?"

Off in the distance I could hear a faint squealing, and I knew it was Liam. That serpentine belt in the Chrysler—or whatever problem it is that they don't seem to be able to keep fixed—you can hear it from half a mile away. "All that stuff I just said," I said, gesturing toward Lacroix's camera. "It needs to be off the record. You got that?"

"They were mistaken," said Lacroix.

"Theo." I snapped my fingers at him, the way I do at Jack when he's daydreaming. "The correct answer is yes. 'Yes, Jessica, I'm going to delete it.' *Capisce*?"

"*Capisce,*" he said. "Your secrets are safe with me, Jessica."

"For Christ's sake," I said. "They're not—" I was going to finish: *secrets.* But the squealing from Liam's car was getting louder. He was almost to the driveway, and all I wanted to do was get Lacroix down from the roof before Liam found us. I didn't want to have to explain to Liam what the two of us were doing up there. Over the past week or so, Liam and I have reached some sort of détente, and something told me that this would ruin that.

But it was too late. Lacroix went down first (so slowly, Arthur, so excruciatingly slowly), and by the time I slithered down to the ground after him, there was Liam, standing there with his laptop under one arm. He was looking at me and then Lacroix and the ladder like they were puzzle pieces he was trying to fit together.

"Ah, the spaceman returns," said Lacroix. "I tried to call you earlier. Elle should be returning from her countryside ramblings around two. That means three Elle time. I was hoping we might come to shoot you and Tristan and some of the others unpacking the new equipment in the lab around sixteen hundred hours. Will that be too late?" As he was talking, I could see that he had a few leaves nestled in his hair, and I had to resist the urge to reach over and pull them out.

"That's fine," Liam said. He had stopped squinting up at the eaves and was studying us now, trying to decide how exactly to play along. "I hope Jess didn't have you up there collecting footage of the sad state of our roof. It should have been replaced five years ago. I keep telling myself, one more serious storm and—" He let out a whistle, which was intended, I suppose, to indicate the top of our house sailing merrily away in the wind.

"I didn't even notice," said Lacroix. "Your wife and I were gathering some fresh air. Admiring the view. Having a nice philosophical chat."

"Is that right?" said Liam.

"Quite," said Lacroix. "You picked a good one. She's sharp as a tack." He reached up and pulled one of the leaves out of his hair and smiled at me. "Now. If you'll excuse me."

As soon as he turned away, Liam grabbed my arm. He couldn't say anything out loud, so he mouthed it at me instead: *What the hell?* All I could do was point to my head and twirl my finger.

Speaking of which—I have to go too—More later—

From: Jessica Frobisher <jesspfrobisher@yahoo.com>
Sent: Wednesday, July 9, 2014 12:01 am
To: Arthur Danielson <art.danielson2010@gmail.com>
Cc:
Bcc:
Subject: Re: As Guest, that would be gone—

Yeah, I know. That was a very Emily Dickinson sign-off. Also, an appropriate line choice. Kudos for that.

Thanks to some schedule wrinkles, the night Lacroix was supposed to film us at dinner got pushed back again to tonight. I'd been at the lab all day, trying to catch up on some overdue genome sequencing, and after racing across town at light-warp speed to pick up Jack and Corinne from day camp, cooking was the last thing I wanted to do. All I wanted was one of those dinners that

171

Jack and Corinne and I have when Liam's out of town—the kind where I heat up a pizza and dump out a bagged salad and then the three of us sit around the table, each of us with our head stuck in our own book. Remember how I told you that I was never going to do that? That's exactly what my mother used to do with Paula and me, Arthur—she was always sticking her head into Austen or Tolstoy or Eliot and teleporting away. It was like she had unlocked the back door and slipped out without telling us. "You'll understand some day," she used to say. When Paula and I got into college, when we got to that age where we had figured out everything about her that she was too obtuse to figure out for herself, we used to take turns translating that phrase: *You'll understand what it's like to have children ruin your life. You'll understand what it's like to be menopausal and bitter. You'll understand how to take the passive out of passive-aggressive.* We thought we were hilarious. It never once occurred to me that she might turn out to be right.

I decided to make salmon and roast potatoes. With the heat from the broiler, the kitchen felt like blazing summer out on the veldt. I'd ditched my jeans for a lightweight (and casual yet tasteful) cotton dress, and the sweat was still trickling down the back of my legs. Everywhere I turned, there was either Elle or Lacroix hovering with a camera lens.

Our kitchen, Arthur, was built before everyone (or, ahem, their husbands) needed to buy things like the latest espresso makers and self-cleaning blenders. Even with just me, it's none too spacious. Now there was Liam, suddenly motivated to tinker with a raspberry vinaigrette he hasn't concocted in years. (He's a good cook, precise and meticulous as a chemist, if not inspired like you, Arthur.) And there was Jack running back and forth in heart-stopping zigzags with handfuls of flatware and plates. (In honor of the occasion, I had decided to ditch the Corelle, and bring out my beloved flea market china with the orchids around

172

the rims.) And there was Corinne pliéing in the corner. (Maneuvering in a not-so-subtle effort to stay in Lacroix's frame.) Yet somehow there were Lacroix and Elle, negotiating their cameras through the chaos, like the old hands they are. You would have no idea, looking at stiff, stocky Lacroix, that he had that kind of dexterity.

Somehow we managed to get ourselves situated, and then there we were, sitting at the table, the spaceman and his earthly nearest and dearest. As I sat there looking around at my family, Arthur, I had another one of those moments I keep experiencing lately. It's like I'm not one of us, as though I'm an outsider or an impostor. I could see how beautiful they were, how extraordinary and oblivious. There was Corinne with those ephemeral butterfly tattoos flaking off her arms. There was Jack. His soccer jersey was still shimmering with red-gold soccer dust, like some precious mineral traces, collected in its wrinkles and seams. And Liam, who I will pass over here without comment. It was the feeling I had the first day you kissed me. (Ten indiscretions, ten fingers. You can count them on both hands.) I came home, and I sat at the table, still feeling the traces of your lips seared along my neck and clavicle, and I watched them carry on with their mundane acts of eating their carrots and drinking their milk, with a feeling of love so overwhelming that it made me queasy, and I couldn't eat a thing.

For several minutes it was quiet. It was becoming readily apparent that spacemen don't have much more to say at dinner than anyone else. I could have told Lacroix that. That after a while the glamor wears off everything. Even CIA operatives and lion tamers and those people who fall out of planes wearing nothing more than those nylon wings must eventually come to the dinner table and have nothing of interest to tell anyone.

My plan was not to speak until directly spoken to, and then as little as I could get away with, but I could see Liam fidgeting in his chair. He couldn't stand our sitting there like some sort of monotonous still life (working title: *Disappointing Family at Dinner, Dullsville, 2014*) while the film rolled in Elle and Lacroix's cameras. I knew eventually he wasn't going to be able to stop himself from breaking the silence. And then, sure enough, he did. He turned to the kids. "How was camp today?"

"Fine," said Jack.

"Boring," said Corinne.

Out of the corner of my eye, I could see that Elle had wandered away to the window and was filming something outside. It could have been one of those deer that keep coming and eating my roses. I keep going out there and finding red petals all over the ground. It's a smorgasbord out there, Arthur, but for some reason they don't seem to be tempted by anything else.

Liam shrugged apologetically at Lacroix, who was still standing in the corner, heroically filming away. "We aren't exactly in rare form tonight," he said.

"You don't have to *do* anything," said Lacroix. "You can just eat. Just pretend we're not here."

It was right then that Corinne decided to pipe up: "It used to be more exciting back when our house was on TV all the time," she said. "I really miss those days."

"I bet you do," said Lacroix.

"Corinne," said Liam.

"After those people died," Corinne said.

Behind me, Elle turned away from the window and pointed her camera back toward the table.

"Can I be excused?" said Jack.

"You may not," Liam said. "Corinne, that's enough."

"I'd really like to be excused," Jack said. Then he went for his fail-safe tactic: "I have to go to the bathroom."

"You're not done with your dinner," Liam said.

"One of them had a dog," Corinne said. "I saw a picture of it on Dad's phone. He was yellow, and one of his ears was missing a big piece. Like half." She took a bite of her potatoes and chewed thoughtfully. "I think something bad happened to it, but no one told me what."

"You don't say," said Lacroix. He was speaking so gently, Arthur, that it was impossible to tell whether he was just being kind or egging her on. I didn't dare look at Liam. I didn't dare look anywhere. I was sitting straight in the camera crossfire, so all I could do was sit there and pick at my salmon skin, searching for edible bits as though my life depended upon it. There was a bee crawling on the rim of Corinne's glass, searching delicately for something with its antennae, but she hadn't seen it yet.

"I'm not hungry," Jack said. "I can't eat when Corinne keeps blabbing. It's killing my appetite."

"I don't even know what that means," Corinne said. "So you're not hurting my feelings."

I reached out, put my hand on Jack's knee under the table, and spoke as quietly as I could: "Just a few more minutes, Jack." This was a trick that once worked almost without fail, Arthur. I could put my hand on his back and he would calm down, soothed like a puppy by nothing more than my touch. Liam never got the hang of it—and yes, I took a little evil pleasure in that. The Jack Whisperer, I called myself. Only at some point the trick stopped working, Arthur. At some point he was onto me.

He shrugged me off. "I'm leaving," he said, and stood up, almost throwing back his chair in the process.

"Can you please turn that off?" I said to Lacroix and Elle.

"Of course," said Lacroix. But he pulled down the camera slooowwwly. The eyepiece had left a red groove around his right eye, like a monocle. The five of us listened to Jack thunder his way up to his room, pausing on each stair to stomp for emphasis.

"I think that went well," I said.

Liam's jaw was set the way it is whenever he's thinking murderous thoughts, but he turned to Lacroix and managed to give a convincing smile. "You'll have to excuse Jack. Every now and then, he likes to start practicing for his surly adolescence. He's normally a pretty easygoing kid."

"Of course," Lacroix said. "Sometimes, the camera . . ." He shrugged apologetically. "It changes the dynamic. Observer's paradox and all that."

"Exactly," said Liam.

I stood up. I'd had about as much of this little charade as I could stand. "Will you excuse me?"

Elle was back at the window with her camera, filming the deer, who were, just for the record, eating my rosebushes.

The only thing I have left to say is: What the hell?

Jess

From: Jessica Frobisher <jesspfrobisher@yahoo.com>
Sent: Saturday, July 12, 2014 1:00 am
To: Arthur Danielson <art.danielson2010@gmail.com>
Cc:
Bcc:
Subject: shades of Lacroix, part . . . I've lost count

I don't know. I think I'm finally starting to adjust to having him around—further proof that, given enough time, a person can find pretty much any situation normal. Take you, for example, and those birds singing their hearts out an hour before midnight.

It does help that he has that rare instinct for being helpful. Example: Last night he filmed Corinne dancing around in the backyard for almost *thirty minutes*. Do you realize how long that is? Half an hour of Corinne's look-at-me time is like one and a half hours in regular time. Liam and I *combined* don't have the patience for that.

Plus, I'm starting to think that Liam's overly optimistic first impression may have been right after all. The man really is some sort of savant, Arthur. Not only is he up on all his rocket lingo, he's an amateur naturalist. He can name almost all of the flowers in the greenhouse-in-progress, plus a smattering of the insects and birds that have started moving into what's become my own miniature preserve.

I interrupted him in the middle of his nature-watching yesterday afternoon. When I opened the dining room door to nowhere, there he was, smoking and watching a beetle crawling along some of the false indigo I got to lure in the butterflies. (My plan is to put it outside the greenhouse, flanking the foundation.) There was lightning off in the distance and a silvery, diaphanous rain was sprinkling his hair with droplets, which he kept brushing off absentmindedly between puffs. He looked so absorbed that he didn't seem to hear me when I jumped down and reached over my head to push the door shut behind me, so I waited a minute before I said, "Storm's coming."

"It certainly is," he said.

"Just so you know, I hid the ladder," I said. "In case you were thinking about going to play Benjamin Franklin on the roof. Liam said you should be banned for life, so management has revoked your privileges."

"Ah," he said. "It sounds like management is trying to save me from myself. You know what Elle would tell you, don't you? She would say, 'Good luck.' She almost divorced me after an incident involving a disgruntled hippopotamus and a Zodiac outboard motor. Which it turned out, upon closer inspection, was defective." He tucked the cigarette into the corner of his mouth and lifted his camera hand to train it on the flashing sky. (It's like the camera is a physical extension of his arm, Arthur. I've taken to referring to him as the Bionic Man, a joke Liam refuses to find funny, because he refuses to find any of my jokes funny these days.) "I had to promise to make it up to her. There was groveling to end all groveling."

"And did you?" I said. "Make it up to her?"

"Of course," he said. "I always do."

I was dawdling. I didn't want to go inside and try to think of what to make for dinner, so I dallied there, watching Lacroix follow the lightning across the sky. One of Jack or Corinne's astronaut helmets was lying on the ground, and I leaned over and picked it up and wiped the rain off the visor. Liam got them at a conference last year. They're not your average dinky kids' toy, Arthur—they're realistic-looking mock-ups and not cheap ones either. How Liam wheedled them away from the vendor, I don't know. Probably he regaled him with some fantastic specs about the rocket Spaceco was building: its weight, its maximum velocity, its payload capacity, its state-of-the-art booster rockets. The helmets have special shields that can be pulled down to protect against glare, and I hate when the kids wear them. It makes them look like strange little specters from the future, their faces beaming back the world to you, dwindled trees and clouds, and behind that full of secrets they won't, or can't, tell you.

"Exquisite," said Lacroix. He dropped the camera to take another deep and poisonous inhalation from his cigarette. "I am dying to get up there and see these storms from space. Your husband tells me it is an unbelievable sight."

"So I've heard." I scuffed my feet on gritty slate and sighed. "What's the deal with the launch anyway? Have you found your victim yet?" I can't remember if I told you this, Arthur: Lacroix and Spaceco have been working on finding another person to come up with him and Elle as part of the film, a guinea pig, someone they can film and interview about the experience. They've been talking to candidates for the past two weeks, a few people on Spaceco's decimated client list. Some of them are more unsavory than others, and the ones Lacroix likes, the Spaceco-ites hate. I overheard Tristan talking to Liam about one of them—some Eastern European businessman who had allegedly, *allegedly*, made at least some of his money running guns into Somalia. What Lacroix thought of *him*, I don't know, but the Spaceco board, not surprisingly, vetoed him on the spot.

"Not yet," said Lacroix. "These people who want to go into space, it turns out most of them are crazy."

"You don't say." I imagined you, Arthur, nodding your head in agreement. "And what about Elle?"

"What about her?"

"How much groveling does it take to drag her all the way into space?"

"I don't drag Elle anywhere Elle does not wish to go," Lacroix said. "My wife may have her own ideas about things, her own"—he waved his hand around, searching for something—"her own very specific vision. But she is game for anything." He looked at his cigarette, maybe trying to gauge how much smoke was left in it. "I pitched this film to her, and do you know what she said? Yes. Yes. Yes. No hesitation. She knows if one has a chance to see something extraordinary, one should take it. Bring whatever you can of it back to the world. Don't roll your eyes."

"I'm not," I said.

"Liar." He stubbed out his cigarette and put it carefully in his pocket. "And you?"

"What about me?"

"You would go if you had the chance, yes?"

"I used to think so. It seemed very glamorous."

"And now? Perhaps the accident made you afraid?"

See, here you have a perfect example of a Lacroix vicissitude, Arthur—specifically how he can go from charming you to getting on your nerves in an instant. "I'm not afraid," I said. "It just strikes me now as extravagant. Maybe selfish. You know how many gallons of fuel it takes for one launch? Tons. Literally. And, *poof!* It's obliterated in seconds." I thought of those college kids marching, futilely marching, outside the Spaceco office. "Maybe those people were right."

"What people?" Lacroix said.

"Come on, Theo," I said. "Try not to be so full of shit. You know who. I know even you take a break from fighting off angry hippos to watch some TV."

"It's true," Lacroix said. "There's no way around it."

There are more anecdotes I have about Lacroix, but this is probably about all you can stand. I hope you're enjoying your brief foray into civilization.

Sleep well, sleep tight.

Jess

From: Jessica Frobisher <jesspfrobisher@yahoo.com>
Sent: Monday, July 14, 2014 12:42 pm
To: Arthur Danielson <art.danielson2010@gmail.com>
Cc:
Bcc:
Subject: Re: murmurations

No. I've never seen anything like that, not anything close to the extent of what you've described, although I've heard of it happening. They say there can be hundreds or thousands of them up in the sky all at once. It sounds heart-stopping. What makes them do that? How on earth can we ever know?

I worry about you, you know. Not just because of the poetic descriptions (e.g., "a dark cloud of God"), not just because you're writing about God at all (I feel that urge too—like you, I'm the atheist hunkered down in the gritty black muck of an emotional foxhole), but because I know what it's like to wander so far away that you don't think you can come back. Come back, Arthur. We'll work it out. I'll browbeat Thom into switching my office to the Herbarium. We'll limit our exchanges to nods in the hallways. We'll keep our hands in our pockets. There has to be a way to still redeem ourselves, to salvage a piece of something good from all this wreckage, although I'm not saying it will be easy.

I have something else to tell you, and you're not going to like it. But I don't have time to go into it now.

so consider yourself warned, i guess.

Jess

From: Jessica Frobisher <jesspfrobisher@yahoo.com>
Sent: Wednesday, July 15, 2014 3:22 am
To: Arthur Danielson <art.danielson2010@gmail.com>
Cc:
Bcc:
Subject: dirty laundry & digressions

I'm getting to it, but you have to listen to this story first.

Since before we got married Liam has had this habit of putting
things into his pockets and leaving them there. Screws, ball
bearings, microchips—you name it. And those are just the things I
can identify. One time I found two pesetas mixed in with his
quarters, like he'd made a quick trip to Spain for his lunch break.
When I asked him about them, he told me that he'd spotted them
in the tip jar at Amer's, so he'd picked them out and replaced them
with dollar bills—a more than fair exchange rate, by his math.
Something about the color or the weight of the coins made him
curious about the alloy, and he wanted to run some tests to see if
he could calculate the components. He had a guess, and he
wanted to prove himself right.

Maybe it's a heritable behavior, because Jack does it too. It took us
losing one washing machine to a rock collection (and two hours of
Liam's time to dismantle the broken machine and fish pebbles out
of its guts because Jack was "100 percent sure" that he had
identified one of his latest acquisitions as a "precious or
semiprecious gemstone"), but I learned my $400 lesson. I now
perform thorough pocket inspections on all clothes before they go
into the wash.

I was in the upstairs bathroom yesterday, digging through the
laundry hamper, carrying out aforementioned rifling duty, when I
found something in a pair of Liam's khakis.

Normally, I wouldn't have paid any attention to it. I stopped scrutinizing the contents of his pockets—almost all of it completely unidentifiable—a long time ago, and started dumping it on the top of his dresser. But this particular thing was wound up carefully in a handkerchief, almost like it had been bandaged, which I suppose is what made me stop and unwrap it.

What I found was a long, thin piece of silvery metal, shaped like a blade, and so light that it weighed practically nothing. When I held it under the bathroom light, I could see that it was scorched faintly black around the edges and inscribed with hundreds of fine scratches like hatch marks. It was twisted, although you could tell that it had once been flat. Even a nonphysicist like me could tell that something with incredible force had torqued it.

To my inexpert eye, it looked like titanium or some sort of amalgam. This is just one of the contradictory quests of Liam's line of work, and of spaceships in general. They require materials that weigh nothing but can withstand anything, the unholy heat and friction that engulfs any kind of projectile attempting to escape the hold that Earth exerts upon it—I'm writing this in spite of the fact that Liam has always resisted the personification of what he reminds me are mere physical forces. "Don't make everything so personal" has always been his mantra. I don't know when it turned from a consolation into a criticism. I think it started early on and happened faster than I realized, the way inevitable things do.

You've probably guessed what I'd found. It actually could have been a thousand things, but I knew. I knew immediately that I was holding a scrap of what used to be the Spaceco *Titan* shuttle. What I didn't know, Arthur—don't know—is how long my unsentimental husband has been carrying it around with him, this token of guilt or grief, or what it means exactly.

I'm not sure how long I stood there, ankle-deep in the dirty laundry, inspecting this sharp-edged artifact, turning it carefully over in the palm of my hand, before I heard footsteps coming down the hallway.

"Jessica?" a voice said. Lacroix's head appeared in the crack of the open doorway. Caught in the act of—what exactly?—I shoved it into the pocket of my sweatshirt. The point of it sank right into the fleshy mound at the base of my thumb, and I didn't need to pull out my hand and look to know that it had drawn blood.

"What?" I said, trying, unsuccessfully, not to wince. "*What?*" I kept my hands in my pocket and tried to give him the same evil eye that I give Jack and Corinne when they interrupt me when I'm on the phone. Clear and direct signals. That's what Paula recommended, that's the best way to deal with someone with boundary issues, which is what she informed me Lacroix has.

"Everything all right in here?" Lacroix glanced curiously around the bathroom. No doubt he was taking it all in—all the private, revealing particulars of our laundry: Corinne's tiny, ethereal pink ballet tights, Liam's T-shirts with their trail of sweat and grease stains, Jack's thermals with the cuffs all nervously picked at, my (as you know) disappointingly unsexy cotton underwear.

"Great," I said. I could feel the palm of my hand slowly filling up with blood, and I was trying to hold it at just the right angle so as not to spill it. I didn't want to make a mess, not in front of Lacroix.

"Someone's at the door with some papers. He needs you to sign for them. Liam isn't here." He cocked his head at me. "I don't think I'm allowed. Since I'm the third-party voyeur."

"I'll be right down."

Still that damn man kept lingering in the doorway. He pulled his bifocals down, settled them on his nose, and peered at me through them. "You sure you're all right?"

"Theo. For God's sake. I'm fine. Can you please go voyeurize somewhere else?" Although the truth, Arthur, was that I was starting to break out into a sweat. I was getting a little light-headed, and I could feel my heart beating, not in my chest, where it was supposed to be, but somewhere down in my thumb. It wasn't from losing blood—I wasn't that bad off—but from thinking about it, or maybe from trying so hard not to. It's embarrassing to admit, but I've fainted twice in my life, and not because I was injured—it was just from looking. Once was when Liam fell off his bike and shattered his tibia. The other time was actually worse: Jack was walking across the top of the monkey bars last spring when his foot slipped through and he slammed his forehead on the way down, splitting it all the way down to the bone. I managed to stand up off the picnic bench, and take about three steps toward his lifeless-looking body . . . and then I woke up with a mouthful of woodchips and a panic-stricken woman screaming in my ear. I had no idea where I was, and all I wanted was for someone to shut her up; I recall that my first coherent and uncharitable thought was that she sounded positively histrionic.

More than anything, I did not want to faint in front of Theo Lacroix. "Go," I said. "And for God's sake, take that camera with you."

"Yes, yes." Lacroix held up his hands in a gesture of exaggerated surrender that I'm coming to know and loathe. "I'm leaving. But you know what I think?" He tapped his forehead. "I think that you, Jessica, are a liar."

And with that very astute observation, he finally left me to bleed in peace. My hand was shaking, but by holding my breath, I managed to ease it out of my pocket and lean over the sink without spilling any gore on myself. I stood there running water over the wound and pressing on it, trying to make it to stop. It wouldn't. At first it seemed a little worse than I had originally thought it was, then I dropped the *little* and decided that it was just plain worse. I had cut myself all the way down into the muscle, a smooth, surgical-looking slice that ran almost from my wrist across my palm, straight through all those love lines and life lines that psychics use to predict a person's so-called fate. This seemed exactly like one of those signs you would tell me to ignore, Arthur. So I did. Someone, somewhere off in the background, was making a weird rhythmic hissing noise, and then I realized it was me, sucking my breath in between my teeth over and over. "Mom," screamed Corinne from downstairs. "The man is waiting for you. I think he wants to leave."

"Just a second!" I called back. I was fumbling around under the sink, with one hand, for the gauze. We needed those papers, Arthur—for reasons that you'll understand if you'll let me explain them—so I was torn. I had promised Liam I'd get them. But I also had no desire to go staggering downstairs like a blood-spattered woman out of a horror movie. The kids have been through enough.

I managed to wrap up my hand—more or less—and then, stuffing the whole mess into my pocket, I made my way downstairs carefully. The double vision made it seem like there were twice as many steps as there really were, and it was tricky telling where the real steps ended and the phantom ones began. I signed illegibly for the papers using my left hand. No one seemed to notice, especially not the delivery guy, a hipster with thick black glasses and mustache, who seemed to be distracted from his modus operandi of bored disdain by the impressive piles of filming equipment in the living room.

As soon as he left, I sat down in the armchair next to the front door and tried to think. I needed to figure out what to do with the kids. Because a couple of things were becoming clear to me. Mainly:

1. I needed to get to a hospital;

2. I wasn't going to be able to drive myself; and

3. I didn't want to call Liam.

It should tell you something about my level of desperation that the person I finally settled on was our neighbor, Beth.

"Beth, hi," I said when she answered the phone. "Jess Frobisher. I'm sorry to bother you, but I was wondering if I could ask you for a favor."

Immediately she fell quiet, but I forged ahead anyway. "I have a little bit of an emergency situation, and I was wondering if I might be able to drop Jack and Corinne off with you for a few hours, while I . . . take care of something."

The silence continued for another few seconds, so long that I pulled the phone away from my ear to make sure that the call hadn't been dropped. Perhaps she was praying for guidance, checking in with God to find out about the blowback that might come from offering aid to the wicked. I was thinking of a biblical verse myself right then, the one about pride going before a fall.

"Oh, Jess," she said. "This really isn't a great time. I'm supposed to be meeting Jim downtown in a little while, and I—"

The piece of the spaceship was still down in my pocket, like a piece of shrapnel, and I didn't dare touch it. "Beth," I said. "I'm going to level with you. I had a little mishap, and I need to make a trip to the emergency room for some stitches. I'm bleeding right now. As we speak." I paused to let this sink in. "I am asking that you set aside whatever issues you may have with my husband's— business associations—and help me. I don't want to freak out Corinne. She is—" I cast around for the direst adjective I could invoke. "Terrified of blood. Please. I'm begging you."

Christian duty won out. "All right," she said. "Let me call Jim."

I rounded up the kids and sent them on their way. It's a clear shot from our house to Beth's, no streets. From the upstairs bedroom window I watched them cutting through the trees in the backyard. Jack was holding Corinne's hand with a protective tenderness that, at another time, would have brought tears to my eyes. They disappeared for a moment, and I blinked, one long, woozy blink, and then they appeared out on the other side on Beth's perfectly square lawn. I waited until I saw Beth's back door open and close, and then I peeled my face off the windowpane. It took a bit of effort, and I observed—with the same kind of detachment you feel while noting measurements in the lab—that it was getting harder to stand up without leaning on something. There was only one thing left to do, and that was to go find Lacroix.

He was sitting in Liam's study in front of his giant, glowing screen, wearing an enormous pair of air-traffic control headphones and clicking through some footage. In it, Liam and I were walking across the lawn together, which struck me, in my dim-witted state, as strange, because I couldn't place when it would have been taken. The scene was shot from behind. As soon as Lacroix heard me come in, he hit pause, just in time to catch a peculiarly synchronized turn of our heads: Liam turning to look at me, me turning to look away. The sun was setting in front of us, and we both looked like we were on fire.

"Yes?" said Lacroix, glancing up at me and smiling, and then he caught sight of something and whatever it was made him stop abruptly and push back his glasses. When I looked down at myself, I could see that I had bled through the reinforcements I had added to my makeshift bandage, and there were several dime-size spots of blood on my sweatshirt—like I had been standing next to someone who had been shot.

I pulled my bloody hand out of my pocket and held it up for him to inspect. "I need you to help with me something," I said.

Your

Jess

From: Jessica Frobisher <jesspfrobisher@yahoo.com>
Sent: Thursday, July 17, 2014 7:08 am
To: Arthur Danielson <art.danielson2010@gmail.com>
Cc:
Bcc:
Subject: Re: Bush-beating, foot-dragging, and other kinds of bloody hell

Wait. Let me finish. I didn't mean to cut off abruptly. It's just hard writing epic e-mails when you only have one thumb to space with.

I'm fine. Apparently there's a vein that runs up the wrist into the base of the thumb and I just nicked it. It only needed fifteen stitches, but it was enough of a slash job that the ER doctor—a no-nonsense ex-military guy with a no-nonsense crew cut—felt obligated to send me upstairs for a psych consult to make sure that I hadn't been trying to halfheartedly off myself. Of course it didn't help that I *was* lying, and not very convincingly. An alibi that involved a dull butcher knife and a sweet potato was the best I could come up with—just not for the reasons they thought.

"A yam?" repeated the young Indian woman, writing down something on my chart. She looked about twenty-four, an intern was my guess, probably young enough to still believe that there's no despair in life that cannot be conquered with the help of a little self-acceptance and a few good pharmaceuticals.

"Yes," I said. The jagged piece of the spaceship was still in the pocket of my bloody sweatshirt, so I had to sit with my arms awkwardly out in front of me, so I wouldn't accidentally shred anything else. "I'd forgotten how tough those things are. Next time I want soup I'll just buy the organic stuff in the can. I don't know what I was thinking, messing around with this homemade crap." I rolled my eyes, in a way that I hoped came across as agreeable—ditzy, but not to the point of complete derangement. "All that *work*, and for what?" It was the exact same story I had tried out on Lacroix in the car, and the same spiel I would be giving Liam back at home, after I had smuggled the piece of shuttle back upstairs, wrapped it back up in its handkerchief, and set it carefully on top of the dresser as though it had never been touched. He didn't believe it either. He held on to my wrist while I talked, examining the Frankenstein stitches, but before I could finish, he cut me off. He shook my arm and said, "If you're not going to tell me what happened, Jess, then don't bother."

"Mrs. Frobisher," Dr. Patel said, leaning forward on her stool and refusing to crack a smile. She was clearly a good doctor, one who took her job very, very seriously. "I understand that accidents happen. We just want to make sure that you're OK. Now there are a few questions that I'd like to ask you before you go. Have you experienced any feelings of hopelessness or despair lately? Any difficulty concentrating or problems sleeping?"

"Yes," I said.

"Yes?" She looked up from her clipboard and frowned a little. "I'm sorry. . . . Yes to . . ."

"To all of them." I gave myself a one-handed boost to my feet. There was a clock ticking on the wall, and all I could think about was Lacroix downstairs in the waiting room, wandering around, getting into God knows what, talking to God knows who. "Look, I appreciate your concern, but are we done here? I really need to get going."

"Mrs. Frobisher—"

"Dr. Patel." I had to resist the urge to call her *sweetheart*, which she surely would have taken as an insult, and not at all the way I meant it. "I appreciate your concern, but the logistics we're talking about here aren't that difficult. If I wanted to slice my veins, I would have just done it. "

Ten minutes later I was down in the waiting room with Lacroix, signing out.

There's one more part I want to tell you, but I have to stop here/now.

Later,
Jess

From: Jessica Frobisher <jesspfrobisher@yahoo.com>
Sent: Friday, July 18, 2014 12:32 am
To: Arthur Danielson <art.danielson2010@gmail.com>
Cc:
Bcc:
Subject: Re: please tell me you're kidding

I guess I thought you would find it funny. I mean, come on, me as a suicide case?

Don't get me wrong. It's not that there aren't days when a shot of Thorazine and a peaceful padded cell with a few ivy tendrils twining picturesquely around the sunlit iron bars of my window sound like a kind of perverse bliss. But who, Arthur, would remember to feed the kids? Who would act as Jack's personal hygiene gestapo? Who would teach Corinne how to wrestle her way into a pair of panty hose? Not Liam. He's become so embattled that I'm not sure he'll ever be able to go back to tinkering with rockets. I'm afraid his passion has been ruined, that it's like something that's been dragged through the mud, that it might be beyond the possibility of repair.

It's about midnight now as I'm typing this to you. I wasted the last hour or so wandering around the house, admiring all its idiosyncrasies, both the ones other people have put here (the bathroom wallpapered in parrots) and the ones we can claim for ourselves (the planets Jack painted on the laundry room ceiling, and labeled with fantastical names). I was thinking that maybe it's a good thing Lacroix came and filmed here—that maybe along with his heroic spacemen, he's going to capture and preserve a tiny piece of our life on the brink, the way an ethnographer comes in to take notes on some obscure tribe out in the bush, just before the loggers and miners come in to strip the land out from under them. He just doesn't know it yet.

Or maybe he does.

As I was pacing around like the madwoman in search of her attic, I was making halfhearted efforts to compose this e-mail to you— although in actuality it was just more procrastinating. Because I know you're going to hate it. You're going to fucking hate it when I tell you what I've been putting off telling you for over a week.

Which is this: that I've agreed to go up into space with Lacroix and Elle next month on Spaceco's first trip since the accident. There's plenty more to the story, obviously, but I'm not sure if you want to hear it, so I'm stopping here.

There you have it at last, Arthur: the truth passed as painfully as a kidney stone. Nothing for me to do but take some Ibuprofen and go upstairs to try to sleep.

I'll be flying over you, and I'll tell you what those forests look like from space. But only if you want to know.

Your star-bound

Jessica

From: Jessica Frobisher <jesspfrobisher@yahoo.com>
Sent: Sunday, July 20, 2014 11:09 am
To: Arthur Danielson <art.danielson2010@gmail.com>
Cc:
Bcc:
Subject: Re: Jess, tried to call, check your voice mail

Hey,

I saw the strange number on my cell last night. I knew it was you before I even heard the message. Please, please don't call me again, Danielson. There are things I have to do here, and I'm afraid if I hear your voice again, it will undo me.

You know those papers that delivery guy brought to the house the other day? They were consent forms for the spaceflight, with my name pre-typed by Spaceco's legal department in all the appropriate "I, the Undersigned" blanks. The information packet they gave me was the size of a novella. Death. Dismemberment. Blood clots. Severe anxiety attacks. All the things that can go wrong, and all the possible ways in which they can transpire—it's all spelled out in single-spaced eleven-point font. There's no way you can say you weren't warned. So I won't.

I met Liam at Amer's during my lunch hour to sign them. Lacroix wanted to get some footage of me signing the paperwork, so there the three of us were. Liam and I hunched over the tiny, sticky table while he pointed out the places where I was supposed to initial or sign, "Here, here, here" in the most expressionless voice he could manage, while I signed excruciatingly slowly again and again and again with my left hand, leaving behind a scrawl that was completely unrecognizable as mine. Lacroix was staring into that fucking camera, dead and gone to everything going on in his peripheral vision, including the people who were standing in line waiting to order their lattes and passing the time by watching our little *folie à trois* with expressions of mild curiosity. The table was gimpy; I had to keep my heel clamped down on one of its metal feet to keep it from wobbling.

"You are official now, Jessica," Lacroix said, when I had finished the final, painful signature and began shaking the cramp out of my hand. "How does it feel to be the next woman going into space? Tell the camera. For the record."

I took a long swig of my chai and let out a loud *ahh*. If Jack or Corinne had made that noise, I would have told them to knock it off. "Honestly?"

"Honestly."

I stared straight into the camera and smiled, trying to show as many teeth as possible. "It feels fantastic."

"Are we done here?" Liam pushed his chair back from the table. "I have to get back to the office."

"Don't forget these." I tapped the papers with my latte cup. "I just signed my life away, after all. You'll want to make sure you get them into the right hands."

Liam didn't say a word, Arthur. He just cut his eyes toward the camera and then looked back at me. You could see his jaw working. Finally, he said: "Right you are." He picked up the papers and tucked them under his arm. "See you at home."

Lacroix kept the camera trained on his back while he walked to the door, pulled it open, and disappeared. Finally he pulled the camera away from his face and saw me looking at him. "What?"

"Nothing," I said.

This is all a long way of saying that the ink's on the page. It's a done deal, and you can't change my mind now if I wanted you to.

Go ahead and call me an ass.

~j

From: Jessica Frobisher <jesspfrobisher@yahoo.com>
Sent: Tuesday, July 21, 2014 9:01 pm
To: Arthur Danielson <art.danielson2010@gmail.com>
Cc:
Bcc:
Subject: Re: fucking insanity

That's EXACTLY what I thought you were going to say. Which is fine. I know I deserve it.

But leave Jack and Corinne out of it.

From: Jessica Frobisher <jesspfrobisher@yahoo.com>
Sent: Thursday, July 24, 2014 10:17 pm
To: Arthur Danielson <art.danielson2010@gmail.com>
Cc:
Bcc:
Subject: Re: re: fucking insanity

Do I know how what looks? You make it sound like someone's holding a gun to my head. Think what you want, Arthur, but no one's *forcing* me to do anything.

Can I also point out that you're not the most objective party here? I know how you feel about Liam's line of work. You made it clear without ever opening your mouth.

And yes, you're entitled to your opinion.

But I've had more time than you to mull this over. Think about what a chance I'm being offered, Arthur. There are only a handful of people who have gone where I'm about to go and seen what I'm about to see. If it weren't me, it would be somebody else. You had your chance, and you took it. You went off to the end of the world without looking back. Now I'm going to take mine.

Jess

From: Jessica Frobisher <jesspfrobisher@yahoo.com>
Sent: Saturday, July 26, 2014 12:49 am
To: Arthur Danielson <art.danielson2010@gmail.com>
Cc:
Bcc:
Subject: Fine

Here are the gory details:

Two Sundays ago I was outside in the proto-greenhouse, washing down the new slate floor, sometime around dusk, when Liam came around the side of the house.

"What brings you out here?" I thought but didn't add: *to enemy territory.* It was strange to see him standing there next to one of the gardenia trees. Lacroix, Elle, Abah, Ikenna, a baffled Tristan, have all been found wandering around through our house's ever-expanding jungle. Jack and Corinne used to avoid it, but eventually they started playing in there. They poke around the half-laid stone floor, like it's some sort of ancient archaeological dig site, and run around in their astronaut helmets through the elaborate system of trellises I've jerry-rigged, using string and stakes and my gravity-defying willpower. It's part of a game with rules that are mysterious to me. They involve disappearing into the foliage and then letting out what I heard Jack refer to as "a transmission"—a long, bloodcurdling scream. It's like having a shot of adrenaline delivered straight to the chest. Liam and I have both threatened them with the pain of death, but that doesn't stop them.

But Liam hasn't set foot in the place once. As soon as I looked up and saw him loitering there in his running T-shirt, damp with sweat, I knew that some sort of necessity must be behind this incursion. Liam may be pissed when he leaves for a run, but usually when he comes back he appears, if not relaxed, then whatever passes for relaxed these days. Businesslike. Perfunctory. Since the accident, his runs have been twice as long as they used to be, and I imagined that the whole biochemical process behind his physical exertion had changed. That instead of converting sugars to energy, his body was fueled by rage or grief or regret, or some other potent emotional propane with a long, slow burn.

Whatever that process was, it had clearly failed. He still looked pissed—I could tell by the way he was kicking his feet around too hard, making the high-tech reflectors on his sneakers wink in the gloom.

But he was trying to play nice. "I just wanted to see what you were working on," he said. "For once." He was twisting one of the gardenia buds around, but he caught himself before he broke it off. "Don't you have a light out here? I don't know how you can see anything."

"I do," I said. "I mean, I just need to go buy one." The electrician put in miles of wiring for all the lighting the greenhouse is going to require. Up by our door to nowhere, there's a whole slew of covered sockets, enough that we could probably power a whole fleet of spaceships, but I haven't installed any of the fixtures yet. Still, Arthur, I am making progress. I added, "I think I've acquired a taste for the dark."

"Yes, well," Liam said. He shifted again and sighed. "Actually, I need to talk to you about something. We've been hammering out the details of Lacroix's launch. It's now tentatively scheduled for August 16."

"Fine with me," I said. I was determined, Arthur, to be agreeable for once. "What is that? A Friday?"

"It's a Saturday."

"So Sunday to Sunday you'll be gone." We were losing the last bit of the light, and so I went back to sponging.

"It'll be more like two weeks. Lacroix wants to film all the preparations and he wants me to be there the whole time. Since I'm the main person he's been tailing. Relentlessly." There was still that odd, slightly aggrieved note to his voice, Arthur, and I was trying to think if I'd done something earlier to antagonize him, something I'd forgotten but was now going to have to pay for. He had started attacking the innocent bystander gardenia again. "Jess, will you stop that and listen to me? You need to listen to this."

"OK." I put down the sponge and wiped my hands on my shirttails. "I'm listening."

"I thought you might come with us."

"No." I picked the sponge back up. "Come on, Li. That's not going to happen. Who's going to watch the kids? We've completely tapped out Paula. There's no way I can—"

"Jess, for the love of God," Liam said. "Will you let me finish?"

With great effort I shut my mouth.

"Lacroix wants you to go. Do you understand what I mean by that?"

I didn't, actually, so I just stood there, silently looking at him.

"He wants you to go up with him and Elle on the spaceflight. He wants you to be the third person."

I looked down at the dripping sponge. I was startled to find myself still holding it. "That's what he said?"

"Yes."

"Wow." I leaned down and swirled my sponge through the bucket at my feet, then held out my hand. "OK. Pay up."

Liam frowned. I'd managed, for at least a second, to make him confused instead of annoyed. "Pay what?"

"I told you he was crazy, didn't I? You didn't believe me." I edged forward, feeling for the next stray clump of potting soil with my sneakers, a mess I could no longer see but knew was there. The day before I'd been ripping a bag of the stuff open, only to discover as it came pouring out that it was infested with hookworms—and in a moment of panic, I'd flung it. "What did you tell him?"

"I told him I would ask you." Liam reached out and gingerly prodded the light-fixture wires where they were sticking out, their bare ends wound up in duct tape.

For a second there was nothing but the sound of the crickets chirping while I stared incredulously at him. I remember one of my first thoughts was, *Arthur is not going to believe this.* Part of my mind was already racing away from the moment, thinking how I would describe it to you: the insect din, the glittery bracelet from Corinne that's been chafing my wrist for days, a better synonym for the word *dumbfounded.* All this in a millisecond, a few synaptic firings, before I came back to my senses and realized how fraught, how fucking fraught, all the explaining would actually be.

"You can't be serious," I said. "It doesn't even make any sense." I was stammering, The questions were so obvious that they were difficult to even form. "Why me?"

"I know," Liam said. "I asked that question too." He was still flicking away at the loose wire, harder now, and using his Serious Engineer voice, the one he uses professionally with strangers. It was so perfectly modulated that it sounded almost like he'd been practicing, and I thought suddenly that maybe he had—in the car on the way home, perhaps, or in front of the mirror earlier that morning, while he was stripping the lather off his jawline in indignant, jugular-endangering strokes. Or maybe while he was running home to come talk to me, while he was slogging his way up the last torturous hill, stewing about how he would have to approach me, with his hat literally in his hands.

"I offered to go. He doesn't want me. He doesn't want Tristan, or Jeff, who all but begged on his hands and knees. He says he wants someone who doesn't know the ins and outs of how it all works. An outsider. Someone to whom the experience is new and *revelatory*." His imitation of Lacroix's accent was passable. "He vetoed all the candidates we suggested. You, on the other hand"— he smiled faintly—"he seems to have taken quite a shine to."

"Trust me, the shine is unrequited," I said, although I wasn't sure if that was strictly true. I remembered Lacroix the other day, the rain in his hair, filming that lightning so intently, like his life depended on it.

"I know," Liam said. He gave the wires another flick. "Anyway. You don't have to answer right now. You can think about it."

"I don't need to," I said. "The answer is no."

"Jess," he said.

"No," I said. "No." I squeezed my eyes closed. I know you think I'm afraid, Arthur, deep down, that I just won't admit it. But it wasn't that. I'm not afraid of dying in an exploding spaceship. I wasn't afraid of being drawn into Lacroix's clutches either—although maybe I should be. I was thinking I didn't want to be a party to something unsavory, to one more thing I'll regret, one more thing that will wake me up at three in the morning with pangs of doubt, something that feels like a heart problem gone undiagnosed. I know you know what I'm talking about.

"Jess," said Liam. "Forget Lacroix. We need this to work. We have a lawsuit pending, remember? There's the house, and—"

"We talked about this." I took the sponge and began wringing it out as hard as I could. "You agreed we might be able to manage—"

"Fine. Then do it as a favor," Liam said. "I'm asking you for a favor. For me. You know that you owe me. Don't pretend that you don't."

The light from Jack's room, just above our heads, flicked once and went out, and then we couldn't see each other at all.

"You should just spit it out," I said. I know what you think, but sometimes there really is no choice, Arthur.

I heard him laugh a little in the dark. "Where to begin? That you were sleeping with someone else? That you made so little effort to hide it?"

The smell of the gardenias in the wind was suffocating.

"You know, in the meeting yesterday, when Lacroix was making the case for you, he kept talking about your je ne se quoi," Liam said. "He was going on about what an expressive face you have. No one else in that room gave a shit, of course, because Lacroix's artistic aesthetic is the last thing anyone has time to worry about. Except for me. I was sitting there thinking, Damn right. You can read it like a book."

There was a long pause while we listened to the sponge in my hand dripping onto the stones, and I stared at the stars trapped in the bucket next to me. I seem to remember that there were four of them.

"Like I said, you can sleep on it," Liam said. "I would." A second later, I could see his shoes flashing away into the dark.

There you have it.

Jess

From: Jessica Frobisher <jesspfrobisher@yahoo.com>
Sent: Monday, July 28, 2014 2:23 pm
To: Arthur Danielson <art.danielson2010@gmail.com>
Cc:
Bcc:
Subject: Re: suicide missions: pros and cons

Yes, well. Ask and ye shall receive.

Arthur, I think it's too bad fate led you to me instead of Paula. (For many, many reasons, actually.) You and my sister have a lot more in common than I originally realized—right down to the exact same turns of phrase. At least Paula doesn't ask me if I am OUT OF MY FUCKING MIND in ALL CAPITAL LETTERS followed by a string of !!!!s and ???s. (One of each would have been perfectly sufficient.) I think her professional training prohibits her from asking that question.

When I called her up to see if she might, hypothetically, be able to come back to Michigan to watch Jack and Corinne for a few days in August, so that I could go get shot up into space, she paused for a long moment, and then said, in the way only Paula can: "This isn't some sort of deeply sublimated death wish, is it, Jess? You would tell me if it was, right?"

"You know, people keep asking me that," I said.

"Well?" she said.

"The contractor came back and upgraded all the switches in the new shuttle at no charge, you know," I said. "They wouldn't let Lacroix film it. You should have seen him. He was storming around the house in high dudgeon, and Elle was trying to console him. It was all in French, but I think she was saying 'Fuck them. Fuck those American pieces of shit,'" I said.

"That's not what she was saying," Paula said.

"How do you know?" I said. "You haven't seen this woman. She looks decorative, but peel away all that pretty and there's nothing underneath but these steely teeth. You get the feeling that if it was you and her stranded together in a lifeboat, and only one piece of tenderloin steak—"

"Why is there steak in the lifeboat?" Paula said. "That doesn't even make sense."

"It's like flying right after a plane crash," I said. "Or after some asshole tries to blow up a 747 with a bomb in his diaper. You know how it's ten times as safe because everyone is double- and triple-checking everything?"

"Oh," said Paula. "Well, in that case." I could picture her, standing in the pristine kitchen of her condo, with its alphabetical spice rack, winding the hem of her T-shirt around her nonphone hand. It's a gesture of exasperation that we share. I only noticed this the

206

last time she was here. You're an only child, Arthur, so you probably don't understand how disorienting it is to see your expressions play across someone else's face or hear your own inflection coming out of someone else's mouth. For a few seconds you know exactly what you look like to everyone else in the world.

"For God's sake, Jess," she said. "You're his wife. The world must be full of nutjobs who would take your place in a heartbeat. Tell him no. Tell him to find someone else."

For a moment, Arthur, I considered coming clean. I leaned over and buried my face in the mason jar stuffed full of flowers on the table. In spite of all the rain we've been getting, everything in the greenhouse area has been flourishing in the way only the wicked is supposed to. There's been such an abundance that I've been going out almost every other day to hack things back. I gave away some of the surplus orchids and basil to Lacroix a few days after he drove me to the ER. I piled them up in one of our old Easter baskets and left them out on the step of his trailer. The offering was a bizarre expression of gratitude and resentment—one part "Thanks for your help" and one part "Fuck you." I'm pretty sure this is something Paula would have understood. She once told me that there's nothing we're not of two minds about if we dig down deep enough. Ambivalence is the bedrock of human existence, she said. Face it.

But then I chickened out. "I can't," I said.

The point of this anecdote is . . .

OK, I forgot what the point was. But there's this: Has it occurred to you, Arthur, that I might actually want to go?

j

From: Jessica Frobisher <jesspfrobisher@yahoo.com>
Sent: Tuesday, July 29, 2014 9:59 pm
To: Arthur Danielson <art.danielson2010@gmail.com>
Cc:
Bcc:
Subject: Re: facing it

It absolutely is a test. And, yes, I'm going to do my damnedest not to fail.

But that's not what I was asking. I was just asking you to consider the possibility. It's a free $250,000 ticket, Arthur. To see space. Every time I think about it, my stomach drops, which is about once every ten minutes. I haven't felt like that since—well, never mind. But I've gone back to swigging Pepto.

I'll try to take some pictures. Seriously, Arthur. They'll be absolutely stunning.

Jess

From: Jessica Frobisher <jesspfrobisher@yahoo.com>
Sent: Thursday, July, 31 2014 6:52 am
To: Arthur Danielson <art.danielson2010@gmail.com>
Cc:
Bcc:
Subject: Funny thing happened on the way to the office

Arthur,

I have a story for you.

It opens on a dull note: Me in the Nat Sci building. I'm knocking on Thom's office door.

It continues with Thom inviting me in. Me getting some paperwork signed. Thom and I make small talk. It goes something like this: Pregnant-with-twins Olivia is doing great. Jack is doing great. Corinne is doing great. (This is still boring, I know, but bear with me.) We do not discuss Liam. Liam, obviously, is not doing great. Thom knows this. I know this. Neither one of us lies that well; we have this in common. We don't want to even try.

I turn to leave. I make it all the way to the door, and Thom clears his throat. (And here's where things get interesting. Are you ready?)

"Ah, Jess," Thom says.

I am still holding on to the doorknob. I turn around. What Thom says next is this:

"Sorry to hear about Arthur."

"Excuse me?" I say. My first thought is that there has been some sort of accident, that you, Arthur, have died, and no one has told me. The reason I say "Excuse me" is not because I have a hearing problem. It's because all the blood has just rushed up to my head, and I need that extra second before I let go of the door and try to make it to the chair. I really and truly am afraid to move. I am afraid I might collapse on the way.

"About his taking the job at Duke," Thom says. "I know you two were close." He is watching me with those mild blue eyes of his, and pretending not to notice a thing, and I realize in a sudden and sad and blindingly obvious way that he knows what he knows. There isn't an ounce of malice in his voice. There is just a regretful sympathy that might, in another life, have disarmed me. The me in this story can't be disarmed, though, because I am still in something like shock. This is a good thing. It prevents me from saying something unwise, something that I will later remember against my will, and be forced to squirm at for years to come.

Thom continues valiantly talking, continues valiantly pretending. "I tried to bribe him to stay," he says. "I offered him all the meager filthy lucre I had on hand, but I got the impression he was eager to shake the Ann Arbor dust off his feet." He is fiddling apologetically with some paper clips on his desk, like he's untangling them, although you and I both know, Arthur, that those paper clips have been snarled together for years, and they are never fucking coming apart. Thom says, "He was playing hardball. You know how a person bargains sometimes in that way that tells you that he doesn't really want his mind changed?"

I don't remember how I respond. There is a very loud ringing in my ears, and I'm not sure that whatever I say next makes any sense. Maybe it's "Why wouldn't he?" Maybe it's "Who would?" The power of movement has returned. More than anything I want to get back to the safety of my office. When I finally escape I pass Moira in the hall, and she says, "God, Jess, take it easy." It occurs

210

to me—and not for the first time—that in her loud, stupid way Moira is the most astute person in this entire department of scientists, and what does that say about us?

That is the story.

So tell me now, Arthur: what do you think?

Jess

From: Jessica Frobisher <jesspfrobisher@yahoo.com>
Sent: Saturday, August 2, 2014 1:03 pm
To: Arthur Danielson <art.danielson2010@gmail.com>
Cc:
Bcc:
Subject: Re: explanations

It's not the same thing, and you know it. The whole spaceflight will take 2.5 hours from start to finish, and then I. Am. Coming. Back.

When were you planning on telling me? Were you going to wait until a week before the semester started, and then send me an e-mail: "Oh, by the way, I've moved to North Carolina, so good-bye forever. P.S. Have a nice life"?

From: Jessica Frobisher <jesspfrobisher@yahoo.com>
Sent: Sunday, August 3, 2014 9:09 am
To: Arthur Danielson <art.danielson2010@gmail.com>
Cc:
Bcc:
Subject: Re: re: explanations

Point taken. You don't owe me anything. I've only been your best friend for six years. Have a great time in North Carolina.

Jess

P.S. Have a nice life

From: Jessica Frobisher <jesspfrobisher@yahoo.com>
Sent: Sunday, August 3, 2014 10:09 pm
To: Arthur Danielson <art.danielson2010@gmail.com>
Cc:
Bcc:
Subject: Re: amends

Yes. T minus 14 days. I haven't started packing yet. There's actually not that much to take. Mostly just long underwear for under the space suit. A doctor's note, declaring me to be physically fit—and not pregnant. Sunscreen. That's about it.

When are you headed down to North Carolina?

From: Jessica Frobisher <jesspfrobisher@yahoo.com>
Sent: Monday, August 4, 2014 10:24 pm
To: Arthur Danielson <art.danielson2010@gmail.com>
Cc:
Bcc:
Subject: treehouses

Arthur, please. I get it. You were just being honest. There's no need to say anything else, so please do me a favor and don't. I've just been taking some time to resign myself, that's all. Resignation is something I've never been very good at. I should be grateful to you for giving me the chance to practice.

Gripe of the day: Lacroix has switched from calling me "Jessica" in his sexy-making accent to referring to me as "fellow astronaut." He's been trying to get some more shots of me on the home planet doing mundane Earthling things, so this morning he and Elle tagged along with me and Jack and Corinne on our trip to the park. We're all sick of the one near our house (which has a hideous postmodernist jungle gym that Corinne's afraid of), so we went to this place on South Wagner Road. It's where I used to take Harley before he died. It was the best off-leash pooch park you've ever seen. Most of the dogs would congregate in the middle of the field next to the parking lot, in a yappy, swirling mass, but Har-har and I would steer clear of them. We'd head down into a drainage ditch and tack around the edge of the lot until we reached the safety of the woods on the west side. The two of us had an understanding. Harley was as eager to avoid the exuberant hip-checking and humping of his fellow canines as I was to avoid small talk with their latte-clutching owners. Liam was right about Har. He was one ornery little muttski. But there are moments when, out of nowhere, I'm still jolted by how much I miss him. I'll be standing at the stove, say, frying up a batch of bacon, or straightening up Jack's boots in the corner where the ratty

213

corduroy dog bed used to be and *has not been for years*, and I'll feel it—a sudden stab that makes me say out loud, "Holy shit," or some other non sequitur that's just as profane.

Nobody takes dogs there anymore. It was only a matter of time. You could have predicted it: someone got bitten a few months back, the company that owned the land revoked its laissez-faire approach to leash laws, and people started trickling away, saying they knew it all along, that it was too good to last.

Now the field's all quiet, reverted back to its natural savannah-like state. In places the grass practically comes up to Corinne's neck. Whenever she stooped down to clutch at a grasshopper, she would vanish. Then reappear. Then vanish again. The grasshoppers really were everywhere, flying up around us like showers of sparks, and landing with sad little sizzling sounds on our bare arms. I concentrated on naming all the wildflowers I could see, yelling out the species and genus when they came to me. I knew that I was hamming it up, Arthur, being as obnoxious as the kids, but I didn't care. It helped me stop thinking, for a few minutes, about what is coming next. We trooped along, stepping over fossilized dog turds with Elle and Lacroix trailing behind us, turning their cameras this way and that. Fortunately the park was empty. We only passed one runner, a lanky, half-naked college girl who slowed down to stare at our strange little entourage, but when she saw Lacroix turning the camera toward her, she picked up the pace and disappeared back into the grass.

This is the place where Jack and I go to climb trees. The last time you and I talked face-to-face I was still letting him win, but no more. The two of us are now dead equals. He's lighter, so he's hauling less weight to the top, but I'm still taller, so I've got a better reach. Our handicaps balance out us perfectly, but they won't stay that way for much longer. The physics is working against me; I can feel it, even if Jack can't. He's getting strong, and I'm getting old.

I wasn't in the mood for a strenuous scramble, but Jack desperately wanted to race me—and Jack doesn't want desperately to do anything these days. Corinne had wandered away to go stomp down some monstrous toadstools she'd discovered, but we coaxed her back and bribed her into being the starter by giving her Elle's periwinkle scarf to wave as a flag. (Corinne has—maybe it goes without saying, Arthur—no interest whatsoever in climbing, or in roaming around anywhere other than on solid earth. She's been wearing an old paper crown from Burger King. It's her accessory of choice these days. I'm sure she's imagining she has royal blood running through her kindergarten veins, that some secret arrangement has placed her with a pair of commoner guardians, disgraced astronauts, that she's only biding her time until a horseman comes to take her back to the castle where she belongs.)

We took our places by our respective trees. Jack was circling around the trunk, staring up into the branches, eyeing them the way you would study a horse you were about to bet on—a trick he learned from me, thank you very much. Lacroix was fiddling with his camera almost frantically, and kvetching about the piss-poor light. "Don't go, don't go," he kept saying.

Fortunately though, Corinne, like time, waits for no man. "Ready . . . SetGo!" she screamed, waving Elle's scarf.

"Wait, wait," Lacroix said.

But Jack and I were already off to the races. I stared straight up at a patch of blue through the branches and scrambled upward toward it. The light was piss-poor, like Lacroix said, but up above me there were clouds and birds flying and a jet, leaving an elaborate feathery plume across the sky. That's the thing I remember seeing the most clearly, as I struggled upward through that glimmering, rarefied forest light, gasping for air, sucking in the smell of those corrupted pine trees, that's why I was crying a little, in spite of all my best efforts not to. It was like—and please don't turn all doomsayer on me when I tell you this—a preemptive pang of homesickness. I want to ask Lacroix if he feels it too, and once, a few days ago, I almost did, but then I stopped myself, remembering that I have to be careful what I say, now that I'm no longer flying under the radar.

So I tried asking Liam instead, if he knew what I was talking about. He didn't. "Please don't get sentimental about this, Jess," was what he said. "You'll come back. We'll get on with things."

To make a long story shorter: I lost. It wasn't even close. When I got to the top, I had to stop and catch my breath, and Jack went up past me and all the way down again. Lacroix caught his victory on film, preserved for all posterity. And piss-poor light or no, he knew I'd been crying. "Fellow astronaut," he said. "Those aren't tears I see, are they?" But I managed to wave him off.

Try as I do or try as I don't, I still think about that day at the Arb, Arthur. About that stupid bet. How many minutes did I say it would take me to make it to the top of that maple and back down again? Was it two or three? Was that streak of paint on the face of that ancient wristwatch you used to time me blue or green? Was it the week before finals or the week after? All of these details remain so inordinately important to me, but they're slipping away from me anyway; I wake up, and another one's gone.

If you could do it again, would you have chosen different terms for our wager? Would you have said, "You lose, and the next Zingerman's lunch is on you," or "You lose, and you owe me twenty graded blue books?" If you had, maybe you would be in

216

Ann Arbor right now, as I write this, puttering around in the kitchen of your fixer-upper house that you never seem to get around to fixing, and I wouldn't be on my way into space. If you had, I can tell you that I would have won that bet hands down or died trying.

But you didn't. You said, "If you lose, then you have to let me kiss you." And then you smiled like it was a joke, except not really, because your mouth trembled on the very last beat. I don't know if it was what you said or the way you said it that handicapped me, Arthur—weakened my knees, weakened my resolve. I still remember how difficult it was to grab the branches above my head and haul myself up. My palms were so damp, and I was shivering so hard with desire that I felt a little sick. By the time I got to the top, I knew it was hopeless. So I took my time on the way down, and when I dropped onto the bottom branch, I lingered one more second before I jumped. I was watching you watch me, I was marveling at your expression—its striking amalgam of joy and ravenous triumph. It made you look, for just a second, like someone I'd never met. And now here we are.

Maybe you know this. You probably do. You were right, you know. I'm not your best friend. I'm not even, as you once said, "the beloved thorn in your side." I'm just the thorn, period.

The point is, you don't have to apologize for anything. I hope you love North Carolina. When you get there, send me your address, and I'll send you $100. It'll make up for all the coffees I owe you. You can take some new colleague, or whoever, out for some of that to-die-for barbecue I hear they have down there.

Yours,

Jess

From: Jessica Frobisher <jesspfrobisher@yahoo.com>
Sent: Wednesday, August 6, 2014 4:22 pm
To: Arthur Danielson <art.danielson2010@gmail.com>
Cc:
Bcc:
Subject: Re: yellow and shades of the inevitable

Yellow. That's right. I remember now.

Speaking of the inevitable: word about my upcoming trip has gotten out at work. My first guess was Thom. I put off telling him that I was going to miss the meeting on the fourteenth, and then I mumbled something about a "last-minute family thing." I've been careful, borderline pathological, about not divulging any details.

But it's too hard to picture Thom blabbing. It makes more sense to think that someone read about the upcoming launch and put two and two together. A couple of news outlets, including the *Times*, ran the story about the Lacroix/Spaceco collaboration. (Kramer bylined the story, which was pessimistically titled something along the lines of: "With Respected Filmmaker Along for the Ride, Spaceco Takes a Final Shot at Redemption.") This is page A100 news now, thank God, but Lacroix has been recognized a few places in Ann Arbor. Some Banff festival fanboy ran into him and Elle outside Seva last week, and according to Elle, the guy wouldn't shut up: "This man, he talk, talk, talk, until my ears"— she made a gruesome gurgling noise—"they are practically bleeding."

Anyway, I didn't discover this until this morning. I took Lacroix to campus because he wanted to get a couple of shots of his "astro-botanista" at her day job. (Me: "That's not a word." Him: "It should be." Me: "Has anyone told you you're a pain in the ass,

Theo? Like epically so?" Him: "Yes. Almost every single person I know. Everywhere I go. For my whole life.")

I hustled him through the Diag, past the orientation groups and a few sidewalk scribblings about the social injustice du jour, past the windows of the Nat Sci greenhouse. (They're all glazed over now, of course, but soon the students will be back and writing messages in those frosty white panes. Two seasons of greenhouse graffiti you've now been away.) Some kid in a pair of gym shorts was tightrope walking across a cable that he'd managed to string up between two trees near the Hatcher, and I could tell Lacroix was dying to whip out his camera and capture this latest tidbit of conspicuous local weirdness, but he restrained himself. I'd made him promise that he would only film in my office, and maybe the lab if no one else was around. I repeated it with those italics I've gotten the hang of: *if no one else is around.*

And he stuck to his promise. The filming in my office didn't take long. I showed him BioSys and attempted to explain the genetic sequencing. I was trying to channel you, Arthur, but with not much success. Practice hasn't made me any less terrible on camera. I have to sit on my hands to keep myself from waving them around while I talk. They take on a life of their own—and they want nothing more than to scratch my nose every twenty seconds like clockwork. Only once did I forget myself. It was somewhere in the middle of my explanation about how the mapping we're doing will enable us to understand the genetic diversity in plant species and how that will help us predict what's likely to survive the looming shit storm of climate change and what won't. And so on and so forth. You already know the spiel, Arthur, and so do I. I should be sick of it by now. But I'm not. Every time I start talking about it, I'm filled with that old urgency of our crusade, the feeling that it matters more than words can possibly describe. I told Liam once that I understood why people stood on street corners with signs and screamed. He thought that was appalling, but I knew you understood. I didn't even have to ask.

I suppose it was this fleeting unselfconsciousness that made me open my mouth and say: "For example, take my colleague, Arthur Danielson"—before I remembered who I was talking to. Don't be too horrified, Arthur. I was leading up to something totally germane. I would have barreled straight through to my point—only it felt so strange to say your name out loud after all this time, in this context, as though I barely knew you, that I was briefly thrown back on my heels. Someone chose that opportune moment to go thundering down the hallway, as though he was running for his life, and so I was able to glance away and then straight back into the camera with a smile that seemed to me preternaturally composed and say, "I'm sorry. I completely forgot my train of thought."

We would have made a clean getaway, except that we made a quick stop in the Greene Lounge to get Lacroix one of the Diet Cokes he's addicted to. When I pushed open the door, with Lacroix right on my heels, I discovered that there were four people sitting around the table. It was still a little before nine a.m. What they were all doing there, I have no idea. You know that everyone's at the lake or out of state this time of year, enjoying their last few days of freedom before the drudgery of the semester starts.

So all I could do was march over to the soda machine and wave a hello to everyone. A few of them glanced quizzically at Lacroix as he swung his camera bag and took in the lay of the land. He was clearly with me, but I was damned if I was going to introduce him.

I had just managed to coax the machine into taking my dollar bill when Carl called out, "Hey, Jess, so when's the big day?"

"Excuse me?" I said. I wasn't playing dumb, Arthur. I was genuinely confused. In the moment I was only thinking of work and hoping there wasn't a deadline for something important that I had forgotten. I in no way connected it to my secret double life, to my upcoming stint as an astro-botanista.

Carl's sunburned face and vestigial beard told the story of a long, carefree summer. "Sam told me that you're going up into space. Did I hear that right? What day are you blasting off?"

The room fell silent, just in time for us to all hear the Diet Coke can clunk to the bottom of the chute with a deafening thud. Lacroix cleared his throat, and I handed him his soda. I had to fight the urge to sink my fingernails into his hand as I passed it off.

"No kidding," said Moira, sipping her coffee. "There's no way you would catch me doing me that. I'm perfectly happy right here on the home planet."

"I'd do it," Carl said. "Are you kidding? It's a once-in-a-lifetime opportunity. I'd definitely do it." He scratched his sun-gilded stubble and reconsidered. "I'd probably do it. Anyway, good for you, Jess."

"Well, take pictures," Moira said. "You'll get some amazing ones."

"Thanks!" I said (with an exclamation point!). That thing you said about Moira's mouth being her tell (was it the left side that supposedly twitches or the right one?) is bullshit. I still can't tell when she's being passive-aggressive, so I just pretend to take everything at face value.

OK, I'm done for now.

Jess

From: Jessica Frobisher <jesspfrobisher@yahoo.com>
Sent: Thursday, August 7, 2014 11:58 pm
To: Arthur Danielson <art.danielson2010@gmail.com>
Cc:
Bcc:
Subject: Packing up

Almost ready to go here.

I finished the umpteenth load of laundry for Jack and Corinne,
We are now stockpiled with enough clean T-shirts and shorts to
clothe a midget army for the rest of the summer. I finished ripping
the old luggage bar codes off my suitcase handles, most of them
emblazoned with codes for airports I couldn't even remember
having passed through. I finished printing out a list of child care/
plant care instructions for Paula, three single-spaced pages she
won't bother to read because she already knows how to do
everything perfectly.

Then I went outside to soak down the greenhouse plants for the
last time. I mindlessly waved the hose around in figure eights
while I stared up above the tree line at the stars, which were
starting to glimmer into view, one by one, like someone,
somewhere, was working his way through a series of switches.
There were butterflies dozing on the indigo, and you could see
their wings upright and alert, even in their sleep, ready to launch
themselves into the air, to flee toward safety, wherever their
instincts told them that might be. The monarchs arrived
yesterday, while Corinne and I were wandering around the
backyard in our flip-flops, in what can only be described as a
swarm from nowhere. Like messengers. Corinne was delighted to
the point of speechlessness when one landed on the back of her
hand and clung there with its tiny, tenacious claws, refusing to let
go. I was speechless too, but for other reasons. All I could do was

stand there with my hands balled up in my pockets and wait the moment out, wait for the feeling to pass. When it did, I turned my head, and there was Lacroix with his camera, his truth-telling machine. He was frowning, maybe with concentration, or maybe with something else. That goddamn sixth sense he has will be the death of us.

It's been insanely hot here, Arthur. Even at ten tonight, the thermometer I installed next to the greenhouse was reading 88F. I was filthy and sweating through the back of my T-shirt. Lacroix and Elle were probably dying out there in their sans-AC trailer. If not, then maybe they were enjoying some pre-space fucking, the weird conjugal celebration of two adrenaline junkies. In spite of the bell-jar humidity, though, I was still shivering like crazy. Who knows why? Maybe I was thinking that in another two weeks I'll be right back here, in my life. I'll be buying school clothes for the kids and yet another belt for that accursed minivan. I'll have to start wading through the bank statements that I've left piling up next to the microwave and collecting all the stray bits of radiation. I'll have to total up precisely how much we've spent over the past five months and figure out how we're going to pay off our exorbitant credit card bills. Whatever we owe, we'll have to pay it. There isn't any point in asking if it was worth it. The money's gone; we spent it a long time ago.

Or maybe it was this: I can't believe you're not coming back, Arthur. It's like a sucker punch that doesn't quit. I get my breath back, and—*wham*—out it comes again.

I was packing tonight, chucking a bunch of stuff into the suitcase that didn't make much sense—pens, flash drives, chandelier earrings, expired tooth-whitener strips, my hiking boots. At the last minute, I pulled out the silk shirt you brought back from your trip to China, and then I stood there for a minute, tossing it from hand to hand. It's such a beautiful silvery thing, and Arthur, it was such an unforgivable extravagance. I admire it almost against my will. You probably thought I didn't want to wear it, but that's not true. I did wear it once. I was standing in the bubble tea place, putting in an order for Jack and Corinne, when a sorority girl came up and rubbed my shoulder without so much as a how-do-you-do. "Gorgeous shirt," she said. The angry lurch it caused in my chest I took as a warning. I kept thinking I would take it to Goodwill so it could find a more appreciative, less conflicted owner, but I could never quite bring myself to do it.

I can't see the shirt, of course, without thinking about you telling the story of its acquisition. How you made the rookie mistake of fingering the cuff, just once, and then you were doomed. How the fire-breathing saleslady wouldn't let you walk out of the stall without buying it. How she blocked the door, and then you had to haggle for it because you knew there was no other way out of there alive—if you didn't, she wouldn't let you leave, you'd miss your flight, you'd be stuck in Beijing until the stores closed, everyone went home, and there'd be no one to rescue you.

Your impression of her was dead-on, Arthur. You had the accent down. You performed the broken English of her relentless commandments flawlessly: *You buy for your wife. You buy for your wife.* And the way, when you broke the news to her that you were lacking in that department, she switched without a missing a beat. *You buy for your girlfriend. You buy for your girlfriend.* And how, when that tactic failed, she delivered the punch line: *You buy one for your wife AND one for your girlfriend! Only need different colors.* And how she then began stuffing your hands full of shirts.

It should have been fucking hysterical—it *was* hysterical. That's your chronic problem, your curse disguised as a blessing. You can't, for the life of you, tell a story straight, Arthur. So can I come out and say it now? I knew you were lying. No ball-busting Chinese saleslady browbeat you into buying that shirt. Even as I was doubled over the Zingerman's table, wiping my eyes, I was struck by the pathos of your fictional anecdote. I was literally laughing myself sick. I drove home from campus that night with white knuckles and clenched teeth, promising myself that I would let you go.

I ended up laying the shirt on top of the zipped-up suitcase. So you see now that all of this was a spectacularly indirect way of telling you that your shirt is coming to Arizona with me. I realize that I could have told you this in about three sentences. But I guess I'm killing time, trying to distract myself from what's coming next.

 Not long now.

Jess

From: Jessica Frobisher <jesspfrobisher@yahoo.com>
Sent: Friday, August 8, 2014 2:42 pm
To: Arthur Danielson <art.danielson2010@gmail.com>
Cc:
Bcc:
Subject: Dallas to Tucson

Arthur,

We just made the last leg of our flight. Some asshat at Spaceco
scheduled the flights with the sole goal of maximum cheapness.
The result was three layovers, three 400-meter concourse dashes,
an airline change, and two separate trips through security. Thanks
to the Lacroixs' foreign IDs and carry-ons filled with expensive
electronic equipment, our TSA experience was even more of an
ordeal than usual. During one particularly lengthy interrogation, I
found myself wishing that Elle would condescend to smile at the
agent. One half-flirtatious laugh would have expedited the
process. But no. Elle is a Serious Artist. She's not going to
condescend to act cute, and certainly not for a sweaty twenty-
two-year-old *fasciste* (*fascist* is a French/English cognate, as it
turns out—I'm learning something new every day) in a TSA
uniform, not if our flights depended on it.

Nevertheless, here we are. Or rather, here I am—in the back row
of the airplane, the one with no windows and nonreclinable seats.
My back is flush against the lavatory wall—it's Delta's unofficial
steerage class. The final asshat saving came from breaking up our
seats, so Liam and the Lacroixs are sitting several rows ahead of
me. When he saw my ticket, Liam offered brusquely to take my
seat, but it was clear that the gallant gesture was mostly for show.
His long legs make it hard for him to sit anywhere in coach other
than the exit row, and I didn't want him sitting there, gritting his
teeth. I'd be able to hear the grinding from fifteen rows away.

It's actually a relief to be sitting alone. Li's been in a terrible mood since we got up this morning. When the alarm went off, both of us were lying flat on our backs, not doing anything that remotely resembled the act of sleeping; he reached out with a stiff arm and slapped it off on the first bleat. "Let's just get this over with," he said. I didn't know if he was talking to himself or to me, so it seemed pointless to tell him that we were both in agreement on this point.

It didn't help that we were running late. It also didn't help that Jack made a scene before we left. Corinne was perfectly content to bestow a parting gift upon me—a pair of pink flip-flops she had bought with Paula yesterday at Target that I was instructed to wear into space—and one kiss on the cheek. She was losing interest before we had picked up our bags. But Jack came barging out through the screen door and clutching at the back of your silk gift shirt. He hasn't done that since he was three or four, when I would go to leave him at the sitter's and the anxiety would turn him all clammy and octopoid. It was like he had eight damp little hands instead of just two.

"Don't go," he said.

"Jack, don't," I said. He's so much bigger and stronger now than he was then, Arthur. It gives his fears a new kind of force, makes them harder to ignore—it compels you to stop and reckon with them. The seams on the shirt were starting to give.

I dropped the suitcase and turned around. "Jack," I said. "Hey. It'll only be a few days. I'm coming back. It'll be just like what Dad did. Remember? How he had all those great stories for us?" When Jack's upset, all his freckles stand out, almost black, like tiny periods, or ellipses. I've always adored those freckles, Arthur, and the way they complicate his face. When he was little, when they started dappling his perfect toddler skin, I studied them. I

227

thought I would memorize their scheme by heart. I staunchly, jealously, believed that, as his mother, I would know him better than anyone, better than his far-in-the-future wife or any of his lovers. "Remember him telling us how he flew over Michigan and he saw that archipelago out in Lake Huron—all those little white islands that he had never seen on a map—remember? And then he realized they were clouds? Remember how someone spilled that bottle of water, and it broke into all those little pieces that were swimming around like fish? Remember—"

He was shaking his head so hard that I had to stop.

"No," he said.

"No what?" I said. "Jack. *Jack*." I reached up and took him by his darling Dumbo ears. I was trying to keep my voice down, because I could feel the men standing right behind us: Lacroix, pretending not to listen while straining to hear, and wishing that he hadn't packed away his camera, mourning another revealing moment that was going, going, gone forever. Liam, drumming his fingers on the hood of the van, resisting the urge to pull out his phone and confirm for the fifteenth time that we were, in fact, late.

"You could *die*," he said.

I wasn't prepared for that, and I did exactly what I shouldn't have: I visibly flinched. Jack has a natural aptitude for dramatic pronouncements. Over the years I've learned to steel myself against them—because something about their passionate conviction can fool me into almost believing them, like prescient half truths, even though I damn well know better. I told you about the time we drove by that three-car pile-up on 69, didn't I? How Jack, who was all of five at the time, kept insisting that the woman in the van was dead, was dead, was dead? We were so packed in by semis that he couldn't have seen a thing, let alone a woman, dead or alive or somewhere in between—and how would he, a painstakingly sheltered kindergartner, have known it if he had?

The thing is, I looked it up later, and a woman did die—although not there, on the side of the road, not until hours later in the hospital. I'm perfectly aware that this doesn't prove a thing. But it took months before I was able to rid myself of the unpleasant superstitious shiver associated with the memory.

I stood up and shouldered my bag. My hands were shaking, but I kept my face perfectly calm. I think that being under the omnipresent eye of Lacroix's camera has started to give me a few tricks. "Be good, Jack," I said. I said it with all the love I could muster, and then nothing else, because I didn't trust myself.

"So what was the crisis exactly?" Liam asked me once we were in the car. Seat belts strapped on, speedometer at 55 mph. There was no going back.

"What's always the crisis?" I said. "Jack being Jack," I said. Out of the corner of my eye, I thought I saw him appraising something—possibly my earrings, possibly the silk shirt with Jack's handprints now wrinkled into it—with a pissed-off expression.

Arthur, we're getting the ding, and the announcement to turn off all electronic devices, so that's all for now.

More when I get a chance,

~jess

From: Jessica Frobisher <jesspfrobisher@yahoo.com>
Sent: Saturday, August 9, 2014 6:36 pm
To: Arthur Danielson <art.danielson2010@gmail.com>
Cc:
Bcc:
Subject: skulking

Arthur,

Greetings from the lobby of the Desert Paradise Motel. Apologies
in advance for any typos. I'm typing this while simultaneously
hiding in the corner behind a potted cactus. Multitasking at its
finest!

Liam and the Spaceco strategists chose the DPM specifically
because it's about twenty miles away from the Spaceco launch
facility. The strategic thinking here was that it would be a good
place to "lie low" (Liam's phrase) and/or "skulk" (mine.) It must
be a slow news week, though, because we arrived yesterday to
find a surprising number of reporters prowling around the lobby,
stalking the evasive Wi-Fi signal, and pillaging the soda machines
in an attempt to sate their urge for caffeine. Liam and the Lacroixs
opted to hang out in the car while I strolled casually into the
lobby and checked in using my credit card.

The check-in process took an agonizingly long time, and while
I waited I picked up the motel brochure and leafed through it
with faux nonchalance. This place advertises itself as a "step
back in time to a Golden Age [*sic*] of travel," and it appears that
this slogan is actually a clever ploy that the management has
implemented to get out of upgrading the decor from its original
1950s design. Everything is a tacky—excuse me, *retro*—
throwback, from the ever-so-slightly skeezy chenille
bedspreads to the teal-tiled bathrooms to the cast-iron AC

window units, which shudder to life with unearthly squeals as though all they really want is someone to put them out of their misery and send them on their way to the Great Landfill in the Sky.

I was so busy feigning interest in motel literature that I jumped when the teenage hotel clerk said my name out loud. It turned out that the Visa had been declined. "No big deal," I said. I sauntered back out through the lobby and across the enormous parking lot. All the DPM parking spaces are huge—perhaps nostalgically oversized for those old Golden Age [*sic*] Chevys that could double as pontoon boats. I knocked on the driver's window and asked Liam for his AmEx.

 "You have a $10,000 limit," Liam said. "I don't get it. How is that even possible?"

I shrugged. "I've been buying . . . things." On my stroll across the asphalt, I had done some quick math in my head, and the total made me a little queasy. "Things" included greenhouse slate. Concrete for the knee wall. Half of the flowers at the Carpenter Road Home Depot. If I keep this up, Arthur, there isn't going to be anything for Robert Kahn to squeeze from us.

"Well, we can't do anything about it now," Liam said. "Here." He dug out his wallet and handed his card to me.

My worry that Liam's name on the card would blow our cover turned out to be a non-issue. The clerk was so busy flirting with one of the facility boys that she barely even glanced at the card. I could have been checking in with Al Capone's AmEx for all she would have cared. Our rooms were in the back, so we were able to sneak around and unload without attracting any attention to ourselves.

Arthur, it looks like my hiding space has been breached. Some guy interrupted me just a second ago to ask me which publication I'm here reporting for. He was clearly trying to make conversation, so I think that's my cue to head up to my room.

Have a good night/afternoon.

Jess

From: Jessica Frobisher <jesspfrobisher@yahoo.com>
Sent: Sunday, August 10, 2014 9:02 pm
To: Arthur Danielson <art.danielson2010@gmail.com>
Cc:
Bcc:
Subject: Re: re: skulking

Nope. I keep looking around, but I haven't seen her. I doubt *New York Times* staff does the dirt-cheap DP Motel. At the very worst, they're probably at a Holiday Inn Express somewhere.

Liam and I have both been skipping the crappy continental breakfasts and taking the back way around the building, hoofing it through the prickly landscaping. This has led to at least three close encounters with scorpions, but yes, so far we've been successful at staying under the radar. More or less, anyway. Elle can't blend in anywhere she goes. She sticks out like an exquisitely lovely sore thumb. It's here that her preoccupied scowl works to her advantage, though, discouraging anyone from striking up a conversation with her. Last night, while we were at the diner, one fratty-looking guy dared to ask her where she was from, and she practically shriveled him up on the spot.

And thanks to the handful of TV people running around, no one has been paying any attention to Lacroix and his camera. That's bound to change, though, if Lacroix doesn't stop . . . being Lacroix. He keeps wandering off, Arthur, taking his camera and making these little forays off into the empty desert behind the Desert Paradise parking lot. Yesterday morning I got up, pulled open the curtains, and spotted Lacroix off in the distance, wandering through the tumbleweeds with his camera. The exact same thing happened this morning, except that this time he was lying flat on his back, perfectly still, filming the fiery sky over his head. I must have stood there for at least five minutes watching him until finally I couldn't take it anymore, and I started banging on the window, quietly and then louder. I didn't even notice that Liam had gotten out of the shower and was standing next to me.

"He can't hear you," Liam said. But he was pulling a T-shirt over his head. Whatever was bothering me, he felt it too. "I'll go get him."

I think the crazy might be catching. I came back to the room last night after e-mailing you to find Liam scooping his hair out of the bathroom sink. While I'd been out, he had shaved his entire head. The effect was so startling that when he popped out of the bathroom, I went lurching backward. Liam had to grab me to keep me from impaling myself on the TV antennae.

It took a second for the power of speech to return. "What did you do to yourself?"

"I don't know." Liam shrugged. "I was thinking it might help me go incognito, you know? No one will recognize me." He turned around, peered into the cloudy mirror, and gingerly touched his naked scalp. It was like even he couldn't believe what he had just done. "You're not a fan, I take it."

"That's one way to put it," I said. I couldn't stop staring at him, Arthur, at the harsh white glare of his head, the unfamiliar dips and indentations of his skull that some phrenologist would once have had a field day with, the new hard muscles along his jawline. Gone was Liam, and here in his place was a pale-eyed commando stranger. The most shocking thing was how fitting the look was on him. "No one is going to recognize you, that's for sure. Especially not the kids. You're going to terrify them. You realize that, don't you?"

"The kids'll be OK." Liam was looking past me, still studying his shocking new reflection. "A week or two, and you won't even be able to remember what it used to look like before."

I watched my reflection shake her head. "I don't believe that for a second."

"Jess," he said, "I promise."

But I was already leaving. Elle was sitting cross-legged out in the hallway, reading a book, and she rolled her eyes when she saw my face. "Men," she said.

As bad as things are at Desert Paradise, I still prefer it to being at the launch site, though. I was out there for ten hours today, Arthur, and close to eight hours the day before that. The logistics of getting in and out of there are an ordeal, but it's not even that, not really.

Plus I forgot to put on sunscreen this morning, and I charred to a crisp out on the launch pad today. Liam's out on a run for aloe and beer, but I think I'm past the point of salvaging. I'm going to peel and peel and peel, and no amount of cover-up is going to make me look normal on camera. Lacroix is going to have to change my credit. It'll be "Lobster Lady: played by herself." Which means my name won't be associated with this film at all. And that would be perfectly fine with me.

Your barbecued

jess

From: Jessica Frobisher <jesspfrobisher@yahoo.com>
Sent: Monday, August 11, 2014 11:08 pm
To: Arthur Danielson <art.danielson2010@gmail.com>
Cc:
Bcc:
Subject: Re: suggestions re going incognito

No, see, that's the problem. I was the one person in the group that didn't *need* a disguise—the nondescript middle-aged woman with the androgynous haircut. Now I'm the flaming red woman with a conspicuously bald husband. It's not the ideal setup for subterfuge.

The twenty-mile drive to the launch site isn't so bad. It's a straight-shot road with only a few four-way stops, and local custom seems to indicate that drivers can take them as optional. When I said getting in and out, I meant getting in and out of the launch site itself. There's no maintained road. It's just a dirt track that used to be surrounded by ghostly serene, empty terrain as far as the eye could see. It's still ghostly, but now when you look out the windows, you can see a smattering of cars and trucks dotting the horizon, flickering like mirages.

There's also a motley group of unshaven and slightly deranged protestors who are braving the rattlesnakes and the javelinas to camp out and make their disapproval of Spaceco known. Jed tells me that they're super-Christians from some wingnut church north of Phoenix, and all their members reject modern technological advances, because they think it's going to lead us to the End of Days. But you only have to listen to Jed for sixty seconds to know that he's full of shit, and I'm not sure he has any idea who these people really are or why they're here. Now that they've seen our van go in and out of the gate, they have identified us as the enemy, and they run after us holding up signs, one of which announces that Spaceco kills babies. They may be crazy, Arthur, but there's no way to joke around it—their menace is absolutely real. The first time it happened, Lacroix rolled down the window to stick out his camera, and one of them—a wiry guy running alongside the van in a grimy bandanna and a T-shirt that read "Apostasy Now"—took a swipe at it and damn near got it in his clutches. All the veins in his neck were bulging out, and you could almost feel the air around him crackling with rage. Elle, cool-as-a-cucumber Elle, actually screamed, and Liam leaned forward and told the driver in a low voice to "step on it now, please." This morning, a new van came to pick us up, one with black-tinted windows. But that doesn't help anything. I sat on the floor anyway, and closed my eyes while the potholes slammed the hell out of my tailbone for twenty miles. It was a long time to try not to think.

No one's been able to get rid of these people, Arthur—and it hasn't been for lack of trying. Spaceco's compound sits like a little island in a sea of land owned by the Bureau of Land Management, so it's all public and, technically, no one is trespassing. There's some endangered beetle that lives out here, and the Spaceco people have called BLM to tell them exactly how many crazies and East Coast reporters are out there wandering around, probably squishing the poor bugs with their tires and poisoning them with exhaust fumes, but BLM will. not. respond.

And it's not just the crazies. I can't believe how much the place has changed since I was here last May. The whole 5.2 square miles of the site was surrounded by nothing more than a hurricane fence with a few No Trespassing signs. If you didn't know the truth, you would have guessed that it was probably some property owned by an eccentric millionaire. A nudist colony for fat exhibitionist retirees, maybe. Or a doomsday prepper with four hundred cans of kidney beans stashed in an underground bunker. Half the people in Sierra Vista didn't even know exactly what was going on thirty miles down the road. I think that most of them assumed that Spaceco had ties to the capital-G Government, that they were carrying out some sort of top-secret military work related to the base there, that the Spaceco guys were operatives posing as overly friendly nerds.

Here's another story I never got to tell you: when Liam and I were out here last spring, we went to get breakfast at this diner near Hereford. Liam had been out doing a prelaunch inspection, and he was still wearing his gray Spaceco jumpsuit. As soon as we stepped through the door, a hush fell across the restaurant. No one would make eye contact with us, not the hulky trucker sitting at the counter, not the parents with their toddler in their booster seat, not the hostess who, in spite of her tender years, looked hard-bitten and world-weary. Liam was practically exuberant: smiling, asking questions about the dismal menu, complimenting the food, tipping extravagantly. I could tell he was enjoying the fact that everyone had mistaken him for a man with a touch of mysterious danger.

Now that's no longer funny. The whole place has a different feel to it. It's not just the beetle habitat that's been laid to waste, trashed with Starbucks cups, or that the saguaro cactuses have been felled by cars and exploded to pulpy bits under the tires. They've turned it into the compound that the conspiracists always theorized it was. Spaceco has reinforced its entire perimeter with razor wire and bought motion-sensor lights that terrorize the jackrabbits. They've hung up signs to warn trespassers about the lethal voltage in the electric fence and issued employees badges that everyone is required to show in order to gain entry. The worst part is the two uniformed guards they hired to stand at the front gate and keep the crazies—and who knows what else—at bay. Actual men with bona fide guns. "Just to be safe," Liam said when I brought them up.

Even though looking at them makes you feel anything but.

I have to go now, Arthur.

Forebodingly,

Jess

From: Jessica Frobisher <jesspfrobisher@yahoo.com>
Sent: Wednesday, August 13, 2014 11:48 pm
To: Arthur Danielson <art.danielson2010@gmail.com>
Cc:
Bcc:
Subject: Cabin fever

Jed is one of the guys who's going to be taking us up in three days. The other *Goddard* pilot is named Bruce. They're nice enough, both ex–Air Force. You can see that in Bruce—he's got the crew cut and the impeccable posture, and instead of "yes" he says "affirmative," but I don't see any of those indicators in Jed, who looks as though he's ridden in on a surfboard. I'm not kidding, Arthur—blond highlights and all. He also doesn't look a day over twenty-five.

Lacroix did his interviews with them this morning, and after he had gotten the footage he wanted of our awkward small talk, the five of us, plus our official Spaceco minder—a neckless guy named Kent—went out to the launchpad, so they could show us the *Goddard*, which had finally been taken out of the hangar and set up on its booster rockets. It's the new-and-improved version of the *Titan* shuttle, this sleek, finned marvel of engineering. I suppose you could even say that it's beautiful, if, like Liam, you had an aesthetic appreciation for those sorts of things. Someone in the design team decided not to paint it white like the *Titan*, and it's a decision that now seems fortuitous. (It was unfortunate enough that they had decided to emblazon the phrase "Space 2.0" on the tail, right above the American flag. After the accident they had to ask the contractor to blast it off.) They just left it with its smooth titanium alloy finish—a burnished silvery hull that makes it look like an H. G. Wells creation. The *Goddard* is downright dinky compared to the NASA monoliths, Arthur, but it still makes a pretty staggering impression. The sun was glaring so ferociously off its side that you could barely look at it. As we approached it, Elle stuck her head out the window and stared up at it through the flickering golden maelstrom of her hair, and Theo whistled a little between his teeth.

The booster rockets are supported by this elaborate scaffolding. In order to get to the shuttle cabin, you have to climb up a near-vertical flight of stairs. While we huffed and puffed our way up to the top, I half listened to Lacroix asking Bruce about his time flying in the military. I've listened to Lacroix do enough of these to understand how they work. First he starts off by asking the obvious, innocuous questions. Then he starts gradually wandering off-topic. I was waiting for him to drop some sort of existential bomb, but he appeared to be showing remarkable restraint.

There was no chance to admire the view at the top of the stairs. Kent had clearly been given orders to keep us strictly on schedule, so he unlocked the cabin door and tried to usher me—since I was first in line—inside the cabin.

The blast of oppressive air that came rushing out into my face couldn't be called *tomblike*—it was too searing and arid, and it was infused with the gritty smell of the desert—but that's the word I thought of, Arthur. I thought I would rather be suffocated than shoved into that burning hot spaceship. "No, thank you," I said. I said it quietly at first, hoping not to have it picked up by the camera, but Kent kept pushing me until finally I had to say it louder: "Stop it."

"Jessica?" said Lacroix, distracted momentarily from grilling Bruce. "Is there a problem?"

Elle piped up then. "You mean besides the fact that *that man*"—the two syllables were laced with disdain—"keeps trying to shove her like she is a chattel?"

"You mean cattle?" said Jed.

"I mean a cow," said Elle.

"It's fine," I said. I leaned out over the railing, fanned my face, and concentrated all my willpower on trying not to sweat. It's funny, Arthur—if you see the launch pad from a distance, it doesn't look like anything fancier than a parking lot for some industrial project that's been abandoned. It's not until you look down on it from above that you can see all its arrows, and arcane symbols, and the gleaming surface of steel-reinforced concrete, consecrated by the fire of rockets. I remember that from last time I was here—one of the many things I filed away to tell you and then never got the chance. "I've seen it before, so someone else should really have a look." I glowered into Lacroix's camera. "For God's sake, Theo, watch where you're pointing that thing. You're going to fall off the edge."

"I'll go," said Elle. She grabbed one of the handles and swung herself in, camera first.

There's not much to see inside—that's another thing I remembered correctly. There are four passenger chairs in the center and two up front in the cockpit. You could mistake them for airplane chairs, except they have decent padding on the headrests and more straps on the seat belts, and the barf bags are much more prominently displayed. There are several windows on either side, like portholes. The walls of the doomed *Titan* were the same blue color—I remember that too. They were also quilted into a diamond pattern with this silver industrial thread.

Perhaps I shouldn't tell you that the far-and-away most impressive part of the cabin is the control panel. But it is. It's as wide as two car dashboards and covered in screens and dials. There are whole banks of glowing orange buttons on the ceiling above the pilots' heads—dozens of them. Each one of them presumably performs a discrete function, but to my leery, untrained eye, Arthur, they all look the same. Each pilot is also equipped with a joystick that looks, somewhat disconcertingly, as though it came straight from an Xbox. It was impossible to look at the whole dazzling array and not wonder which tiny piece had so catastrophically failed, which of those buttons Liam had so fatefully signed off on. The computer systems in the Spaceco shuttles are so mind-bogglingly sophisticated that they run almost entirely on autopilot. The pilots are primarily there for appearances—laymen being much more willing to trust their lives to the judgment of their fellow human beings than they are to the calculations of machines. I certainly felt that way once—back when Liam went up, back before I could have had any clue how laughably, how sadly naive it was to take such a notion for granted.

And this I did tell you, didn't I—that I made Liam update his will before we came out here last spring? It was half serious, half a joke.

Lacroix turned back to Bruce. "Are you married?" he said.

"You bet," said Bruce. "Ten years. She's an ER doctor in Tucson, and—"

"What does she think of your job?" said Theo.

Here we go, I thought. I glanced over at Kent, who had turned his eyes away from Elle's disappearing rear end, and was now paying attention to the interview again.

"She thinks it's great," said Bruce. "She loves being able to tell people that her husband goes into space and—"

"So she doesn't have any concerns about your safety, then?" said Lacroix.

"Well, of course she has *concerns*," Bruce said. "There are certain risks inherent in—"

I could see Kent giving the throat-slash signal behind Lacroix's head.

"*You* don't have any concerns?" said Lacroix. "Say, for example, when you're hurtling up through the atmosphere at six thousand miles an hour toward the abyss, you don't have a moment where you wonder what compels you to do such a thing?" He was on a roll. "It doesn't cause you to reflect—"

There was a clang as Elle stepped back out onto the platform, and we all jumped a little. Bruce looked relieved, or as relieved as it's possible for a stoic ex-military spaceman to look.

"I think I got it all," Elle said. She shrugged. "Not bad."

Listen, Arthur, I want to (carefully) shower before I try to call Jack and Corinne, so that's all the day's report that you're going to get.

If you have the draft of your paper, can you send it to me?

Your medium-to-well-done

Jess

From: Jessica Frobisher <jesspfrobisher@yahoo.com>
Sent: Friday, August 15, 2014 11:07 pm
To: Arthur Danielson <art.danielson2010@gmail.com>
Cc:
Bcc:
Subject: Good Friday

Favorite former colleague (hereafter referred to as FFC),

Back at the Leave It to Beaver Hotel, waiting while Liam finishes up one last meeting. This place may be stuck in the 1950s, but the minibar is impressively contemporary. If you were here instead of roughing it up in Canada, you would probably be gloating at how the tables have turned, at the sight of Goody Frobisher stashing her empty bottles in the trash can under the bathroom sink.

Fair enough, but if you were here, I'd tell your hypothetical ass to cut me some slack. It's been a long, bad day, FFC, and I have a sinking feeling that it's only about to get worse. So I'm trying to steady my nerves—how's that for a retro term?

Today, Arthur, was space suit day. Getting what Spaceco guys call "geared up" isn't normally done until the morning of the launch, but Lacroix wanted to film it, which makes every procedure take ten times as long, and nobody wanted to leave it until the day of. So Liam picked me up from the motel at eleven and drove me to the Spaceco launch site. There, in a gloomy, warehouse-like room, blazing with Lacroix's klieg lights, one of the techs looked at the height and weight listed on our physical reports, disappeared for a few moments, and came back with several jumpsuits draped over her arm.

The suits aren't really necessary. The cabin is pressurized; you could technically go up in a pair of jeans and a T-shirt. (Not the flip-flops Corinne offered me, alas. The tech told me that in zero G, they'll float off—all clothing has to be firmly attached.) But since customers are paying a premium for a seat, Spaceco wants to deliver all the effects.

And the suits are effects all right. After we zipped ourselves, we all practiced walking around for a few minutes, wandering through the blinding puddles of Lacroix's lights, listening to the whispery whooshing noise of our own steps. Even Elle paused in front of the full-length mirror to admire her superheroine reflection. They are stunning costumes, Arthur, sky blue, made out of some futuristic fabric. The closest thing I can think to compare it to is the stuff of ski jackets—the expensive ones. They're practically weightless, with just a little bit of a velvety feel if you run your fingers against the grain. We're supposed to wear long underwear under them. That was on the list of items we were instructed to bring. This is for two reasons, the tech told us:

1. People get cold in the cabin. This isn't because of the temperature. The cabin is heated to 20 degrees Celsius. It's a psychological reaction to the dark. All that black, she said. And not nighttime Earth black. *Black* black.

2. People tend to sweat a lot during liftoff. The tech said, "It can be a pretty intense—"

"Over here, over here," said Lacroix, gesturing impatiently. "Can you look into the camera while you say it?" Lacroix is getting more obsessive by the day, Arthur. You get the feeling that he must sleep with his camera pressed against his face. There's a little shadow under his right eye, a faint gray-green bruise from the constant pressure of his eyepiece. He paces back and forth relentlessly in his dusty T-shirt, trying to appropriate every stray remark and gesture and channel it into his lens. I'd feel sorry for him, if he wasn't getting so fucking domineering.

The tech sighed. She was a young woman in her twenties with a shellacked ponytail, pretty much the only female in the whole place as far as I could tell, and here she was, playing the role of a glorified costume director. She looked seriously fed up. "I said," she repeated slowly. "It can be. Pretty intense. For some people."

"It's all part of the experience," Liam said. "You have to understand that the people who sign up for this kind of thing— they're not the cruise ship demographic. They're in it for the adrenaline. They're people who want to actually . . ."

He had been helping me tighten the adjustable cuff around my wrist, and as he spoke, he had gotten distracted and was cinching it to the point of pain.

"Who want to what?" Lacroix said. He was pointing toward his eyes with his free hand, mouthing, *Look at the camera.*

"Who want to actually feel something," said Liam. "You know, beyond the usual. The status quo."

"What is that? The status quo?" said Lacroix. Possibly the term had been lost in translation, Arthur, but I'm not sure.

"It's . . . ," Liam said. I think he was suddenly at a loss, Arthur. I was afraid of Lacroix's all-seeing camera, but I couldn't help myself, I turned to look at my husband anyway.

But he didn't get to finish, because right then Kent stepped in. "Let's get a picture of Mom in her space suit for the kids," he said. A couple of people pulled out their phones. "Get Dad in the picture," someone else said. "Closer." Liam reached out and put his arm around me.

"Make sure you get the flip-flops in for Corinne," I said. I could see the two of us on the monitor. We were standing under one of the kliegs, both of us frowning out into the dark. All the blood was flooding back into my hand, and it felt like it was on fire. "Closer," someone said. "Look like you like each other."

"Well, Jessica—" Lacroix turned the camera toward me. "What do you think? T minus 24 hours to liftoff. How does it feel?"

On the wall behind Lacroix's head were snapshots of the crews that had gone into space. Someone had put up a shot of Kelly Kahn and Uri Katamatov and Daniel Goldstein and Joseph Connelly. They were in their space suits, and someone had posed them in the exact same way Liam and I were standing—with their arms around one another, as though they were the best of friends instead of strangers. They all looked positively ecstatic, even the steely-eyed Kelly. You would never have guessed that they didn't have more than a few hours left.

"I'm sorry," I said.

From: Jessica Frobisher <jesspfrobisher@yahoo.com>
Sent: Saturday, August 16, 2014 12:42 am
To: Arthur Danielson <art.danielson2010@gmail.com>
Cc:
Bcc:
Subject: Good Friday (cont'd)

Sorry, that was Liam coming in. I panicked and made an erroneous click. Too many tiny bottles of wine have appearantly impaired my ability to distinguish between the Save and Send buttons.

Dear Husband arrived in a weirdly ebullient (possibly sloshed?) state. He had run into a couple of "reporters" in the parking lot and had chatted with them for several minutes. Not a single one of them recognized him. Li chalked this feat up to his badass shaved head and his ability to converse fluently about the Diamondbacks, a topic that almost no one from Michigan would know anything about. He even got them to tell him all about the upcoming launch by playing dumb.

"Which must have been no easy feat for you," I said. But he didn't get what I meant, or he didn't want to. He leaned down and gave me a loud smacking kiss on the crooked part of my hair.

"Almost there," he said.

Which means, I guess, that my betrayal hasn't been discovered yet. It'll stay hidden until the unlucky grunt in Spaceco's legal department who's charged with reviewing all of Lacroix's footage discovers it. That was part of the agreement, you know, in Lacroix's haggle-fest of a contract. That anything filmed at Spaceco's launch site would be reviewed by Spaceco personnel. Liam told me this. The reason, he said, was so that nothing proprietary would get released. But the real reason, of course, was that they want to control the truth.

Who knows? Maybe it will stay hidden forever. Sometimes things do. It's a platitude that the truth always comes out, but there's no way of knowing the ratio, right, FFC? The truths unearthed to the lies that stay buried? This morning, as we were driving into the compound, we passed a couple of leathery hicks with metal detectors. I pretended they were looking for gold—maybe bits of treasure dropped by illegal immigrants during their hasty northward trek to a brave new world. But I knew deep down that they were looking for pieces of the blown-up shuttle. Some of those titanium alloy smithereens are no bigger than a dime, but you can sell them on eBay, like pieces of silver. One step to the left or the right could have meant the difference between pay dirt and plain dirt for those profiteers, but of course there was nothing to guide them, so they just had to shuffle along and pray. Half a mile down the road you could still see them, the plaintive dusty clouds of their making being swallowed up by the turquoise sky.

FFC, I think I'm forgetting what my point was. Getting drunk the night before going into space is actually one of the things Specifically Forbidden on our packet. It's No. 3 on the list of proscriptions: "Avoid alcoholic beverages and get plenty of rest." And yet here I am breaking both of those rules. (To what peril, I don't know, and FFC, there's no one here I can ask.)

I'm sitting out on the balcony watching all the unfamiliar Arizona insects commit suicide against the porch lights, missing Corinne and Jack. I want to be back at home with them, hovering outside their rooms, listening to them breathe, the way I used to right after they were born, when the simple biological act of their respiration seemed miraculous to me, a function just as likely to cease as to continue steadily on. I keep picturing all the beautiful things about them. It was Liam who found constellations in Jack's freckles, you know. Cassiopeia and Leo and Perseus and Orpheus. Our son's face is adorned with the stuff of ancient Greek legends, of valor and loss. If she didn't know better, it would almost be enough to make this jaded astro-botanista believe in some sort of grand design.

That's what I would have told Kelly Kahn, back when we were in my dream together, if I could have just found the words. Then I would have taken her hands and helped her unzip her way out of that stupid space suit. I would have said, *Stay*. I would have said, *Wait*. I would have said, *Don't go*. But of course by then it was already too late.

FFC, I have many more run-on thoughts to share with you, but I should probably cut myself off before I forget how to use punctuation altogether. I think Liam's asleep now, which means maybe I can sneak back into bed without his noticing I ever left. Thank you, darling, for reading this.

Your slightly drunken, favorite (admit it!) former colleague,

Jess

From: Jessica Frobisher <jesspfrobisher@yahoo.com>
Sent: Saturday, August 16, 2014 9:02 am
To: Arthur Danielson <art.danielson2010@gmail.com>
Cc:
Bcc:
Subject: Re: serious missing data points

Fuck, Arthur—I don't have time. Just—shit.

I'll explain more later, maybe.

From: Jessica Frobisher <jesspfrobisher@yahoo.com>
Sent: Saturday, August 16, 2014 2:32 pm
To: Arthur Danielson <art.danielson2010@gmail.com>
Cc:
Bcc:
Subject: storms

Hey Arthur,

I'm glad to hear that my folly is entertaining reading for your morning coffee, but I think that's a sign that you're desperately in need of a newspaper, if only to help you start preparing for your return to civilization. I know you've been away, so let me be the one to fill you in: global warming is only the half of it. We, as a species, are seriously fucked.

And speaking of seriously fucked, when I got your reply this morning, I had to go back and read (or try to) my e-mails from last night. I was so out of it that at first even I couldn't figure out what I was talking about. And then, unfortunately, I did.

We were supposed to blast out of here at ten this morning, but the launch has been pushed back because of storms moving in. (The clouds out in the desert are like uberclouds. They are holy clouds, Arthur. They go upward for miles. They put our drizzly, ho-hum midwestern clouds to shame.) So here we are back at the hotel again, listening to the charming vintage leak dripping from the charming vintage faucet, and watching the sky brighten and fade, brighten and fade, brighten and fade, taking its time while it decides our fate.

So until that time, there's nothing to do but chew on my fingernails and try to avoid Lacroix. He's already barged into our room once this morning, right after he heard the news about the storm delay. He wanted to get a few stats from Liam about rain delay and the dangers of storms for shuttle launches. I was sitting on the bed, jiggling my feet. As soon as I saw the camera, I tried to get up and make my way stealthily toward the balcony, but Lacroix caught me just as I reached for the slider handle.

"Astronaut Jessica." He pointed the camera toward me. "Let's get *your* reaction. The launch may not happen until tomorrow. Are you disappointed? Impatient?" Even without turning around, I could feel him zooming in. It's a kind of ESP I've developed. "Maybe you're secretly relieved? Come on, you can admit it to us."

As always he was talking in that grandiose, slightly croaky inflection of his that he uses only for narrating, when (you can tell) he's thinking about his imaginary audience, waiting somewhere out there in the future, and how he's going to shape the story for them. If you end up watching this movie, someday in North Carolina, or wherever you go, you should know that he doesn't actually talk like that. In real life, he actually sounds much less flamboyant, sometimes matter-of-fact, and sometimes even kind. But only sometimes.

The truth is, Arthur, I'm full of nothing but dread. But there wasn't anything I could do other than turn around to face him head-on and put on my best hungover smile. "Looking forward to it," I said. Hoping to redirect Lacroix, I turned to Liam, who was standing in the bathroom doorway, brushing his teeth. "Li, what's the quote the Spaceco guys always use? It's some appropriately rousing Shakespearean—"

"Right," said Liam. "'Once more into the breach, dear friends, once more.'" There was a profound melancholy to his voice that startled me, Arthur.

"Ah," said Lacroix, still keeping the camera trained on me. "You know the first thing that came to my mind was the quote from *Julius Caesar*. I always forget how it is said. Something like: 'Cowards die many times before their deaths; the valiant never—'"

"That sounds right to me," said Liam.

"*Julius Caesar*," I said, "was always my least favorite play." I was staring directly into the lens, trying to get Lacroix to peel his face away from that damn camera and look at me so I could read his expression, but he wouldn't. It was like a game of double-entendre chicken. He was daring me to talk about what he had seen me do yesterday, to bring it up in front of Liam.

What he saw, unfortunately, Arthur, was me talking to Melissa Kramer. No, wait, let me back up. We have at least two hours before launch time, if we go at all.

So here it is:
I did tell you yesterday about trying on our space suits, right? Gearing up was on our itinerary from eleven to one. After that, we were supposed to have lunch in the Spaceco cafeteria (referred to, for some possibly pretentious reason, as "the mess

hall"). I wasn't hungry and I had a headache, so I decided to go for a walk instead.

I didn't actually tell anyone where I was going. Now keep in mind that there's an explicitly stated rule against Spaceco customers wandering around the premises on their own. It's No. 1 on our list of proscriptions, printed in bold and italicized font: "For safety reasons, Spaceco passengers and their guests are prohibited from wandering around the restricted areas of the Spaceco launch site without the accompaniment of Spaceco staff." As Liam's wife, though, I fall into a kind of gray area. I'm assumed to be smart enough to read warning signs, to keep my hands off wires. I'm also assumed to be loyal—whose motives could be purer than mine? That's why what happens next in this little narrative is funny. In an ironic, unfunny sort of way.

Since I'm not allowed to explain anything to Lacroix's future audience, Arthur, I'm giving my explanation to you. I would like to say, for the record, that I never set out to betray anyone. In fact when I saw the front gate, and the TV vans sitting there, I deliberately changed my direction. I turned around and started walking back toward the safety of Spaceco's fenced-in wilderness. Liam and I may not have much in common these days. (I can probably count all the things we do on two hands, Jack and Corinne taking one thumb apiece). But our loathing of reporters is one of those solid points of agreement where we present that solid unified front Tristan has exhorted me to aspire to.

To be perfectly honest, I had no plan at all. At least, nothing beyond finding one of those amazing prickly pear cactuses so I could take a picture of it for Jack and Corinne—a sort of alien life form they could marvel at. (And maybe for you, Arthur—they're like the antithesis to your conifers. You know how much I like to play devil's advocate. Who will I play against when you're gone?)

I don't know how long I shuffled on for. All I had on was Corinne's flip-flops, and at first I was trying to keep an eye out for rattlesnakes or endangered, pincered beetles, but after a while I stopped. There was a weird heaviness to the still, bright air, like grief, but all the overrated "dry heat"—it was evaporating the tears right out of my eyes.

At one point I saw the launch pad in the distance. I could see a few guys puttering around, so I gave it a wide berth. Whatever questions they might ask me, Arthur, were questions I sure as hell didn't have answers for.

This is all just a convoluted way of saying that all my instincts have been blown to hell, Arthur. They say *Go* when I should stay. They say *Stay* when I should go. When I hit the fence again, when I looked through and saw the crash site on the other side, I should have turned around and gone back before I was missed. But I didn't. I found a loose flap on the fence. (There are signs posted all over that read DANGER: HIGH VOLTAGE, but thanks to Liam, I know they're a lie.) When I should have stayed put, I wandered out into enemy territory. I believed I was safe. I had shed my Spaceco space suit before lunch, and now I was just in my shorts and your silk shirt. I thought I could pass as pretty much anyone. A city slicker, dressed badly for the desert, say. Or a tourist bored with TV tragedies and looking for a taste of the real thing. Or a kooky rubbernecker local.

The main crash site was marked off with caution tape stapled to a ring of plywood stakes. It was still intact, despite months of wind and the occasional desert rains, although most of the letters have worn away, so now there's a smattering of faint runic A's, U's, and O's. Inside there were a few orange cones, a few little triangles with numbers, tipped on their sides. Someone had stapled some roses to one of the stakes. If you didn't know, if you had to guess, you might think the place was some sort of archaeological dig site, that some ancient civilization did something significant here. Celebrated, maybe, or buried their dead. You might mistake the black scorch marks in the sand for the remains of fires built for a feast or for lamentation. When the *Titan*'s pieces landed, most of them were on fire, and they actually fused the sand together. I read somewhere that one of the chairs came down almost intact, with one of its buckles still buckled. I overheard Lacroix asking someone about it, and they told him that the story was apocryphal. The atmosphere devoured almost everything.

But I'm digressing again, Arthur. I was talking about staying versus going and going versus staying, wasn't I?

A car was parked a short distance away from the crash site. I had just stepped over the tape ring, and bent over to examine the little numbered triangles, wondering if Liam had put any of them there, when Melissa Kramer opened the door of that car and got out.

Even from a distance I recognized her. (There's something about her long, boyish strides. They're unfeminine and yet somehow still graceful in their own distinct, leggy way.) It was clearly a *go* situation, and yet for some reason I didn't. I stood there, jiggling the handful of loose change in my pocket and watching her make her way toward me. At the moment, I do remember thinking that it was strange to see her, but in hindsight, Arthur, it seems less so. We're both traveling along an orbit around the same tragedy. Why shouldn't we brush shoulders from time to time as we hurtle past one another? Why shouldn't we wave a brief, simultaneous hello and farewell?

She greeted me with equal nonchalance: "Dr. Frobisher, hi. I thought that was you."

Her newest ensemble included a Yankees hat and a pair of hiking boots—definitely more rattlesnake retardant than my footwear.

She looked as at ease in them in as she had in the blazer she wore to my house that morning back in April. It made me think, Arthur, that she really must be damn good at her work. There's more to it than her self-possession or her willingness to ask the precise question that no one wants to answer. She's also endowed with the ability to arrive at a place and effortlessly assume its dress and customs. Whatever her sympathies or allegiances are, you have no way of guessing at them. A moment of purely idle curiosity made me glance down at her wedding ring hand, but I couldn't see it because she was holding a large container of McDonald's French fries. Like I said, Arthur: When in Arizona. The woman had it down.

She held out the fries to me. "Fry?"

Instead of leaving, I took one. I said, "Wherever I go, there you are."

"I know," she said. "It's this story. My editor won't let me get away."

I reached out and helped myself to another fry without asking. "Do you want to?"

"No." She picked up a ketchup-laden fry and considered it for a moment. "I like to see things through to the bitter end."

Instead of leaving, I asked her another question. "Are the endings always bitter?"

She shook her fry, flinging the excess ketchup away into the dirt. I noticed that she turned a little to the side as she did so, to keep the droplets from falling inside the cordoned-off area in front of us. The wind had picked up; everything was blowing a little at a slant. "I never say *always*," she said. "If the answer was *always*, this would be a pretty depressing job."

The wind was blowing the black dust all over the tops of my feet, starting to turn the pink straps of Corinne's flip-flops an ugly dusky color. Instead of leaving, I stayed put and watched them darken. "I kind of assumed that was the case."

"It has its moments." She had her head tilted and was looking at me with her eyes squinted. "Word on the street is there's another shuttle launch tomorrow."

I took another French fry. "Are you guys hanging around to see if there's going to be another spectacle?" I said.

"If I said no, I would only be 90 percent telling the truth," she said.

"You could do worse." The fries were delicious, and they were making me ravenous, but I knew it was only a matter of time before they hit like a ton of bricks, like some sort of gastrointestinal revenge. When I stepped woozily back over the tape, I caught my toe, and she had to grab my shoulder to make sure I didn't fall.

Instead of shaking her off, I grabbed her hand. Instead of turning around and booking it back toward the fence, I leaned in toward her ear, as though someone were close by, hanging on to our every word. "You know they were lying about that control panel switch, don't you?" I said. "They knew it was a bad idea. I mean, they didn't *know*. They thought it might be risky, but they decided to go for it anyway."

"I know." With a gesture so careful it seemed composed of the utmost kindness, Melissa Kramer took my shoulders and steadied me. "Well, my bets were on something like that." She glanced back over her shoulder toward the shuttle hangar. "I don't suppose there's any way I'm going to convince you to go on the record with that, am I?"

I closed my eyes for a second and tried to think. "I bet you already know the answer to that question, don't you, Melissa?"

"I have to try," she said. "I can't help it. Here. Just in case." With her free hand, she was digging around in the pocket of her jeans. "Let me give you my card. Come on." She held it out to me. "Just take it. You can always pitch it later. It's 100 percent recyclable, I promise."

As I was reaching out to take it, she said, "Who's your little friend?" She jerked her head to the side, back over toward the fence.

I turned around and looked back. If you've been reading all the way through to this point, Arthur, I guess that I don't have to tell you who was standing there. I still have no idea how he'd managed to escape his Spaceco minders, but there he was. *All big mistakes are made up out of a thousand little ones.* Is that you I'm quoting, Arthur, or am I misattributing? When Lacroix saw me, he didn't stop filming, but he lifted his face from behind the camera and stared straight at me. Even from a distance I could read it, its fatal expression of dispassion, and my knees went a little weak. I don't think it dawned on me until right at that moment that I had just done something I could not take back.

I wasn't aware of doing anything, of having moved so much as a muscle. But I must have looked stricken, because Melissa Kramer put her hand on my shoulder again. She was talking to me, in her steely rational voice, I remember, saying something about how Lacroix was too far away to have caught anything from our conversation, that the wind was blowing against him. But I was already shaking her off and running across the sand toward the man with the camera, as fast as I could in my dirty pink shoes, oblivious to the rattlesnakes, the endangered beetles, the fundamental fact that I was in a dangerous place where you need to watch every step.

Lacroix had already put down his camera and ducked back through the fence. I could see him through the chain link, swinging his camera a little as he walked, hefting the weight of his compact, powerful equipment with each step. He wasn't hurrying, or trying to evade me, Arthur. You'd have thought he would have looked pleased—what with having just captured this latest dramatic plot twist on camera. But he just looked like a man who wanted to go home, back to his beautiful wife and his quiet hotel room. I caught up to him just after I got through the fence, and I tried to grab his shoulder. I was moving so fast that I accidentally punched him in the back. But he barely flinched.

"Easy does it, Jessica," he said.

"Theo," I said. "Stop. I want to explain."

With a faint sigh, he turned around. It was the first time I had ever seen him look tired. He was looking up toward the clouds, and then, with some effort or annoyance, he lowered his eyes and looked at me. "The answer is no," he said.

"Theo," I said. "I am begging you."

"I can't," he said. "I hand everything off to them when I leave the premises. You know the arrangement." He looked down at his camera and sighed a little. "I'll see you at dinner."

Arthur, the storms have been clearing off, and I just got a call a few minutes ago that the launch might actually be happening after all. My presence is being requested at the launch site. It

259

looks like we may be space bound today after all. Li's going to be here in a minute to pick me up, so I have to go.

Onward and (maybe) upward,

Jess

From: Jessica Frobisher <jesspfrobisher@yahoo.com>
Sent: Saturday, August 16, 2014 4:01 pm
To: Arthur Danielson <art.danielson2010@gmail.com>
Cc:
Bcc:
Subject: blasting off

Hey Arthur,

Storms have moved out, and Central Command has given us the go-ahead, so we're launching in an hour. I have to go get geared up and give the kiddos a quick call.

If you can get out of the trees and go someplace where you have a clear shot of the sky, you should look up. I'll give you a wave when we fly past.

See you on the other side.

Jess

Sent from my iPhone

From: Jessica Frobisher <jesspfrobisher@yahoo.com>
Sent: Saturday, August 16, 2014 10:38 pm
To: Arthur Danielson <art.danielson2010@gmail.com>
Cc:
Bcc:
Subject: Touched down

---

safely at dusk. A landing time of 20:29. Exactly as scheduled.

Yes, I have an answer to that question, but I need to think on it.

So more later. I think.

Love,
Jess

Sent from my iPhone

From: Jessica Frobisher <jesspfrobisher@yahoo.com>
Sent: Tuesday, August 26, 2014 2:24 pm
To: Arthur Danielson <art.danielson2010@gmail.com>
Cc:
Bcc:
Subject: Re: well?

Hey Arthur,

I don't know what you read, but it wasn't as bad as they made it sound. Lacroix is fine. The man was once chomped on by a (doubtlessly provoked) hippopotamus, for Christ's sake. He's going to outlive us all. Last time I saw him he was at the hospital in Sierra Vista, involved in a heated argument with the nurses about his right, or lack thereof, to film on hospital property. There was one of him versus three of them, and he was giving back as good as he got. When he saw me, he took a time-out to ask me if I would agree to a postspace interview. Of course I said no. But he has my e-mail address, and he's going to harass me until I cave in or ask the university to change it.

Lacroix wasn't the only casualty. There were other things that were damaged . . . and unlike our obnoxious filmmaker, I think it's safe to say that they're beyond fixing.

But I don't want to talk about them right now. The truth is, I'm a little distracted by all the epiphanies I'm having. They're keeping me up at night. I'm told that these symptoms—mania, sleeplessness—are common aftereffects for people who go up. I'm told they don't last.

As for your question . . . you know as well as I do that it's a sore subject. Maybe we should just leave it lie?

Your prudent, sleepless

Jess

From: Jessica Frobisher <jesspfrobisher@yahoo.com>
Sent: Thursday, August 28, 2014 3:18 pm
To: Arthur Danielson <art.danielson2010@gmail.com>
Cc:
Bcc:
Subject: Re: seriously now

Danielson, I seriously don't *have* to tell you anything. If you're dying to know how it all went down, then maybe you'll just have to bite the bullet and shell out $10 to go see the movie in a theater when it comes out. What with everything that's happened, Lacroix's gotten such good publicity that the film may make a run in the mainstream theaters, not just the artsy-fartsy ones like State Street. But I sure as hell hope not.

Besides, I signed so many nondisclosure agreements that I'm no longer sure who I'm allowed to tell what. I don't need a lawyer to tell me that all these missives I have been sending you are a huge liability. Actually, I knew that all along. E-mail isn't secure, as my newly estranged husband used to remind me. Who knows who could be reading this?

How about if I told you the expurgated version I told Jack and Corinne? It went like this: My trip out into space was an exciting adventure. Our planet is a lot smaller than you would think. And more staggeringly beautiful than you can possibly imagine, but in a terrible sort of way.

There's the longer, trickier unabridged version that I'll need to tell them eventually, of course. I've spent a few of my sleepless nights trying to think about what I'll say, someday in the future, when they have sins and failures of their own, and they have a better grip on the terminology, and a better chance of understanding.

But I have some time, I guess, to practice.

Re the northern lights: heartbreaking in a good way or just heartbreaking?

Jess

From: Jessica Frobisher <jesspfrobisher@yahoo.com>
Sent: Thursday, August 28, 2014 3:20 pm
To: Arthur Danielson <art.danielson2010@gmail.com>
Cc:
Bcc:
Subject: p.s.

It looks like I'm getting your 265 section, so thanks a lot.

From: Jessica Frobisher <jesspfrobisher@yahoo.com>
Sent: Sunday, August 31, 2014 11:43 pm
To: Arthur Danielson <art.danielson2010@gmail.com>
Cc:
Bcc:
Subject: practice run

Yes, you read that right.

I wasn't being coy. We haven't even figured out what we're telling Jack and Corinne about the separation.

As for my trip . . . it's just hard to describe. That's all. My first day back on campus, I ran into Moira on the steps of the Hatcher. I was coming back from your office with an armful of your indefinitely checked-out library books. Your days of abusing your faculty borrowing privileges are over, I'm afraid. And Krasinski's taking your office. The decision was made the day before I got back, so I couldn't call dibs even if I wanted to. If I weren't trying to cut back on my daily dose of paranoia, I would say that this was a strategic move—to spare everyone the unseemliness of my name being brought up so close to yours. But perhaps not.

The first thing Moira said to me was, "You survived." She laughed after she said it to make it a joke, although I swear she sounded a little disappointed.

The second thing she said was, "How was it?"

I smiled and gave her the most unsatisfying reply I possibly could. "It was fine," I said. There was nothing else to do after that except for us each to go our separate ways. Her to the lab. Me to drop off your books, to divest my life of the last few traces of you.

Are you ready, Arthur? The real answer goes something like this:

Everything was a little crazy when we arrived at the launch site. Even though Spaceco was doing their damnedest to keep the launch "low-profile," it was clear that someone had "accidentally" leaked the time of the launch, and the entire dirt track was covered with TV vans and cars, which meant Jed didn't have a chance to show off his action-hero driving skills again. All he could do was creep along like everyone else, one hand on the horn. Every now and then he had to veer off the road, and we all had to reach out and put our hands on the windows to brace ourselves. Elle was sitting in the front seat, filming the general chaos, while Lacroix sat in the back, zooming in and out on Liam and me. He was hoping to capture, I imagined, some final bit of earthly domestic drama, maybe the moment where I broke down and sobbed, and owned up at last.

If that's what he was hoping for, he was in for a disappointment. But the tension in the car was cranked up so high that it was almost as audible as the hum of the air conditioner. Liam had taken my hand and was kneading my fingers a little, a camera-perfect gesture that looked like comfort. But it wasn't, Arthur. I think he was goading me on, warning me not to back down.

But most importantly there was the matter of Liam's phone. It had started ringing not long after we left the hotel. Every five minutes, like clockwork, the Imperial Death March would start up (thank you, Jack), and every five minutes, after a beat or two, Liam would glance down at it and turn it off. Finally I couldn't take it anymore. "Li," I said. "Will you *please* answer that thing?"

"It's Chris," he said, "from Legal. I told him that I would call him right after the launch. I can't imagine what his problem is. He's always like this. Everything is a crisis. Crisis-a-minute Chris is what Tristan calls him." He turned to look at Lacroix. "That's off the record, by the way."

"Of course," Lacroix said. Whether he had turned the camera on me or not, I don't know, Arthur. Everything had slowed down, suddenly jumped into exquisitely sharp relief. Through the van window, I could see the flies lifting up and touching down in their drugged, intricate loops. "Everything hangs in such a delicate balance," you said in that PBS interview. Can I be a know-it-all and say this, Arthur? You have no fucking idea.

"Are you cold?" Liam asked. It was like his voice was coming from far away. "Hey, Kent, can we turn down the AC?"

"We're almost there," said Kent.

But it wasn't the AC. I proceeded to shiver while I got geared up in my long underwear and space suit. I proceeded to shiver while I paced around the shuttle hangar, watching Elle and Lacroix run back and forth across the launch pad, holding up tiny little meters to the sky, doing last-minute checks on lighting.

I shivered while I called Jack and Corinne. Jack refused to take the phone when Paula tried to hand it to him. Corinne, true to form, wouldn't shut up. Both of the hermit crabs had died the night before, in one final skirmish that was years in the coming. There were legs *everywhere*, Corinne reported, and— She paused for a minute, distracted from her gory blow-by-blow.

"Are you in space right now?" she asked. I think it was the guttering reception, Arthur, that made her think I was even farther away than I actually was.

"No, sweetheart," I said. "I'm still in Arizona."

"Oh," she said. "You sound like you're in space. Like you're a thousand miles away. No, a million." And then she went right back to talking, saving me the trouble of saying anything more. Which was a good thing, Arthur, because I was starting to cry a little. I had to hold the phone away from my mouth. On the other side of the launch pad, a man was waving impatiently at me. *Time to go, go, go.* It seemed like everyone was manhandling me. Someone was practically pulling the phone out of my hands. The rule is that you can take phones with you, but they have to be turned off and secured in one of the million pockets of your space suit until you reach your low-orbit cruising altitude of about 120 miles up. Someone else was jerking on my watchband, making sure it was secure.

"OK, bye," she said nonchalantly. "Have fun in space."

And then, in spite of all the urgency, there were a few more minutes of milling around. Liam had been swallowed up by the crowd, but suddenly he reappeared. "Everything's going to be fine," he said. "We just ran through the last test sequence. It went perfectly."

"That's good," I said.

He held out his hands and then dropped them helplessly back to his sides. Our time was almost up. "Jess, can't we—"

But I never learned what he was about to say, because right then his phone rang again. "For the love of God," Liam said. "He's like one of those pit bulls that latches on and never lets go. Just give me two minutes, Jess."

"Take all the time you need," I said. But he was already walking away and didn't hear me.

Lacroix came up behind me. "Jessica. Fellow astronaut. Boarding call. They want us to load up."

"Hang on a second," I said. I was watching Liam, who was still walking out past the shade of the shuttle hangar and into the sunlight, away from the crowd. I remember exactly how he looked—the dread and sorrow of the moment has preserved it in a kind of dusky amber, frozen it, so it will survive the ages. He had the phone against one ear and his finger in the other, trying to drown out all the other sounds, to listen and to understand. When he did, he turned around and looked back at me. I mouthed something at him. This is the part that's hazy to me. It was some two-syllable word; I remember the rhythm of it as it rolled off my tongue. Maybe it was his name. Maybe it was a single *sorry*. Maybe it was just the word *goodbye*.

"It's time to go," Lacroix said.

Jess

From: Jessica Frobisher <jesspfrobisher@yahoo.com>
Sent: Tuesday, September 2, 2014 11:11 pm
To: Arthur Danielson <art.danielson2010@gmail.com>
Cc:
Bcc:
Subject: 3 . . . 2 . . . 1

No, no, I'm not done yet. For God's sake, you know better than that. I'm still trying to get this all down, all the important parts, anyway. This was one of the epiphanies I had the other night while I was out wandering around in my half-finished greenhouse, kicking at the stones I had so painstakingly laid down according to a scrupulous plan: that no matter how much I wish it otherwise, this has become the story of my life. I paced and paced, listening to the cricket din. (Have you noticed, Arthur, how harsh-sounding they get as the summer wears on? It's as though there's nothing left to them but wearisome and bitter truths.) Eventually, I came to my senses and went back inside.

Remember those pictures of the *Titan* shuttle that I subjected you to? It was so small that the first time I laid eyes on it in person, I almost laughed. I couldn't believe that Liam was going to be going 120 miles up in the air in something not much bigger than a tour bus.

And now, here I was. I was the first one up, followed by Elle and Lacroix, who were both wielding cameras. The handrail was scalding to the touch, and the metallic, faintly caustic scent of rocket fuel was hanging in the air like a cloud.

I didn't have time to pause at the top, to try to peek through the scaffolding beams out at the desert and take one last look at Liam, or everything else that I was leaving behind. There were two techs waiting on the platform, ready to maneuver me through the

270

door. One of them took hold of one arm, one took hold of the other. Imagine getting loaded into a sideways tilt-a-whirl car by two carnies, impatient as hell to get the ride started, and that should give you a feel for the logistics. Everything is oriented straight up, so getting into your seat requires you to use handlebars located on the ceiling, and a surprising amount of upper-body strength. By the time I had managed to scramble into my seat, I was panting a little.

The window was to my left. I kept my eyes focused on it, turning my head as far as the plushy headrest would allow. The angle was such that I couldn't see any land at all, nothing but blank blue sky. Because the auxiliary power source hadn't been turned on yet, the cabin was hot as hell. Once Lacroix and Elle had been loaded into their seats, then the Spaceco guys climbed into the cabin, squeezing around us, jerking the straps on our seat harnesses tight. Gone was the solicitousness we'd been handled with all week. We were nothing more than bodies, cargo in space suits. They were barely making eye contact with us, and I couldn't help but feel like this was part of some instructions they'd been given— to keep the conversation to a minimum, to keep us focused, to try as much as possible to suspend any extraneous, personal earthly ties. We were going. They were staying behind. "Barf bags are right in front of you," said one of the guys. "So you can grab one without even looking." Then he turned to the cockpit and said something to Bruce and Jed. I think it was "Don't fuck it up."

"OK, guys," said one of the techs. He was wearing the standard-issue Spaceco polo shirt, but you could see a tattoo creeping out above the collar. It was either a lizard or a mermaid. *Tan* wasn't even the word to describe him. He was a deep weathered brown, like he spent all his free time foraging out in the desert. If he'd been born two hundred years ago, he'd be shipping out for a penal colony somewhere in the New World. Instead, he was working here, manning shuttles at this twenty-first-century port, as close as he could get himself to the last hostile frontier, probably hoping to bum his own passage someday. "It's going to take about ten minutes for the cabin to pressurize and for us to activate the thrusters. Once we start that, we're at the point of no return, so I need everyone here to give me an affirmative that we're good to go."

"Good," came Elle's voice from behind me.

"Good," said Lacroix.

It was right then I realized that I was shivering again—so hard that my knees were banging together. My teeth were chattering audibly, and I had to clamp down and grind them together to get them to stop. I'll say it one last time, Arthur: I wasn't afraid. But it was like my body and I were parting ways, wrestling for control, and I wasn't sure that I was going to be able to get the upper hand.

"Jessica?" said Tattoo Guy.

Even through the thick nylon of his suit, Lacroix was emanating heat. I leaned toward him as much as I could, tried to draw off of him, like a draft.

"Jessica?" he said again.

I managed to unclench my teeth. "Great," I said. Or something that resembled it.

"All right, guys," he said. "Have a safe trip."

Arthur, I have to go now, but speaking of safe trips—I believe you're on your way to North Carolina now, correct?

If so, safe travels,

Jess

From: Jessica Frobisher <jesspfrobisher@yahoo.com>
Sent: Wednesday, September 3, 2014 10:37 pm
To: Arthur Danielson <art.danielson2010@gmail.com>
Cc:
Bcc:
Subject: trial by fire

Is what Liam calls liftoff.

Here's what I remember: It felt like an earthquake. The sky trembled in the windows. It got brighter. There was a shuddering somewhere down under us, a ways off, like thunder, and then it got louder, and then it wasn't like thunder at all. It was too loud, too sustained, and there was a furious, high-pitched screaming, like air shredding, this terrible grief-stricken sound. Then there was a calm moment, like a decision being made. It can't have lasted longer than a millisecond. Somewhere off in the distance, someone was breathing hard, gasping to the point of hyperventilation. It could have been me.

Then we were moving. Moving is the proper verb here, Arthur, but you can't even begin to imagine how far it falls short. We were being pressed down in our seats, flattened, as though something was trying its best to turn us from three dimensions into two. The g-force made it hard to breathe, hard to even blink. My window was on fire; the friction was causing the air to conflagrate around us. "Don't be afraid. This is normal," is what they had told us.

I remember that I was trying to count to twelve, so that I would know the exact moment. I mean the moment when those six people died. Time seemed to slow down. I thought we would never reach it, but in hindsight, I realize that I was just counting badly. I told myself that when the end came for them, it would have happened so fast that they wouldn't have known what was happening. The sky had swallowed them up, devoured them instantly, obliterated all traces. Everything was gone before the tech at ground control had time to lift his eyes from the monitor and say—this was recorded—"Holy mother of God."

I counted to twelve. I counted to thirteen. Then to twenty. Then to a hundred. I remember that there was a lurch as the rocket boosters fell away, and I opened my eyes. There was an eerie flickering in the cabin. It was like I had temporarily jettisoned my body, but now I was coming back. One of the harness straps was cutting into my neck. There was a taste of blood in my mouth. I had apparently bitten my tongue. There was a warm weight on the top of my right hand. I saw that Lacroix had reached over and taken it, although his eyes were closed as though he hadn't noticed I was there.

It takes about eight minutes to reach orbit. Surely Bruce and Jed must have been conferring with one another up in the cockpit, but for the life of me, Arthur, I can't remember hearing a word. All I remember was this feeling of waiting. I think it was the loneliest eight minutes of my life.

All of a sudden, the thrusters shut off.

It was absolutely quiet.

When I looked down, my shoelaces were drifting around, their ends making lazy figures around my ankles. I was so mesmerized by watching them that I barely heard Jed come out of the cockpit

274

and tell us that we were free to unbuckle ourselves and float around the cabin. My seat belt was clinging to me in a needy sort of way, and by the time I had extricated myself, Elle and Lacroix were already out of their seats and pulling their cameras from the lockdown trunk in the back of the cabin. Elle's braid was floating up, winding around in the air, gracefully, like a cobra rising up out of its basket. She was pulling quarters out of one of her zippered pockets and flicking them into the air with her finger. She was—yes, Arthur—actually laughing with her mouth open and her head thrown back. And then we all started to laugh giddily in sympathy with her, even Jed, who kept saying, "See? See?" in response to nobody in particular.

That's all I have time for now, Arthur.

You want me to keep going?

Jess

From: Jessica Frobisher <jesspfrobisher@yahoo.com>
Sent: Saturday, September 6, 2014 2:09 am
To: Arthur Danielson <art.danielson2010@gmail.com>
Cc:
Bcc:
Subject: Re: re: trial by fire

OK, fine. It's just that I haven't forgotten that this isn't your favorite subject, that's all. Don't pretend you don't know what I'm talking about. You didn't want to hear about space last spring, remember? You called me cruel, Arthur. You called me a bitch. You said you'd never met someone so emotionally underhanded. Those terms haunt me, Arthur—in the way of all aspersions that contain a germ of truth. I have been unable to banish them. They sit on my shoulders and mutter in my ears during all my moments of doubt.

I suppose in our seasoned middle age, it's trite to observe that the most fateful days are the ones that arrive with no forewarning, that they are the ones you awaken to obliviously, staring into your coffee while you rub the pillow creases off your forehead. (A side note: is it just me, or are those things getting slower and slower to fade?)

Still. I can't help it. I had no idea, that day I came back after watching Liam get shot up into space, that my time with you was almost up. If I had, I would have done things differently. I would have worn my brown sweater instead of my blue one. I would have put my hair up instead of leaving it down. I would have left off that ridiculous perfume.

I would have concentrated on my assays instead of watching the clock, instead of getting up out of my chair and going to the door every five seconds to see if you had come in yet. When I saw you standing there in the doorway, I would have stayed put in my chair instead of leaping up and flinging out my arms. When you said, "Well, how it'd go?" I would have paid heed to the grudging note in your voice. I would not have said, "It was amazing." I would not have said, "You should have been there." I would not have uttered these things in such a breathless way. I knew better.

Not that these things weren't true. When Liam touched down, it was like he had gotten religion. He was practically speaking in tongues. But everything he told me, as effusive as it was—Arthur, it didn't even come close to doing it justice. All three of us— Lacroix, Elle, and I—crowded around the windows, hanging on the handles next to the sills, and we were all struck dumb. Even Jed, who had been up before, was whistling a little, a thin plaintive sound that filled the quietly humming cabin. I don't know what I'd been picturing, Arthur, but this wasn't it. Our planet was looming in front of us, immense, ravishing, lush, luminous against its black, curving edge of space. (How many synonyms are there for the word *amazing*? I'll bet you $100 I can win the game again.) The windowpane was freezing, but I was pressing myself against it anyway, like one of those dazzled little kids at the aquarium, the ones that look like they want to melt through the glass, like they're about to swoon from an overdose of beauty.

At first it was nothing but overwhelming color. Blues, browns, greens, whites, grays—and none of it made any sense. After a few minutes, though, things began resolving themselves into recognizable shapes. There was some sort of landmass. There were some glimmering clouds—the storm system that had been over us a few hours ago and was now tracking eastward. Sixty seconds and we had passed over it, left it behind. There was a coastline, fissured with tiny dingy cracks.

"The Gulf of Mexico," Jed said. "See those murky spots right along the coast? That's fertilizer runoff. We're polluting the crap out of it. All that shit—" He looked at Lacroix's camera. "All that garbage washes down the Mississippi and creates this hypoxic zone. It's like a wasteland. There's nothing alive, and it's so big you can see it from space. Shit, we passed it." He shrugged. "That's the thing. You see all this awesome stuff, but you have to look fast. Hold on. We're coming up on Florida in a minute. Sometimes that's good for meteorological shit—I mean, weather events. Very picturesque."

We all waited while the long green finger crept slowly toward us. "Damn," said Jed. "It's looking pretty lame down there today. Hold on."

Lacroix had the lens of his camera pressed hungrily against his window. He was sniffling a bit, but no one was paying attention. Why would we have?

"I just wish we could have gotten you guys up here during hurricane season," Jed said. "You see one of those suckers from space, and at even 200K up they're like"—he spread his arms— "this big across. You see a category four or five, and seriously, it can about make you piss your pants. I know a dude who was up in the ISS, back in 2005, and they were going around and around over Katrina for days. He said the guys couldn't get any work done. They kept dropping everything and going to the window every ninety minutes. He said it was like watching a monster in slow-mo, moving in for the kill."

In the cockpit, Bruce cleared his throat. He had his headset on, nodding along to the banter from ground control. I didn't realize that he had been listening to us at all. "We could lighten things up a little, you know, Jed. Let's not make this a tour of ruination and desolation. It's not good for business."

"Among other things," I said.

"He's just being honest," Elle said. "People should be honest. Some things can't be saved."

"Well, I think—," Bruce said.

"This conversation has taken"—Lacroix's voice was even more froggy than usual—"a somewhat dour turn. Now." He let go of the camera and snuffled a little. "I'm fine with that, but Jed, I'd like to ask you a couple more questions about . . ." His voice trailed off for a second, and for the first time, I noticed that he looked a little gray.

"We're crossing over into nighttime now," Jed said. "Now we're going to see some interesting stuff." He pushed himself away from the window and made a practiced grab at the handle above his head to face Lacroix. "What were you going to ask me?"

"I can't remember," Lacroix said. "I think I need to sit down for a second."

The light was fading fast and the cabin lights switched on.

"Theo?" said Elle.

Something dark and red hit the back of my hand and burst.

Other things that I wish I could take back: The night I left the barbecue early. That whole drive back from East Lansing. The phrase "jealousy doesn't become you." ("Become you"? What kind of prima donna uses that phrase, anyway?) That stupid joke about the smell of space. Deep down, I knew you hated it. When I told you that Liam had won the Spaceco employee lottery and that he was going up, that he was going to answer the question once and for all, I heard what you said: "Lucky guy, getting to know something like that." You thought I wasn't paying attention, but Arthur, I was. I don't have any excuse.

So why the hell did you play along for so long? Standing there in my office doorway, watching me babble on about Liam's adventure, about the magic trick of watching Liam get sucked up into the sky and spat back out, 25,000 miles and an hour and a half later, you crossed your arms and said, "So let's hear the conquering astronaut's verdict. What does space smell like?" I was still on a contact high. I held out my wrist and said, "I brought a little Eau de Astronaut back for you." I said, "Come smell it for yourself." If I was smiling as I said it, I swear it was only because there was just one person I wanted, more than anything, to tell my story to, and Arthur, that person was you.

You didn't smile back. You stepped through the doorway without another word. You grabbed my elbow. You forced me back against the desk. Then you bent over my head and pressed your lips against my hair. You breathed in twice, painfully, as if someone had an elbow in your chest, but when you spoke, your voice sounded almost detached. "It smells . . . ," you said, and then you paused, thinking, before you finished your sentence: "*lonely*." You said, "I have to go, Jess," and when you walked out, you shut the door behind you.

I guess there's no need to rehash what happened next. How I went charging after you, how I slammed your door behind me. I thought I had ditched those middle school theatrics a long time ago, but apparently not. You used the word *chickenshit*. You told me to "shit or get off the pot." Not until later did it occur to me that the entire third floor of Angell Hall was listening to every word we said and drawing the worst possible conclusions.

Another small red droplet went drifting across the cabin, and then another. It took me a second to recognize them for what they were: blood. Even then, I wasn't alarmed. I just started looking around, trying to follow them back to their source with a curiosity that wasn't much more than scientific. You have to understand that everything up there follows such different rules. All motion seems to unfold in a dreamy, ethereal way. When I looked at Lacroix, he had a hand over his nose in a way that made it look as though he was trying to hold back an inappropriate laugh. The cracks between his fingers were dark with a ruby stain. He looked more annoyed than anything.

"Tissues, tissues," said Elle. "We need some tissues."

"Some what?" said Jed. "I don't think we have any of those. We have a first aid kit up in the cockpit. It might have some gauze in it."

"I'll get it," I said. I started to run, then remembered I couldn't. I put both hands on the window, smack dab on top of the spectacular view, and pushed. Thanks to all those new digging muscles I have, it was harder than I meant, and I nearly went crashing into the doorway.

"Easy does it," Bruce said. "It's under there."

Both Elle and Jed had managed to swim through the cabin to reach Lacroix. Elle had him by the face and was staring intently at whatever she saw there. Jed had him by the arm and was holding on to the seat to keep the two of them from drifting away. When they floated to the left, I could see the blood creeping up around Lacroix's nostrils in slow, trembling, creepy tendrils, and for a second I forgot what I was doing, Arthur, and just hung in the doorway, staring, until Jed said, "Gauze, please," tersely, and snapped me back out of it again.

The first aid kit was the exact same one we had at home—a cheapo plastic case stocked with a tube of generic Neosporin and a couple of Band-Aids. Liam might very well have pilfered the thing from under our sink. I remember thinking that I would I ask him when I got back to Earth, and then belatedly that such a conversation would happen only if he were still speaking to me. Someone had at least had the foresight to secure everything with strips of duct tape, so they didn't go floating away when I popped open the lid.

"There's not much here," I said. "Three pieces tops."

"Well, throw over it here," Elle said. She was talking to Lacroix in a long, impassioned stream of French, and she paused only to call over to Bruce. "This bleeding isn't stopping. We need to get him down."

"This isn't a crop duster," said Bruce. He was drumming his fingers on the armrest of his chair. For the first time, I could see that he actually looked rattled. "We're two hundred kilometers above the Earth's surface. You do realize that, don't you? I can't just pick a cornfield and plunk us down." Jed had pushed past me into the cockpit, and the two of them had their heads together and were muttering into the radio. The only thing I could hear was "the sooner, the better."

"Elle, go get your camera," said Lacroix. His voice was muffled. "Keep filming."

"Fuck the camera," said Elle. When she lifted her head, you could see the spattering of Lacroix's blood across her neck, just above the collar of her space suit, like a string of delicate red beads.

"Elle," Lacroix said. "For God's sake. Don't let all this go to waste."

"We can't turn around. We can't go back," Bruce said. "It's going to take at least another twenty minutes to complete orbit. Get him strapped down in his seat." He leaned over and fiddled angrily with something on the control panel. "Base, you're going to have to speak up. We can't hear you up here."

There was a gabbling noise, like several people talking at once, and then a ghostly voice crackled through the static. Two hundred kilometers up in space, I recognized it as Liam's. It was radiating a steely calm. "*Goddard*, the consensus here is that you should have him blow his nose gently. *Gently*. We're thinking since things aren't going to be draining, he wants to try to keep his sinus

282

cavities from filling up with blood. No big surprise, the scientific literature on nosebleeds in zero G is thin. Tristan's got a call in to NASA. Thoughts?"

"Hell if I have any," said Bruce. He leaned forward and dropped his voice, but even back in the cabin we could still hear it. "I have to be honest, Callahan. The guy doesn't look so great."

"They're getting this all on film, I assume?" someone said.

"Yep," said Bruce.

"Christ," said Liam. There was a pause while his sigh was beamed through space, and then we heard it, a long scouring sound against the speaker. "How's the wife?"

"Hanging in there, Liam," I said.

There was another pause, and when Liam's voice came back, it had hardened, Arthur, so that it was barely recognizable, and for a second I thought it was someone else speaking. "Jess," he said. "I was talking about Elle."

Of course he was. Liam and I were never going to talk about that first aid kit. We weren't going to be talking about much of anything at all.

I turned and looked over my shoulder. Lacroix had managed to get back into his chair, and he was pressing a sodden, shockingly red piece of gauze to his nose. His eyes were closed. Elle was hanging on to the back of his chair with one hand and holding her camera with the other. She looked poised, but grim as hell. She was whispering to Lacroix, probably telling him to be sensible, reminding him that now would be an extremely inconvenient time for him to conk out and die on us. She was probably telling

283

him that she had never wanted to make this damn movie, that she had known from the beginning that it would be a complete and total disaster.

All of this is projection. Maybe all she was telling him was that she loved him madly, that she always would, no matter how things got botched and ruined, no matter how much blood was spilled. Which is along the lines of what I would have said to you, if I had a do-over, if it weren't too late. "She's doing fine," I said into the faintly crackling silence. "It's almost over. You should call an ambulance, Li. We're going to need it when we get down."

"Affirmative to that," Bruce said.

"That's Africa we just left behind," Jed said quietly to no one in particular.

Jess

From: Jessica Frobisher <jesspfrobisher@yahoo.com>
Sent: Sunday, September 7, 2014 11:36 pm
To: Arthur Danielson <art.danielson2010@gmail.com>
Cc:
Bcc:
Subject: Re: re: re: trial by fire

Well, that was the most dramatic part. You now have the firsthand exclusive. No one else has talked to the press as far as I know—not Lacroix and Elle, who are trying to save all the thunder for their movie, and not Bruce or Jed, whose hands are tied by confidentiality agreements. So maybe you can sell the story.

There really wasn't much to do after that, except wait while, somewhere below us, the world hurtled past in the darkness. We were clocking 7.8 kilometers per second. I remember that I passed the time by watching the numbers tick off on the clock in the cockpit. When Lacroix's camera floated by, I grabbed it, held it up over Jed's head, and tried to get a shot of the Indian peninsula. Tiny, dazzling cities were flicking by. There were storms out in the Arabian Sea, flashes of perfectly silent light that looked like bombs going off. They went on for hundreds of miles. "There they are," said Jed. It doesn't matter when you go up, you always see at least a couple of storms, he told us. It's always lightning on Earth somewhere.

But I already knew that. It was you who told me that poetic little factoid, wasn't it? I know it was, because I remember. The two of us were walking out into the Herbarium parking lot one afternoon, and it was starting to storm. I remember glancing up at you after you said it, at the raindrops in your eyelashes, at your hair ruffling in the passive-aggressive wind, and thinking, How like you, Arthur, to know such a thing. How like you to say it at the right time. You caught me looking and said, "What?" There didn't seem to be any way to say it, so I just shrugged and looked away.

Later, of course, I had lots of things to say. Most of all: Why the fuck didn't you tell me that you were going on sabbatical? I had to find out from your office-usurper, Krasinski. Do you have any idea how dreadful that was? I spent the whole week after our argument with my office door closed, avoiding you in the halls.

That Saturday I came back to Angell Hall to find a dolly of your books next to the elevator. When I asked Krasinski what was going on, he told me about your sabbatical with McGill. It was like I was playing the part of the amnesiac woman in the bad daytime

285

television show. Everyone else in the department had known for *months*. Another confession, Arthur: I ran around the building looking for you. I charged up and down all the graveyard-quiet stairwells. I haunted the doorway outside the third-floor men's restroom, composing a long and eloquent tirade. Which you never heard. I don't need to tell you the end of the story, obviously. You had left.

Where was I again?

Oh, right. The seconds ticked down, and the world started brightening back up again. We had come around through the dark, and back out the other side. It had been enough time for me to start making a to-do list for the rest of my life. I thought I would need to get custody of Jack and Corinne. I would need to trade in the dying Chrysler for some other mode of transportation, something tougher and more reliable. I would hire someone to come plow under the stone floor of the greenhouse before Liam and I sold the house, because I couldn't bear it if someone covered it in tacky patio furniture. I thought I would need to call Melissa Kramer and tell her that she was right, and the story had ended just like she thought.

From way up there, looking out at the world, the ultimate big picture if ever one existed, all these undertakings struck me as not only possible but simple. Even the worst one: to stop writing you. My glorious, omnipotent feeling didn't last, of course. (These damn epiphanies come and they go, and they refuse to stay.) I came back down. But yes, yes, yes, you are right. For God's sake, Arthur, I'm the last person you need to be explaining this to. Let's please not talk like adults, let's please not resort, in our final hours, to being sensible. Rational conversations are horribly overrated. They're the coldest comfort there is; they're no comfort at all.

I don't know what else you read, but our landing was pretty uneventful. There was an ambulance waiting for us out at the launch site as soon as we touched down in the dust. All its lights were on and sparkling, like a calamitous beacon welcoming us home. Off in the distance were dozens of twinkling stars that I mistook, in the dusk, for fireflies. But of course, Arthur, there aren't any fireflies in the desert. No, it was camera flashes. The paparazzi were pressed against the hurricane fence, having caught the scent of death or dismemberment, and trying as hard as they could to capture us as we climbed, blood-spattered and smelling a little singed,* out of the cabin.

Two of the EMTs were there to assist Lacroix, and although you could tell that he desperately wanted to reject their offers, in the end he had to concede. He let them lower him down into the wheelchair, and then he held up his bloody hand in a grudging wave to the insatiable congregation in the distance, while Elle walked behind us, filming him, and me and Jed and Bruce—our laborious progress through the heavy gravitational field we had just returned to. I thought I was exhausted, but Arthur, I must have been euphoric. Even in the dusk, everything looked bright and extraordinary and miraculously new. All the faces of all the people rushing around were unfamiliar to me—even the ones I knew that I knew—so I kept searching and searching for Liam, thinking that I was just overlooking him in all the hubbub. But no. He wasn't there.

Jess

* You were close. I wouldn't say it smells lonely, per se, but there is something a little desolate to it. I can't think of any other way to describe it except to compare it to burned toast. I'm sorry, but that's the best I can do.

From: Jessica Frobisher <jesspfrobisher@yahoo.com>
Sent: Saturday, September 13, 2014 12:29 pm
To: Arthur Danielson <art.danielson2010@gmail.com>
Cc:
Bcc:
Subject: Re: touchdowns, returns, and sundry

Arthur,

I'm glad to hear you made it to North Carolina. I'm sorry to hear
it's a steaming hellhole. I don't think there's anything to say
except that little white lie people always fall back on in these
kinds of situations: you'll get used to it.

I don't know if I told you that we had a drought while I was gone.
Jack deliberately neglected my watering instructions—he's still
mad at me—so I lost half of the greenhouse plants and all the
vegetables. I was ripping all the tomato plants out earlier when
Liam came by to start emptying out the shed. I stopped and
watched him carry out his clamps and washers and load them up
in buckets. When he got done, he asked to borrow my trowel. The
sound of the words coming out of his mouth startled me. He
speaks to me so little these days. It's like sentences are dollars and
cents, and he doesn't want to pay me a penny more than he
absolutely must.

In silence I handed it over. Then he walked back over to the shed
and took something silver out of his pocket. I think it was the last
and final piece of the *Titan* space shuttle. Under the lilac trees, he
gouged out a chunk of dirt and he buried it there. He drizzled the
last little remains of earth over the top of it. He rubbed his hands
over the tiny pile, smoothing it out, and then he stood up and
walked away.

I see you heard the news about Spaceco being kaput. We're earthbound creatures now, Arthur, stuck on this gorgeous, fucked-up planet, just like everyone else.

And although the days of our space traveling are done, I have the feeling that our days of ignominy are still far from being over. Lacroix's film (tentatively titled *Dieu est un astronaut,* or *God is an Astronaut*) is due out in twelve to fourteen months. I guess there's nothing to do except resign ourselves to our upcoming film debut and keep repeating the same white lie I told you: we'll get used to it. At least Kelly Kahn's father has dropped the lawsuit. All he wanted, he said, was to make sure "those people" (that's us) don't ruin the lives of anyone else. And that mission has been accomplished. Astronaut, omnipotent deity, whatever he is, he works in mysterious ways.

In answer to your question: yes. The first time I sent this e-mail, I accidentally sent it to your umich address and I got a bounce-back reply telling me that your account had been closed. I think . . . maybe it would be better if you didn't send me any other new contact information, though. You know where to find me. I know where to find you. Maybe it would be better for now if we left it at that, don't you think?

Jess

From: Jessica Frobisher <jesspfrobisher@yahoo.com>
Sent: Monday, September 15, 2014 6:47 am
To: Arthur Danielson <art.danielson2010@gmail.com>
Cc:
Bcc:
Subject: one last thing

I just want to clarify that not *everything* in the greenhouse died. All those prima donna roses, the bloodred ones I bought a while back? Of all things, they managed to hang on. One good hail-Mary soaking the day after I got back, and they came back from the dead. There's some kind of lesson there, Arthur, I'm sure, some kind of metaphor. I have no idea what it is, but there you have it.

And last of all, Arthur, before the line goes quiet: good luck.

All my love.

Jess

ACKNOWLEDGMENTS

I would like to thank Rayhané Sanders, the best agent a writer could have; my thoughtful and sharp-eyed editor, Rachel Mannheimer; Alexandra Pringle; and rest of the fantastic team at Bloomsbury.

Many thanks to the faculty at George Mason University for their support encouragement over the years: Alan Cheuse, Susan Shreve, Stephen Goodwin, and Courtney Brkic. A huge thank you to my fellow writers at Mason, those of you wonderful people who became my friends as well as my readers: Eugenia Tsutsumi, David Conner, David Rider, Rion Scott, Sara Hov, and Ryan Call.

For my writing-group buddies who gave me their excellent feedback and rooted me on while I sweated through the arduous process of finishing this book—Elizabeth Moes, Betsy MacBride, Tim Rowe, Collin Grabarek, Priyanka Champaneri, and Steve Loiaconi—I can't thank you guys enough.

Thank you to my colleagues at the National Geographic Society Library & Archives who so kindly took an interest in my progress and toasted my successes at several happy hours along the way.

Most importantly, a loving and grateful thank you to my family: my parents, Barbara and Stephen; my sister, Becca; and my husband, Michael. I love you all more than words can say.

A NOTE ON THE AUTHOR

Alyson Foster was born in St. Louis, Missouri, and grew up in Mt. Pleasant, Michigan. She studied creative writing at the University of Michigan and received an M.F.A. from George Mason University, where she was a Completion Fellow. Her short fiction has appeared in publications including *Glimmer Train*, the *Iowa Review*, *Ascent*, and the *Kenyon Review*. Foster works for the National Geographic Society and lives in the Washington, DC, area with her husband.